[**KILL**FILE]

ALSO BY CHRISTOPHER FARNSWORTH

The Eternal World

The Burning Men

Red, White, and Blood

The President's Vampire

Blood Oath

[KILLFILE]

Christopher

Farnsworth

wm

WILLIAM MORROW

An Imprint of HarperCollins*Publishers*

This book is a work of fiction. References to real people, events, establishments, organizations, or locales are intended only to provide a sense of authenticity, and are used fictitiously. All other characters, and all incidents and dialogue, are drawn from the author's imagination and are not to be construed as real.

HarperCollins books may be purchased for educational, business, or sales promotional use. For information please e-mail the Special Markets Department at SPsales@harper collins.com.

FIRST EDITION

Designed by Renato Stanisic

Library of Congress Cataloging-in-Publication Data has been applied for.

ISBN 978-0-06-241640-7

16 17 18 19 20 OV/RRD 10 9 8 7 6 5 4 3 2 1

To Caroline and Daphne,
my dreams come true

[**KILL**FILE]

[1]

I know what you're thinking. Most of the time, it's not impressive. Trust me.

Dozens of people move around me on the sidewalks in L.A.'s financial district, all of them on autopilot. Plugged into their phones, eyes locked on their screens, half-listening to the person on the other end, sleepwalking as they head for their jobs or their first hits of caffeine. The stuff inside their heads can barely even be called thoughts: slogans and buzzwords; half-remembered songs; the latest domestic cage match with whoever they left at home; dramas and gossip involving people they'll never meet in real life. And sex. Lots and lots of sex.

> *<can't believe she tweeted that going to get her ass fired> <meeting at 11:30 lunch at Chaya after> <bastard tell me where to park that's always my spot> <damn those are some tits wonder how she'd look in high heels and bent over> <she woke me up daily don't need no Starbucks> <I know right?> <like it would kill him to do the dishes once just once in his life> <not bad I'd fuck her> <who's got the power the power to read ugggghhh stuck in my head again> <forty bucks just to get my car to pass an emissions test thanks Obama!> <OMG did u see that thing on BuzzFeed LOL>*

<so that's $378 with electric and shit shit shit about $200 in the checking account and Matthew's got that dentist appointment please God don't let him need braces> <Lakers have got to dump Kobe if I was coach I tell you man seriously what are they thinking>

That's what I live with, constantly, all around me like audible smog.

Most of the time, it's just annoying. But today, it makes it easy to find my targets. They're fully awake, jangling with adrenaline and anxiety. They stand out, hard and bright, a couple of rhinestones glittering in the usual muck.

I cross Fifth Street to the outdoor courtyard where the first guy is waiting at a table, empty Starbucks cup in one hand. I'm supposed to see him.

The one I'm not supposed to see is watching from a half a block over and twenty stories up, on the roof of a nearby building. I can feel him sight me through the rifle scope. I backtrack along his focus on me, reeling it in like a fishing line, until I'm inside his head. He's lying down, the barrel of the gun resting on the edge of the roof, the cool stock against his cheek, grit under his belly. His vision is narrowed to one eye looking through crosshairs, scanning over all the people below him. If I push a little deeper, I can even see the wedge he placed in the access door a dozen feet behind him. He taps his finger on the trigger and goes over his escape route every five seconds or so.

They're both nervous. This is their first kidnapping, after all.

But I'm in kind of a bad mood, so I'm not inclined to make it any easier. I get my coffee first—the line is a wave of pure need, battering impotently against the stoned boredom of the baristas—and then walk back out.

Time to go to work.

I take the open seat across from the guy at the table. I dressed down for this meeting—black jacket, white oxford, standard khakis, everything fresh from the hangers at Gap so I won't stand out—but I still look like an insurance salesman compared to him. He's wearing a T-shirt and baggy shorts, with earbuds wired into his skull beneath his hoodie. Nobody dresses for business anymore.

"Seat's taken," he says. "I'm meeting someone."

I put down my coffee and tap the screen on my phone. His buzzes in response immediately.

He looks baffled. He doesn't get it. I try not to roll my eyes. In real life, there are no Lex Luthors.

"That's me," I tell him. "I'm your meeting."

<how the fuck did he know?> <he was supposed to call first> <doesn't matter> <don't let him see it> <stick with the plan> <stick with the plan>

He covers pretty well. He doesn't ask how I knew him, even as he fumbles to shut down the phone. It's a burner. That headset in his ears? It leads down to his personal phone, keeping a direct line open to his buddy up on the roof. If this conversation doesn't end with them substantially richer, he only has to say one word and his friend will blow my head off my shoulders.

So he still thinks he's got the upper hand in this conversation.

"Fine," he says. "Let's get to it."

"What's your name?" I ask.

"We don't need to get into that." *<Donnie>* "All I need from you is the bank transfer. Then the girl can go back to her rich daddy."

I'm already bored. Donnie here has gotten all his moves from TV and movies. He's an amateur who thought he'd stumbled into his own personal IPO when he met my client's daughter in a club two nights ago.

At least I can see why she went with him. He's got catalog-model good looks and, from what I've learned, a ready supply of drugs that he sells at all the right places. She probably thought he was no worse than her last two boyfriends.

But as the gulf between the One Percent and everyone else grows wider, kidnapping idle rich kids has become a minor epidemic in L.A.

Guys like Donnie and his partner—can't quite snag his name yet, but he's still there, watching through the scope—lure one of the many Kardashian or Hilton wannabes away from their friends, drug them up, then lock them down until they get a ransom. The parents pay, and the kids usually come home with little more than a bad hangover. The police are almost never involved.

You haven't heard about this because the parents know people who own major chunks of stock in CNN and Fox. They don't want the idea going viral, and they know who to call to kill a story.

But they also know who to call when they want something like this handled.

My client, Armin Sadeghi, is a wealthy man who had to flee Iran as a child when a group of religious madmen took over his country. That sort of thing leaves a mark. He doesn't particularly trust the police or the government, especially when it comes to family.

"We need to make sure she's alive and unharmed," I say, sipping my coffee.

"She's fine," Donnie says. *<drugged out of her head>* *<Christ, I've seen guys twice her size OD on that>* "But she won't be if you don't give me what I want."

I get a glimpse of Sadeghi's daughter, skirt bunched up over her waist, snoring heavily, facedown on a soiled mattress. Well, at least she's alive.

"So here's how it's going to work," he begins.

I cut him off. "Where is she?"

"What?" The location appears behind his eyes like it's on Google

Maps. A hotel stuck on Skid Row, one of the last pockets of downtown to resist coffee shops and condos.

I lift my phone and start dialing. He looks stunned. "Sorry, this won't take long."

"What the hell do you think you're—"

I hold up a finger to my lips while the call connects to Sadeghi. When he picks up, I tell him, "She's at a hotel in downtown Los Angeles," and recite the address from Donnie's memory. He's got a group of well-paid and trusted security personnel waiting to retrieve his daughter.

"Hold on a second," I say as he's thanking me and God, in that order. "What room?" I ask Donnie.

It pops into his head even as he says, "Fuck you."

"Room 427," I say into the phone. "You can go get her now."

I disconnect the call and look back at Donnie. His confusion has bloomed into bewilderment and anger. "How the hell did you do that?" he demands.

He's desperately trying to maintain some control here, torn between running to the hotel and doing some violence to me. I can feel his legs twitch and his pulse jumping.

I can sense the same anger, the same need to do harm, coming down from above. The scope is still on me.

"I know your buddy can hear me," I say, as calmly as I can. "What's his name?"

"Go fuck yourself," Donnie says. *<Brody>*

With that, a jumble of memories sort themselves into a highlight reel of Donnie and Brody, both of their lives coming into sharper focus. Donnie: the club kid, the dealer. Brody: one of the thousands back from the military, no job, no real family, no marketable skills outside of combat training. A partnership forms. Donnie likes having a badass on his side. Brody likes being the badass. They both like the money.

I hope they can both be smarter than they've been up until now.

"All right. Donnie. Brody. You need to recognize that this is over. You can walk away right now, as long as you never get within a thousand yards of the girl or her family again."

I boost the words with as much authority and power as I've got, pushing them into their skulls, trying to make them see it for themselves.

Donnie hunches down. Even if I weren't in his head, I'd see that he's gone from angry to mean. I'm maybe five years older than him, but he's hearing his parents, every teacher, and every cop who ever told him what to do. His anxiety has a sharp and jagged edge now, like a broken bottle in the hand of an angry drunk.

"Yeah?" he says. "And what if we just kill you, instead?"

Not my first choice, admittedly. Out loud, I say, "You spend the rest of your lives running. And you still won't get paid."

I can sense some hesitation from Brody twenty stories up. But he keeps the rifle pointed at my head.

This close up, a little empathy for these morons seeps in around the edges. Neither of them was raised by anybody who gave anything close to a damn. They're scared by my spook show, torn between the need to run and the need to punish. It could go either way. I push harder, trying to steer them onto the right path. I'm working against years of bad habits and ingrained attitude.

But surely they are not stupid enough to try to kill me in the middle of downtown Los Angeles in broad daylight. They just can't be that dumb.

I try to help them make the right decision. *<Go home>* I send to them, as hard as I can. *<Give it up. Be smart. Please.>*

Donnie stands up. "Fuck it," he says.

I relax, just a little.

Then he makes his choice, like a motorcycle veering suddenly down an off-ramp.

"You tell that bitch and her old man we'll be seeing them," he says. "Never mind. I'll tell them myself."

Triumph spreads through his head like the shit-eating grin on his face. I don't know exactly what he's got in store for the Sadeghis. All I see in his mind is a knife and bare flesh.

And blood. Lots of blood.

"Do it," Donnie says. Talking to his partner, not to me.

I feel Brody begin to squeeze the trigger.

Idiots.

I see it so clearly through Brody's eyes. The weapon, a Remington 700 Police Special he bought online, comes alive in his hands. There's a brief flash memory of test-firing it into dunes in the Mojave. He calculates distance and velocity and timing all by reflex. Brody was a good soldier. He breathes out and the rifle bucks slightly as he sends 180 grams of copper-jacketed lead toward my skull, still neatly framed in the crosshairs.

There's a small explosion of blood and bone and my body pitches forward, dead as a dropped call.

But when Brody looks up from the scope, he notices something off. My body is in the wrong place. He can tell, even from that distance.

He puts his eye back to the scope and sees me there, still alive, coffee still in hand.

Donnie is on the ground, arms and legs splayed out at unnatural angles.

Brody feels something sink inside, like a stone dropping into a pool. He jumps to his feet, rifle in hand, and runs toward the door and the escape route he'd planned.

I can see it as clearly as he does, riding along behind his eyes.

Something strikes his shin just above his foot and he goes flying forward. And instead of pitching face-first into the gravel-topped surface, he finds nothing.

It takes him a moment to realize he's tripped over the edge of the roof. He sees clearly again and realizes he's in midair, hands and legs windmilling uselessly, touching nothing but sky.

He was sure he was running toward the door.

Then he's aimed like a missile at the pavement below and the pure animal terror kicks in. The ground rushes up to meet him at thirty-six meters per second and he screams.

I was far enough into Brody's head to cut and paste his perceptions, editing his vision before it got from his eyes to his brain. I put an image of my own head over Donnie's for the shot. When Brody got up to run, I flipped his vision of the roof, made him think the door was in front of him.

I get out of his mind before he hits the ground, but I can still feel the echo of his fear.

I tamp it down and concentrate on going through Donnie's pockets. A little brain matter and a lot of blood leak from the exit wound. His eyes are empty.

Someone comes up behind me. "Oh my God, what happened to him?"

I hit them with a blast of pure panic and disgust—not too hard at this point—and yell, "Call 911! Get an ambulance!"

They bounce back like they've touched an electric fence.

I find what I'm looking for: Donnie's phone and the hotel room key.

Before anyone else can stop me, I walk away. Not too fast, not too slow.

Around the corner, I have to stop and put my hand on the closest wall to stay upright.

The deaths hit me.

I was too close to both of them. Donnie's last moments weren't too bad: a feeling of victory suddenly cut short, a sharp pain, and then blackness as the bullet tore a gutter through his brain and emptied him of everything he was.

Brody, however, had a good long time to realize that he was going to die. He took a second breath to keep screaming.

I manage to keep my coffee down. I pull myself together and file both deaths away, in the back of my head, for future reference.

Then I call Mr. Sadeghi again. No, he hasn't sent his team to the address yet. They're still getting ready.

"Never mind," I tell him, looking at the hotel room key. "I'm closer. I'll pick her up and have her home within the hour."

I can't read what's going through his head over the phone, but the relief in his voice sounds genuine. Parental bonds are tough to break, or so I'm told.

I hear sirens. The police will be here to collect the bodies soon. My bet is that they'll call it a murder-suicide, a couple of small-time scumbags settling a business dispute.

I wonder if I did this on purpose. If I was just so offended by their arrogance and their casual cruelty that I pressed their buttons and boxed them into this ending.

But it doesn't work like that. My life would be a lot easier if it did. They could have just walked away when I told them. I can push, I can nudge, I can mess with their heads, but despite all my tricks, people still find a way to do what they want. Their endings were written a long time before I ever showed up.

Or maybe that's just what I tell myself.

I get my car and head toward the hotel.

[2]

Three hours in a private jet turns out to be the perfect antidote for the migraine clawing at the inside of my skull. If I could afford it, I'd do this every time someone tried to kill me.

Ordinarily I would take a little longer between jobs to shake off the hangover that always comes from being too close to a violent death—a kind of feedback that echoes around my brain for at least a day.

But this client was particularly insistent and sent a check for my time, along with a Gulfstream to LAX to pick me up. That overcomes my reluctance pretty fast.

The entire flight is blissfully silent. The plane's interior is polished walnut and butter-soft leather, like a set designer's vision of an English library from some BBC period drama. After getting me a drink, the gorgeous flight attendant retreats to the back of the jet and her thoughts vanish into the celebrity mag she brought with her. The pilot's mind is filled with the white noise of altitude and heading and airspeed. The next closest human being is forty-two thousand feet below.

So I drink my drink and stare out the window and try to keep my head as empty as possible. The meeting is with the client's personal attorney, a man named Lawrence Gaines. The client himself wants to remain anonymous. That's not unusual. I did a preliminary check on

Gaines to make certain I wasn't being set up, but didn't go any deeper. I can live with the mystery for now.

And not to brag, but it's not like it can remain a secret once Gaines and I are in the same room.

I am a little surprised by the relative quiet once we hit the tarmac. Airports are ugly enough for most people, but they're side trips into hell for me. Anxiety and anger and exhaustion and pain and loneliness and boredom, all in one convenient location. Most of the time, my teeth start grinding from a mile away.

Here, the usual jangle is muted. When the Gulfstream's door opens, I find out why. This is the smallest, quietest airport I've ever seen. It looks like a toy play set from the 1950s brought to life.

"Welcome to Sioux Falls," the flight attendant says as she hands me my jacket. I get a brief glimmer of interest from her, mixed with cool appraisal. I've worn a gray Armani two-button over a gleaming white broadcloth shirt and solid blue tie for this meeting. But it's only camouflage. I'll be the first to admit I don't look like I belong in this tax bracket.

She's wondering if I'll be staying at the same hotel she and the pilot use. Now I'm wondering too. I thank her for the drink.

Then I go down the stairs and meet my ride: a driver waiting outside a black town car, parked right on the runway. He's a head taller and maybe seventy pounds heavier than I am.

"You Smith?" he asks, as if he didn't see me get off the plane specifically chartered to bring me here.

I catch a wave of animosity coming off him right away. He's not happy I'm here. I wish I'd brought more luggage just so I could make him carry it. I nod.

"Keith," he grunts, and points his chin at the back door of the car. He gets behind the wheel without waiting for me.

I know Keith, even though I've never seen him before. We'd both say we work in the private security field, but that's just being polite. One of the side effects of spending the last dozen years at war is that it produces a surplus of guys trained in the latest government-approved methods of hurting people. Most of them find a way back into normal life, but there are plenty of opportunities for those who don't. There are fourteen major private military companies in the U.S. alone, and that doesn't include all the corporations in other fields that have decided their options should include lethal response.

The result is guys like Keith: basically a hired thug in a suit.

The same can be said of me, of course, but I like to think I'm a little more specialized. And I wear better suits.

I try to sort out his hostility from the backseat, but it's too wound up in a bunch of other irritations: the mushy handling of the town car, the amount of time it takes for the automatic gate to open, the incompetence of every other driver on the road. Anger is Keith's default setting.

He soothes himself with images and lines from a half dozen action movies. I get flashes of him fighting bad guys, complete with a voice-over reading catchphrases: <*He doesn't need a reason, just an excuse. Go ahead, make his day.*> His internal soundtrack is like something from a video game.

I screen it out as best I can and look out the window for the rest of the ride. There really is not a lot to see in South Dakota. Miles and miles of empty space.

I like it.

THE ATTORNEY, GAINES, aims me at a chair after the briefest of handshakes. He's much younger than I expected, about my age, but with fresh-scrubbed pale skin and blond hair that makes him look like he just got out of law school. He's gym-toned and decked out in the usual douchebag tuxedo: sport coat over $500 jeans.

Keith brought me into the building down a hallway lined with offices for firms named WILSON TRUST CO., DALTON FAMILY TRUST, and CARSON GENERATIONAL FUND. Most of the windows were dark. Gaines's office looks part-time, too. The decor includes bull horns on the walls and brands burned into the leather of the chairs. Cowboy rich.

"You like this place?" Gaines asks. "Corporate ghost town. South Dakota state law offers a perpetual trust that exempts money from the estate tax, but you have to have a physical presence here. So you get a bunch of billionaires sheltering their money in empty suites. One other benefit: it also gives us a quiet little spot to meet."

Keith takes up a position by the door, next to another chunk of hired meat who doesn't give his name or speak. *<David>* Only mild curiosity from him. Keith, however, is still on edge, spoiling for a fight.

All I get from Gaines is caution and suspicion. Nothing I haven't felt before.

"John Smith," he says. "Never actually met anyone named that before."

That's what the state tagged me with. I was put in a group home before I was one. I had a blank spot on my records instead of a name. "It could have been worse," I say. "It could have been John Doe."

"Well, Tom Eckert speaks highly of you. He's very grateful for the work you did."

"I'm afraid I can't confirm or deny I've worked for anyone with that name," I say. Client confidentiality is one of the promises I take seriously.

"Oh, don't worry. Tom and my boss go way back. But I appreciate your discretion. We don't want rumors spreading. Like I bet you don't want to talk about that business in downtown L.A. yesterday."

He's waiting for a reaction. I stay neutral. At this level, people spend a lot of money checking me out. I expect nothing less. It means they're willing to invest even more in me.

"I'm sure I don't know what you're talking about."

"Right," he says, with a smile that is absolutely fake. "So. You're a psychic."

Here we go. He doesn't believe I can do what I do. It's not the first time I've encountered this, obviously.

"Actually, most people who call themselves psychics are half-bright con artists using hundred-year-old magic tricks to convince people of things they already know."

"But that's not you." The sarcasm drips from his voice.

"For starters, what I do is real."

"Really. You read minds."

I relax and go into my pitch. I've had a lot of practice.

"You like to think you've got one guy behind your eyes, driving your body like a giant robot, making all the decisions. It's actually more like a whole crowd in there, dealing with a few dozen things at once. What we call the mind is actually a metaphor for all the different processes—memories, physical sensations, emotions, thoughts, and reflexes—bouncing around inside three pounds of tofu in our skulls. Most of the time, we're running what we'd call subroutines—things we don't even think about, like breathing or walking or eating. But we also use our minds to direct our activities, to form thoughts and actions, usually before we're aware that we're doing it. My talent is picking up on all those disparate elements as they happen in someone else's brain, and then translating them into a coherent narrative that I can understand, and even influence to some extent."

"Well, here's the million-dollar question: How do you do it?"

"I wish I could tell you. I've always had a talent. Then I went into the military. There was a program that helped me develop it further."

"Right." He picks up a tablet and taps at the screen. I can't see what pops up. "I've been looking at your history," he says. "You enlisted right after 9/11—good for you, by the way. You weren't even eighteen yet."

"You can sign up at seventeen with a parent or guardian's consent. My foster parents agreed." They were glad to see me go. We'd settled into an uneasy détente by then, but I still frightened them.

"Three tours in Special Forces. Iraq and Afghanistan. Impressive." He's not impressed. He's just being polite. The world is shifting already. The wars are old news to anyone who wasn't directly involved in them. Pretty soon, they're going to seem as distant and irrelevant as Vietnam was to me.

"Says here you were discharged," Gaines continues. "Then there's a blank spot for seven years."

"I was with the CIA. First as an employee, then as a contractor."

"Doing what?"

"That's classified."

"Of course it is. And—if you can do what you say—why did they ever let you go?"

"That's also classified."

He waits for more. I don't offer anything. Like I said: I do take some promises seriously.

Gaines taps the screen again and moves on. "So now you're a private consultant. A very well-paid one."

Even if I couldn't read what he's thinking, I'd hear the tone in his voice.

"I'm worth it."

"Are you?" *<yeah right>*

"I have a specialized set of skills, in addition to my talent. I was trained to handle problems. And I've learned that some people, particularly those who have more money than most state governments, have bigger problems. There are times they cannot use the standard remedies available to regular citizens. They require specialized solutions. I saw a niche in the market, and I filled it."

"You'll forgive me if I'm still a little skeptical. Can you make me bark like a dog, cluck like a chicken, anything like that?"

I restrain a sigh. Everyone wants the Vegas act.

"Unfortunately, it's a lot more complicated than that. I don't like to use this terminology, but it's as close as I can come: if your mind is a computer, I can hack into it, read your emails, trigger some processes, and even overwrite some files. What you're asking, though, would be like reprogramming the entire operating system from the command line. A person's mind is far too complex for that. You've spent your whole life becoming who you are. I can't change all that in a few minutes, or even a few days. People always return to who they are."

"Now it sounds like you're making excuses. Like most psychics. The energy has to be right. Or you need the right subject. Or the planets are out of alignment. Whatever."

"I'm just being honest. I can't control someone else's mind. Not the way you're thinking."

Gaines laughs. "Honest. Yeah. That's a good one."

"What's your problem?" I can see it in his head, but I want him to say it out loud.

"Well, since we're all being honest: I think you're ten pounds of bullshit in a five-pound bag, Mr. Smith."

"You brought me a long way and paid me a lot of money to say that. A phone call would have been cheaper."

"My employer wanted to see you. He thinks there might actually be something to you. Unfortunately for you, I don't. And nobody gets to him without going through me first. I think you are a con artist. I think you've convinced some rich old men and women that you have superpowers, and you've gotten by on luck and—what did you say?—'hundred-year-old magic tricks' until now. But I see no reason why I should allow you to waste my boss's time, or even get in the same room with him."

His self-satisfaction is practically gleaming through that perfect skin of his.

"You want a demonstration?" I ask. "I could tell you that you've got just over sixty-three thousand dollars and change in your checking account, at least as far as you can remember. I can tell you that you forgot to call your wife before I showed up, and now you're thinking you won't get another chance until after lunch. You're still worried about the appraisal on a piece of property in Wyoming that you're considering for a mini mall. And you've got a Glock nine-millimeter in the right-hand drawer of that desk."

The gleam dims a little. He struggles to get it back.

"That doesn't prove anything. I've heard that you guys can read stuff from body language, that you hire private detectives to do your research. You might even have a camera in this room, for all I know."

"All true," I admit. "There are people who do that. But I'm not one of them."

"Fine. Tell me something you couldn't learn from a twenty-dollar Internet credit report. Tell me my boss's name."

It's right there in the front of his head, but I deliberately ignore it. "You asked for your employer's name to remain confidential. I'm going to honor that."

He beams with triumph. "You mean you don't know. You couldn't get that info before the meeting." *<knew it>* *<bullshit artist>*

"We're done," I say. I stand and button my jacket. "There's nothing else I can do that will convince you."

"That's not exactly true," Gaines says.

I feel Keith behind me, suddenly interested, an attack dog straining at his leash. David, the other security guy, is on alert too, but without the bloodlust. They step away from their posts at the door.

"I've asked Keith and David to beat you stupid and dump you off the highway," Gaines says.

Keith's mind is suddenly all sunshine and rainbows. David limbers up, not exactly happy, but willing to follow orders.

Gaines smiles again. "So all you have to do, Mr. Smith, is keep them from crippling you right here on the carpet. Then I'll be convinced."

Keith rushes me first. Waves of glee dance all around him. He's been looking for an excuse to punch someone in the head all day.

He doesn't care that I haven't turned to face him. Fighting fair doesn't get a lot of emphasis in combat training.

David is a step behind. He's still more ambivalent, but I can see the moves he's planning. He's a good, efficient brawler.

Keith's fist comes up to clobber me. I see the back of my head through his eyes.

<smart-ass prick> *<see how tough you are now>*

All right, then. Here's the Vegas act.

I hit Keith with the physical memory of double-port chemo nausea from a late-stage cancer patient. His equilibrium shorts out, and his knees buckle. He's suddenly folded in half on the cowskin rug, retching up the power-protein smoothie he had for breakfast.

I'll pay for that later, but it's worth it.

David wasn't nearly as anxious to slaughter me, so I go a little easier on him. I only blank the visual input from his eyes to his occipital lobes. He's effectively blind in an instant. He screams as I step aside, and he runs into the wall hard enough to bounce.

They're both out of the game. I turn back to Gaines. I feel a stab of fear inside his mind.

"Now you're trying to remember the last time you fired that Glock at the range," I tell him. "And how many bullets are still loaded. And you're especially curious to find out if you can get it out of the drawer before I do anything else."

I take a step forward. He flinches back in his chair.

"I admit, I'm a little curious myself."

A side door to the office opens. An older man stands there in a white shirt and khakis. I knew he was there. He was listening to my audition the entire time.

"That's enough, Mr. Smith," he says. "I believe Lawrence is convinced now."

I'm looking at Gaines's boss. Who also happens to be the thirteenth richest man in America.

"I'm sorry for the trouble," Everett Sloan says. "By way of apology, I hope you'll allow me to take you to lunch."

My steak is big enough to fall over the lip of the plate. Which is actually fine by me. Vegetarians can have their clean arteries. Humans are smart because a bunch of primates on the African savannah developed a taste for raw flesh, and the amino acids in their bellies went straight to their heads and built bigger brains. Two million years later, there's me, reading minds and downing megaloads of protein to refuel. Evolution in action.

Sloan sits across from me at the table, drinking coffee. We have an acre of space in the back of the restaurant, all to ourselves. I'm not sure if this is because Sloan wants it this way, or if this is just the standard lunch hour in South Dakota.

Even so, I pick up the angst as the waitress follows an argument between two friends on Facebook, the boredom of the manager, the stoic acceptance of the cook in the back as he adds another burn to the layers of scar tissue on his right hand.

Keith was still dry-heaving when we left, so Sloan drove us here himself. His hands were steady on the wheel. I know he's in his seventies, but he looks at least a couple of decades younger and stands straight and tall. One of the benefits of having a billion dollars is that time doesn't leave the same marks on you as it does other people.

When I decided to go private, I memorized the names and faces of all the people on the Forbes 500. Future clients, I hoped. Sloan stood out. He's not the richest man on the list, but he might well be the smartest. And yes, I'm including Gates. Forget the software geeks who have gotten rich off stock options because they came up with a new way for teenagers to take nude selfies. Sloan is an actual, honest-to-God genius. He was still a college student at Stanford when he was recruited by the NSA to break Soviet codes in the Cold War. He went to grad school after that, supplementing his meager salary as a teaching assistant by playing poker in backroom card games. Then he found that some of his equations could actually predict the movements of the stock market. He took his paycheck to Vegas and won a poker tournament. He used the prize money to start his own investment firm. Within a year, he was a multimillionaire.

Now he manages about $20 billion in assets, and there are people who'd sell their own daughters for the chance to give him their money.

I've never encountered a mind like his before. Even this close, I couldn't tell you what he's thinking. He's running calculations and modeling outcomes way ahead of anything I can fathom, much faster than I've ever experienced. It's like a wall of ice—cold, flawless, and perfectly smooth. Most of my attempts to read him just slide right off.

"I hope you'll forgive Lawrence," he says. "He tends to be overprotective."

I saw that clearly in the office when Sloan appeared. Gaines's fear wasn't for himself. It was for the old man. He didn't really believe in my talent, but he wanted to protect Sloan just in case he was wrong.

When Sloan and I left, his fear was a bright spark in his head, because now he believes. But Sloan ordered him to stay, so he stayed.

"I've had worse job interviews," I say.

"It didn't appear to be very pleasant for Keith or David either."

"I didn't tell them to attack me."

"No, no, I don't blame you for defending yourself. I'm mainly curious how you were able to do that."

"Have you ever heard of the Kadaitcha?"

He shakes his head. I finish another chunk of steak, then continue. "In some Australian aboriginal tribes, they have a guy who is sort of a cross between a witch doctor and a hit man. That's the Kadaitcha. He's responsible for the tribe's magic, and for enforcing the tribe's laws. There are only a few things a member of the tribe can do to be sentenced to death, but if that happens, then the Kadaitcha carries out the sentence."

Sloan waits patiently for me to get to the point.

"Here's the thing. He doesn't use anything like what we'd consider a weapon. Instead, he carries a sharpened bone. Sometimes from an animal. Usually from a human. A little longer than a pencil. And he points it at the offender. According to the tribe's beliefs, the Kadaitcha sends a spirit out of the pointing bone—like a spear of thought—into the other person. A couple of days later, a week at the most, the offender drops dead. He believes so completely in the spirit and the power of the bone that he actually loses the will to live. He convinces himself that he's dying. What I do, it's a lot like that."

"But nobody in that room believed you had that ability."

"That's what makes me different. I don't need anyone else to believe in me. I can implant the memory of a trauma directly. Your security men were in pain. They were experiencing a physical reality, based on what their minds were telling them."

"So did you break my bodyguards?"

"They'll be fine," I tell him. "It's like any other bad memory. It passes with time."

"And there are no permanent effects?"

"Hopefully just a strong aversion to picking a fight with me in the future."

He considers that for a moment. "You're fairly open about all of this, considering we only just met."

"It's only a trade secret if someone else can do it." What I don't tell him is what that little trick costs me. I can put the idea of a broken leg or a stab wound into another person, but their response echoes in my head as well—so I always get a percentage of the pain I inflict on anyone else.

"But where does it come from?" Sloan says. He really wants to understand. There's a lot of the true scientist in him. He wants to know.

"Psychosomatic implant, delivered through quantum entanglement of consciousness," I say.

And then I restrain a laugh, because for the first time, I detect a hint of confusion in Sloan's brilliant mind. "What exactly is that supposed to mean?" he asks.

I shrug and smile. "Hell if I know. It's a term I heard someone use once when he was talking about me. It was his theory. I'm not sure I can explain it."

Sloan frowns, just a little. "You don't have any idea why you can do what you do. And you're satisfied to leave it at that? You've never looked any further?"

After the Vegas act, this is what everyone wants. They want an answer. They want to know why. And I can't help them. I grappled with the question for years, wondered what made me different, what set me apart from everyone else. Until I decided it didn't matter.

"I've lived with it my whole life," I tell Sloan. "Do you wonder why your legs work? Or your eyes? Somebody told you something about your nervous system once, back in school, and you accepted it. But it doesn't change how you walk or see. This is what I am. I can't change it. So I might as well use it."

He considers me for a moment. "Remarkable," he says. "You know, a man with your talents could make a lot more money doing other things."

When one of the richest men in the world wants to give you financial advice, you listen. "Like what?"

"Blackmail, for starters. You could make a fortune."

"Blackmailers end up with a target on their backs. And it's never a good idea to piss off the people in your tax bracket, Mr. Sloan. Just ask your friend Tom Eckert."

"From what I saw, you can defend yourself."

"I'd rather not live like that."

"Well, if you find blackmail distasteful, why don't you just steal? Pick account numbers or insider secrets out of people's skulls, then use what you find to make yourself rich."

"What makes you think I don't?" I say. "You have a lot of valuable information. Why would you let someone like me this close to you?"

He shakes his head. "You're not that sort of person."

"You're sure about that?"

"I am. Forgive me if this sounds arrogant, but I'm in the business of knowing more than other people."

"Your assistant had a few gaps in his knowledge."

"True. But everything Lawrence knows about you is not everything I know about you. I knew how he would react to you. I wanted to find out how you'd react to him."

"Did I pass the test?"

"It confirmed what I already suspected. I've read your file. It shouldn't surprise you to hear that I have contacts in the government, both from my days in the NSA and from the people who depend on me to make them richer. So believe me when I say: I know everything you did while working for the CIA. I know how you came to them. I know why you left too. That's why I don't feel particularly unsafe with you, Mr. Smith. I know you have a conscience. But perhaps more important than that, I know you have a price. And I know that I can meet it."

I don't say anything. I'd forgotten what it feels like to be surprised. It's almost terrifying.

"How are the headaches?" he asks.

Another surprise. And proof that Sloan really has read my file. Or at least part of it. "Good days and bad," I admit.

"I can give you some respite from them. A place you can go without people. A sanctuary of your own. No other thoughts, no other interference. Just quiet."

He takes out his phone and taps the screen. Then he shows me a map of a small chunk of green in the middle of a field of blue.

"This is Ward Island, located in Davis Bay off the coast of Washington. Thirteen acres. Zero population. There's a fully equipped house there. Twelve thousand square feet, three master bedrooms, wine cellar, wet bar. Solar panels, dedicated broadband cable to the mainland, plus satellite backup if you need it. It's easily accessible by boat. At the moment, it's vacant. I own it."

"You're offering me an island?"

"A ninety-nine-year lease, actually. It would revert to my heirs afterward. Obviously, neither of us would be around to see that happen. But for the rest of your natural life, it would be yours. You can have servants on the island, paid for by me, or, if you prefer, you can simply have supplies dropped off and a cleaning crew on a regular basis. You can come and go as you please for your work, but in between your jobs, complete isolation. A retreat from the world, anytime you want it, with thirty nautical miles between you and the next living human."

I look at the little green shape on the screen for a moment longer. No people. No endless chattering stream of complaints and pains and idiocies.

"That's quite a fee," I say. "I'm listening."

I finally get something concrete from Sloan. A feeling of satisfaction. Once again, it confirms for him that everything has a price. It's not so much that he believes in money as a supreme power above all else, but it restores his faith that everything can be quantified. He lives in a world of absolute limits and measures, and he knows he's found mine: a home of my own, quiet and secure against the constant noise invading my head.

The offer alone is enough to buy my loyalty; he really is a very smart man.

Sloan checks his watch, a vintage 18-karat gold Hamilton Pulsar.

"Then I should probably tell you why I wanted to meet you," he says.

"ELI PRESTON," SLOAN says. "You've heard of him."

"At this point, who hasn't?"

Sloan smiles. "He's been making a lot of noise, that's true."

Eli Preston is not on the Forbes 500 list, but everyone in the financial press says it's only a matter of time. He's the founder of OmniVore Technology, a small, privately held company, which is expected to make him a billionaire once it goes public.

Preston is supposed to be the next Zuckerberg, or at least one of the candidates: smart, ambitious, and insanely rich; lives on bulletproof coffee, energy drinks, and high-protein sushi prepared by a personal chef; lectures about the future at TED one week, then shows up courtside at a Knicks game the next.

He just turned twenty-six. I know this because he rented out the entire Bellagio in Las Vegas for the party. I read about it on Gawker.

I'm not, however, completely clear on what exactly OmniVore does, or why it's worth so much money. So I ask.

For a brief instant, I get a slight weariness from Sloan. His IQ scrapes the limits of the tests made to measure it. He's constantly explaining things, stopping his own personal train of thought and waiting for everyone else to catch up. To him, the rest of us move in slow motion, taking forever to understand what is clear to him in an instant. For a moment, I sense how tiring it must be to be so much smarter than everyone else. To know the answers so long before everyone else does. To see clearly while they're still blindly groping around in the dark.

But he explains anyway.

"OmniVore is what we call a data-miner," he says. "It sifts through massive amounts of information for its clients. You see, most companies are drowning in facts. Thanks to the Internet and cheap digital storage, they have access to incredible levels of detail now—they can track down to the minute the last time you purchased razor blades at the store, and it goes into a little file that contains every other fact about you. Your credit-card number. Your birth date. What car you drive. Your sexual preference. Your favorite flavor of ice cream. Everything that might be considered even remotely relevant to extracting another couple of dollars from your wallet. And they have that for everyone. They can track the number of left-handed divorced women who visit their website, or gauge the reaction on Twitter to their latest ad campaign from Denver Broncos fans or vegetarians or even rape victims, if they want to go that far. But it's all too much. They have more raw data than ever, and they actually know less. It's like drinking from a fire hose, as they say. They can't narrow it all down. That's where OmniVore comes in. It applies its software to the data, and it finds out exactly what the companies actually need to know. It identifies problems before they happen. It learns the patterns inherent in a business, and makes predictions for the future. It discovers threats and eliminates them."

"Threats? Like what?"

"It depends. For a tech company, it could be hackers or industrial espionage, someone trying to steal next quarter's product designs. For a retailer, credit-card fraud or employees stealing merchandise. For a bank, embezzlement or tax fraud. Could be anything. The idea is that OmniVore's software is smarter than humans. It's like chaos theory in reverse: we see a hurricane, but they know where and when a butterfly flapped its wings."

He's dumbed it down significantly for me, but it's close enough.

"And that's profitable?"

"God, yes. Eli is turning away the biggest companies in the world. He's got government agencies, automakers, studios, TV networks—everyone you can think of, really—lined up and waiting on him. Unlike Twitter or Facebook, there are people with deep pockets willing to pay a great deal for this service."

"So what's your problem with him?"

"Not many people know this, but Eli used to work for me."

"That doesn't seem like something he'd be shy about. I imagine it would look good on his résumé."

"We didn't part on the best of terms. I recruited him out of Harvard as an analyst. I thought Eli would be perfect for the job. As it turned out, he got bored very quickly. He didn't care for sitting in an office and crunching numbers. He wanted to be out in front, playing at the high-stakes tables."

Right. Where the hookers and free drinks are. It wouldn't be the first time a young guy thought he could do better than his boss. "You fired him."

"We came to a mutual understanding. A few months later, he had raised enough capital to start OmniVore. And his success story began."

"But you don't think he did it himself."

"You really must be psychic," he says, smiling. I hear that joke a lot. I smile along with him anyway. "Yes. He's built his company—everything he's done since he left—on the strength of my ideas, my intellectual property."

Something about the timeline seems off. I interrupt Sloan. "Let me ask you a question here: He hacked your files two years ago, and you're just finding out now?"

"Do you understand what I do, Mr. Smith?" *<of course you don't>*

He's right. I don't. I'm not ashamed to admit it. "Not even a little."

"You invest in the stock market?"

"Not really."

That surprises him. "Where do you keep your money?"

"In my wallet, mostly." He laughs at that, but it's true. My fees are high, but so are my expenses. I also don't trust money I can't pull out and spend whenever I want. I know it's not very smart, but old habits die hard.

"Well, if this all works out, maybe we can set you up with a starter portfolio," he says. At the same time, in his head, he prepares to give me the Fisher-Price explanation of his job, the one he uses for people he meets at parties.

"Stock picking used to be about people making educated guesses based on the companies," he says. "Profit and loss statements, supply and demand, market conditions—but really, nothing more scientific than throwing darts at a board with names on it. Most investment firms are lucky if they do as well as an index fund—that's a collection of stocks that simply mirrors the market, goes up when it goes up, goes down when it goes down. What I do is different. Have you ever heard of algorithmic trading?"

You don't work for rich clients without picking something up. "You use computers to analyze the market and make stock trades for you."

"Close enough," he says. "I invented it, more or less. I created an algorithm—that's a mathematical formula that you enter into a computer—that analyzes data. Essentially, it was a way to look at any set of data and organize it, and even make predictions based on it. It could find the underlying patterns in the numbers, when a human being would see only a mass of random information. This was something I discovered when I was looking into Sienkiewicz-Moore theorems, a subset of Big Number theory, back when I was still in graduate school."

All I get from that is the ice wall again. He sees he's lost me and tacks quickly back into simple concepts. "So I take a series of facts, translate them into numbers, plug them into the formula, and it makes a series of educated guesses about the future. What made the algorithm so interesting was that the predictions were almost always right. I could take any facts that could be reduced to mathematical inputs—migration patterns of birds, or tide tables, or annual rainfall in the Gobi Desert, for instance—and I would get a very good idea of how those same numbers would turn out in the future. Then it occurred to me, what if I entered something a little more concrete than rainfall estimates?"

I'm starting to get it now. "Like, say, stock prices."

He smiles again, and I sense genuine pride still lingering there. "Exactly. I quickly found the algorithm was a great deal more valuable to me in practice than as a theory published in an academic paper. That's how I began trading. I'd use the algorithm to predict the rise and fall of the market, and I'd make bets accordingly."

"And you got very rich."

Another small burst of pride. "Yes. Other people noticed. They hired their own computer engineers and math professors. Now there's a whole industry of traders and programmers analyzing market data using algorithms and computers. Each firm has something they call their 'secret sauce.' That's a proprietary algorithm that's the heart of their trading. It tells their computers how to interact with the markets. I called mine Spike. To find the spikes in the markets."

He looks at me. I smile, to show him I get it. "Your secret sauce is better."

"Much, much better. Not to boast, Mr. Smith, but nobody else has come close to understanding what I did when I broke that problem back in graduate school. And we're constantly refining the process, feeding more data to the algorithms. Spike, like every other piece of trading software, makes millions of decisions every second. Literally billions of dollars every minute, all moved around by computers. That requires incredibly smart people to analyze market trends, to see risks and opportunities and then translate them into the kind of math that machines can understand. Everyone is trying to beat the odds, trying to get their computers to think a little faster, a little smarter. It's not easy. As I said, most firms are lucky to match the market. The best ones can offer you perhaps a ten percent return over time."

"What's your return?" I ask.

"Eighty to ninety percent," he says. "Even when the economy collapsed, we managed to make a profit. All with Spike. It's simply smarter than anything anyone else can come up with. Other people will promise you pennies. We double your money, or close to it."

Bullshit. That's Ponzi scheme territory. Nobody can guarantee that kind of return. I don't get any active deception off Sloan, but people have a habit of buying into their own hype. After all, it's not a lie if you really believe it.

Some of my skepticism must show up on my face, because Sloan smiles and asks, "You don't believe me?"

I try to be diplomatic. "That's quite a return," I say. "Warren Buffett only manages nineteen percent, and he's supposed to be the most successful stock picker in history."

Sloan smiles again. "Warren's a friend. But he's a very public figure. People follow him. They jump into his stocks when he buys and run away when he sells. We don't allow that. We keep our trading secret. We've got a dedicated dark pool that hides our trades, and we spread them over a variety of market makers. And we control our overall investment. I could have a half a trillion dollars in assets under management if I wanted. I've got the clients lined up outside my door. But then we'd be big enough to tip the market. People would see our trades move the prices. We'd have information leakage, and we'd lose our advantage. I don't need that. That's why we've kept the heart of Spike a secret ever since I invented it."

"And you think Preston stole it from you."

Some anger finally slips past the ice wall. *<little bastard>* "He *did* steal it. He's taken the knowledge I've spent fifty years building, and is now getting rich from it."

"I thought you said he was in data mining. Not stock picking."

"It's all numbers," Sloan says. "The heart of Eli's business is a piece of software called Cutter. It analyzes the data for him. But the engine that drives Cutter is the same one that drives Spike. The one I built. It can be used on any set of facts, provided you can reduce those facts to computer input. Phone calls, credit-card purchases, social-media posts—my algorithm can find the patterns hidden in all of it. Everything OmniVore does, it's doing on the back of my work. That's the genius of my discovery."

"Again, not to boast or anything."

Sloan waves that off. He doesn't have time for false modesty.

"Still doesn't explain why you've waited two years to go after him," I say.

"If I knew he'd stolen from me, I certainly would have done something about it sooner. I thought my security was adequate. There are no records of any breach. The software behind Spike is located inside secure computers that would have recorded any attempt to hack them. Access is strictly controlled. Every email is monitored. My analysts walk through a scanner and a strong magnetic field on their way into and out of the office, which means I would know if they carried any thumb drives or disks from the office, or they would be wiped clean if I didn't. Then, about six months ago, I received information from one of Eli's former employees. Someone upset with his own pay package, of course. He told me that he'd heard Eli bragging to a client that his computer models were better than Spike—that he'd improved them."

"That doesn't prove he stole them from you."

"No. But Eli's security isn't as thorough as mine. This informant showed me several blocks of the source code Eli uses for Cutter. With a few changes here and there, it's the same as Spike. No question."

He takes a manila folder and places it on the table. He opens it and shows two different printouts. One is marked SPIKE and the other is marked CUTTER. They look identical to me, but only because I can't make sense of either of them. Sloan seems pretty convinced, however.

"So if he didn't download it from you, how was he supposed to steal it? Did he break your security system? Pay off one of your other employees?"

Sloan shakes his head. "No. Again, I would have noticed any breach. I have redundant systems and loyal, well-paid people. He might have been able to corrupt one or two, but not all of them. It would have shown up."

"Then how did he do it?"

"He took my ideas out of here the old-fashioned way—in his brain."

That staggers me for a moment. "Is that even possible?"

Sloan radiates ironclad certainty. There's no doubt in him. "He's smart enough, yes. He read the underlying computer code of Spike, line by line, until he found the algorithm, and then he memorized it. He walked out of here and wrote his own version, and then used it to create Cutter."

I suddenly have a new respect for Preston. He's not just another tech-bro, boy-billionaire douchebag. Smuggling an entire software system out by memorizing it would require both an insane amount of discipline and genius.

"I take it you don't want to go to the authorities," I say.

Sloan makes a face. "Please. They couldn't catch Madoff. You think they'd even understand this?"

Fair point. "So use your own lawyers. Sue him."

"You know that would take years. And it would require exposing all my software to his attorneys as well as the court. What's worse, my own clients would react badly to news of this sort of a data breach. I rely on their confidence. If they were to find out that I'd had my most valuable trade secret stolen—"

"They might take their money to someone else," I finish for him.

"Correct," he says. "Even if I won, years from now, what then? Eli still has my knowledge inside his head. He could simply start over. I'd have to sue him again. The cycle would continue, over and over, and the only people who'd profit are the lawyers. I'm already an old man, Mr. Smith. I don't have the time or patience for this to play out inside a courtroom. I know he's stolen from me. I don't need to be paid for it. Forgive me for sounding Old Testament, but I need him to be punished."

"If you're looking for someone to take out his eye, you could send one of your goons. It would probably be cheaper."

Irritation leaks through Sloan's cool detachment for a moment. *<thought a psychic would be quicker on the uptake>* Out loud, he says, "I don't need you to be a hired thug. I want my ideas back. I want you to recover my intellectual property. And then I want you to scrub every trace of it from Eli Preston's head."

"I can recover the software," I tell him. "I could even get inside his mind to find out how he stole it from you. But I can't wipe out someone's memories permanently."

He gives me a long, hard look. "Mr. Smith. Do you think I enjoy repeating myself? I told you: I know more than other people do. Why would I ask if I didn't already know you were capable of it?"

Another secret. This one I thought was buried deeper than Sloan could dig, honestly.

"Then you must know that's only ever happened once. And it wasn't exactly planned."

Sloan taps his phone. He shows me the island on the screen again. "Well," he says, "for what I'm offering you, I expect you'll find a way to repeat that trick."

I look at the green square surrounded by blue one more time. Peace and quiet and a life of luxury. Everything I've ever wanted, right in front of me. It only takes a second for me to decide.

"All right," I tell Sloan. "I'm in."

[3]

Sloan takes his private jet back. He drops me off at O'Hare on his way out of the country, and suddenly I'm Homer Simpson again, down here with the rest of you.

I spent the night at a business-suite hotel in Sioux Falls, along with Sloan's flight crew. The flight attendant and I found each other at the hotel bar, and then she used my body as impersonally and athletically as a StairMaster. In her mind, I was barely in the room at all. Which, honestly, is the way I prefer it.

I should be in a better mood. But I threw up twice this morning—the chemo trick from yesterday catching up with me—and the Vicodin I swallowed with my morning coffee does nothing to shut out the herds of people in the airport. Now there's pain and anxiety and boredom and discomfort from every person I pass, poking me like thorns. I get caught behind a morbidly obese man with a brand-new knee replacement, buzzing slowly along the floor on a scooter. His whole body is a collection of aches and pains and his thoughts are an ongoing obscene phone call. His fat is like a wet wool blanket, hugging every inch of him under the skin. His fake knee is giving me a real limp by the time I manage to get around him.

The doors to the first-class lounge don't screen out the mental noise, but the anxiety level is lower in here, at least. Most of these people are more worried about making their connecting flight than about how they'll pay next month's credit-card bill. Believe me, that's an easier burden to bear. I start looking for my contact.

Sloan was on his way to Switzerland for a high-security retreat with all the other men who run the planet—that's why he needed the jet. He will be locked down and completely out of touch for the next week or two, as he goes off with presidents and prime ministers to think big thoughts at high altitudes. I can reach Gaines if I need anything, but Sloan also provided one of his employees to go with me on the job. Someone to pay for plane tickets, hotel rooms, and any weapons or supplies I decide I might need: a walking expense account and executive assistant. I asked him what my credit limit was, and he said, "I'll expect a phone call if you buy a yacht. Anything below that is DGAF." DGAF is a technical term in finance, for "Don't Give A Fuck."

I sense her eyes on me before I see her. Twenties. Business suit/skirt combo. Tasteful makeup, unobtrusive jewelry. None of which does a thing to hide the fact that she's stunning. She cuts through the crowd and walks over to me. I feel envy from the other men in the lounge like dirt on the floor underfoot.

"Kelsey Foster," she says. "I'm here to help you with your work for Mr. Sloan."

I take her hand and do a quick surface scan, more out of habit than anything else. I get flashes of the self-image that we all carry with us—the tiny chunks of identity and memory that we use to orient ourselves in the world, to literally remember who we are. I see a tidy apartment more like a hotel room, cool and abandoned due to her constant travel; a Mercedes C-class in the garage that she never gets to drive; and a semiboyfriend who's polite enough to call instead of text before he comes over late at night.

For an instant, I see myself through her eyes. I look a lot better than I do in the mirror. There's a charge of attraction from her, but it's quickly shut down. She's remembering chunks from a dossier given to her by Sloan. I know instantly it's not complete—there's a lot that Sloan didn't choose to include. But some of the details are enough, especially the ones about my personal life.

"And no, I'm not going to sleep with you," she adds with a smile.

"Is that some kind of legal disclaimer you have to give to everyone you meet?"

"Just want to be clear. I know men in your position sometimes expect companionship as part of their fee. I'm not paid to be a mattress topper."

"And what if I am looking for that?"

She gives me a look. *<easy there, Romeo>* "I'm sure you can find your own Internet porn."

"I'm sure I can. Thanks."

"As you asked, I've set up a meeting for you with Preston," she says, smoothly moving on from the unpleasant spot in the conversation. "You're going to be a new employee of Mr. Sloan who's tasked with starting our own data-mining division. You're going to ask Eli to consult on this venture. That should give you a chance to see him face-to-face and do . . . well, whatever it is you do."

She comes out with a folder full of materials and hands it over. "I prepared this for you. Eli Preston's life and times. The highlights, anyway."

I open the file. It's filled with magazine articles, financial statements, and a confidential dossier from a high-priced investigation firm. On top of everything else is an invitation for OmniVore's quarterly corporate retreat.

This explains why we're flying to Pennsylvania, not California. Instead of going to Silicon Valley, where OmniVore is headquartered, we're going to someplace called Gun Hill Ridge, not far from Scranton.

"What's Gun Hill Ridge?"

"It's a hunting preserve," Kelsey says. "They import exotic animals, like wildebeests and zebras and such, or buy them from zoos when they're old and dying. And then they charge guys to come in with guns and shoot them. Go on safari without ever using your passport. That sort of thing."

I read the invite. "'Dress for Serious Play'? What the hell does that mean?"

"No idea," Kelsey says. "It's some kind of team-building exercise. So I suppose he wants his people to kill some big game and then take the skins home as trophies."

"Oh good. A bunch of tech geeks with weapons. Nothing could possibly go wrong there."

"It was the only time I could get you on Preston's schedule."

I close the folder. "Thanks for this. But really, I'll get everything I need out of Preston's head."

Another brilliant smile. "Of course you will." *<this guy's so full of shit> <Everett cannot possibly buy into this lunacy>*

"Look. We're going to work together," I tell her. "It will save some time if you just accept that I can do what I do."

"I didn't say anything," she says. "Oh right. You knew what I was thinking."

"That I'm full of shit."

"Well, now I'm convinced. There's no way you could have guessed that."

"Your pin number is 3510. It was the combination on your Hello Kitty bike lock when you were a kid. Your favorite color is turquoise,"

I say. "And you've never really forgiven your dad for leaving your mom when you were fifteen."

Kelsey goes very still for a moment. Inside, I can see her assimilate this new piece of information. A moment ago, her world didn't include people who can read minds. Now it does, and she smoothly integrates the new reality with only a slight pause. It's like watching a drone lose track of a target and then reacquire it with a radar lock. Not many people can do that. Most people go tripping over new facts like potholes in the concrete, eyes fixed firmly ahead, pretending they don't exist. It's got very little to do with intellect; even people with high IQs can have agendas and issues that act like a blindfold. They spend so much time tending their interior damage that they ignore anything in the outside world that seems even vaguely threatening.

Kelsey's smart enough and has a healthy enough ego that she doesn't need to do that. Her self isn't bound up in always knowing the right answer. She always wants to find the right answer, which is not the same thing at all.

This might sound odd, but she has a great mind. Seriously, I see a lot of them, and I could watch her think for some time.

Unfortunately, she doesn't feel the same way. Her smile vanishes. Her guard goes up so fast I can almost hear the sound of doors slamming.

"Oh, can I play too?" She doesn't wait for me to answer, just takes a theatrical look up and down. "Let's see, you get all your fashion tips from *GQ* and *Esquire*, which is probably your way of compensating for the fact that nobody cared what you looked like when you left for school. You're way too impressed by labels, which means you don't know that the really good stuff doesn't come with a tag and a logo. You haven't woken up to the fact that no man in America under fifty wears a suit and tie every day unless he sells used cars. And you put more thought into your choice of shoes in the morning than whoever you climb on top of at night."

She pauses, looks at me.

"How's that? Pretty close?"

Impressive. Hard to argue with any of it. "Dead-on, actually."

"And I don't even read minds," she says.

"You cheated a little," I remind her. "You have access to Sloan's file on me."

"That's right," she said. "We have very good researchers. But I don't need them to tell me everything I need to know about you. I admit, you're a good-looking guy, Mr. Smith. And yes, I might have used your body for a night or two and we both would have enjoyed it—"

She makes sure I pick up on the past tense there.

"—but now I'm thinking that's not a good idea, since you don't know where the line is between professional and personal."

I hold up my hands, as if to ward off incoming blows. "Hey. You wanted proof."

"No," she says sharply. "Actually, I didn't. I'm capable of working with you whether I believe you or not. Mr. Sloan believes you. That's all I need to know. I'm a little surprised that someone who can apparently do what you do hasn't learned this by now, but sometimes people keep things to themselves. You know why? Because they want to *keep it to themselves*."

Despite her tight control, I get a shot of everything behind that speech: Ivy Leaguers who looked down on her public school education; coworkers she technically outranked asking her to fetch coffee; and the self-designated alpha males who saw her as a decorative place to drain their glands. When Sloan offered her a job, it was like clouds parting. She broke for the sun.

Any time anyone condescends to her, underestimates her, or simply violates her personal boundaries, her shields go up, and she gets ready to fight all the old battles again. And I just did all three.

One of the many other downsides to being a telepath: knowing instantly and with certainty when you've acted like an asshole. I broke into her private life to score a cheap point, which is a lot worse than the countless guys who snuck a look down her blouse when they thought she wouldn't notice.

There's only one thing to do: I apologize.

"I'm sorry," I tell her. "You're right. That was unnecessary."

Her guard is still up, but her hostility recedes a bit. She makes a conscious effort to let go of the grudge. I can feel her releasing it, like opening a clenched fist.

"Apology accepted," she says, with a curt nod. "They're calling our flight. We should go."

She walks away without looking back.

Well done, I tell myself. We're off to a great start.

Once we're in the sky, the background noise recedes. There's still a whole plane full of people, but the tension level drops considerably now that we're on our way. Most of the passengers in first class are asleep or close to it. The only people awake and alert are a couple of plastic surgeons on their way to a conference, discussing this year's jawlines.

And Kelsey. She's busy with her computer and the gray slate of detail it presents. So I get a bourbon from the flight attendant and my copy of *Debt: The First 5,000 Years* from my bag.

Books were the first thing I found that helped me. I went to the library in my elementary school because it was usually deserted; it was easier to screen out the thoughts of the elderly librarian than the chaos of six hundred grade school kids and their overworked teachers. To stay there, I had to read. Word by word, line by line, the focus required for reading built a wall between me and all the stray thoughts ricocheting through the air.

That was my only defense until junior high, when some of the older kids in my group home got me drunk on Zima. I could see they thought it was a joke: <*Hey, let's get the weird kid messed up and see what happens.*> I was sort of curious myself.

Turned out, there should have been trumpets playing "Hallelujah." It was a revelation. I could still read others—better than before in some cases. The noise was still there too. I could still feel other people's pain and see their secrets. I just didn't care. I had a nice, warm cushion of apathy for the first time in my life.

Now booze and books are like old friends. Together they make me feel almost human.

Of course, it can't last.

<*come take a trip in my airship*> <*come take a sail 'mong the stars*>

What the hell?

It's a high, childlike voice, but there are no kids in first class. It takes me a second to place it. It's Kelsey.

She's folded away her MacBook and stares out the window. The song repeats over and over in her head as she looks at the clouds.

<*come have a ride around Venus*> <*come have a spin around Mars*>

It's completely unlike her usual internal tone. She broadcasts a sense of peace even as it gets louder. I almost hate to interrupt.

<*AND WE'LL VISIT THE MAN IN THE MOON*>

Almost.

"Could you not do that?"

My voice breaks her out of her reverie. Her full attention comes back online, along with a healthy dose of suspicion.

"Do what?"

"The singing."

"I wasn't—" She stops. "Oh wow. Okay. Now that's really creepy."

"I'm sorry. I wasn't trying to eavesdrop."

"I told you, you don't have to prove anything to me."

"And I'm not. I swear. It's just very—distracting."

She's having a hard time with this. *<what the actual hell>* But on the surface, at least, she maintains her composure.

"I wasn't even aware I was doing it," she says. "It's just something that goes through my head whenever I'm in a plane—"

"Since you were a kid. I know."

"Of course you do."

"That part of you still sounds like a little girl."

"You're really not making it any less creepy now."

Not much I can do about that. "Some things are harder to block out than others."

"My singing is that bad? Even in my head?"

That makes me laugh. "No. It's all music. Any kind. I find it grating."

She blinks twice while she processes that. "You don't like music?"

People have a hard time understanding when I admit that. It's almost easier to convince them that I read minds. Everyone likes music, right?

No. Not everyone. So I try to explain. "I know people hear something else when they listen to it. I mean, I get that. I can see it. But I've never felt it. It's just annoying to me. Just more noise. It always has been."

She's still not quite able to grasp it. "So what do you listen to?"

"I have enough to listen to. Believe me, it's never quiet."

I can see her imagining what it would be like to hear every stray thought, the way I do. She doesn't like the idea much. "So that's why you want the island."

I nod. “Sloan told you about that?”

“I helped draw up the contract.” She turns in her seat to face me. “Do you mind if I ask you a question?”

Honestly, I’d rather skip this. I see what’s forming in her mind. And I know how I’ll respond, and then I’ll see her response before she can put it into words, and so on. It’s tedious.

But we’re stuck with each other for a while, and we could use the repair work. So I put down my book and try to act like a person who has conversations.

“If it’s so painful for you to be around people, why not just move away from them?” she says. “There are plenty of places where you could go off the grid. Why not just get a cabin in Montana? Why do you need a private island?”

“What’s that suit you’re wearing?”

She looks confused, but answers. “Theory.”

“Why so expensive? You’d be fine in jeans and a T-shirt, right?”

She makes a face. “That’s not the same thing.”

“Yes it is,” I say. “Just because I don’t come from money, don’t assume I don’t know what it means. Money offers its own protections. Your boss already knows this. You accumulate enough, and the world starts to bend in your direction. I could find a cabin in the woods right now, true. But it wouldn’t stop someone else from buying the spot next to me. I want more insulation than that.”

“You need a whole island’s worth of insulation between you and the rest of the world?” She says it with a little smile.

“You’ve never been poor, have you?”

Kelsey recoils physically from the question. “I’m not sure what that has to do with anything.”

“It’s got everything to do with it. It’s the same reason you want your doctor to be trained at Harvard instead of a state school. Or why you shop at Whole Foods instead of the corner grocery. If it costs more, it's generally because it's worth more. And every system we have is set up to protect the people who have more. You've never had to think about that because you've always been on the inside of the fence."

"I was just asking you a question," she says. "You don't have to get personal about it."

"I'm just answering your question," I tell her. "I've been poor. I've done without. I've scraped by. I'm not going to do it again. If I walk away from the world, it's going to be on my terms. And no matter where I end up, I am going to make certain I never have to eat Top Ramen or Hamburger Helper when I get there. Does that help you understand?"

"Yeah," she says. "It does."

I scan her for sarcasm, but I don't find any. In her mind, it's the flat, unvarnished truth.

She's got one last question, and again she means it, without judgment or agenda. "So what happens if you ever need a friend?"

I answer her as honestly as I can. "Wouldn't know," I say. "Never had one."

[4]

There's not a lot I want to say about my childhood. I can't tell you when I knew I was different. It took me a long time before even I realized what I could do.

Language is necessary before we can form consciousness. Or, to put it more simply, we're animals until we learn how to talk. Until we begin to grasp words, we're just little screaming, eating, diaper-filling beasts.

So it's hard to say when I knew I was picking up things from inside other people's minds. I had to learn how to read before I realized I could read minds. I had to learn to talk before I realized I knew the things other people wouldn't say out loud. But I believe I always had my talent, even if I couldn't understand it.

Before I knew any words, I saw colors. I think this was because I simply hadn't learned the framework necessary to put my gift to work. I didn't have language, and without it, my brain sent me messages in the most basic building-block method possible.

Red was pain. Green was the color of fear, anxiety, and uncertainty. Anger I associated with deep violet, which would become almost black as it shifted to rage and violence. Yellow always meant greed and hunger, which were the same things to me. Blue was love.

Most of what I remember of my birth parents is violet and green and black, with occasional highlights of red. There is one time I can remember being held in the arms of someone and feeling safe and warm and protected, surrounded by nothing but blue.

That might have been my mother. Or maybe I'm just imagining it.

Either way, they were gone before I was nine months old. I don't say this for sympathy. It's just a fact. It means I don't have any reliable witnesses to fill in the blanks in my memories. I don't know when I started acting differently from the other kids. Maybe it was there from the start, and that's why my parents exited the picture as quickly as they did.

I can tell you that I didn't speak until I was almost five years old—and then I began talking in complete, grammatically perfect sentences—but I don't really remember why. I suspect it was the way I coped with all the stimuli coming into my brain. I had to sit quietly for a long time to sort it all out. Until I did, the adults in charge of my life thought I might be retarded. After that, I tested in the genius range by most measurements.

But by then, I was already deep in the system for abandoned and unwanted kids.

There are many, many people who join the system because they want to do right by those kids. They want to save them, or at least make their lives a little better. And there are those who are more or less apathetic, who joined up because they needed a job and this was what came along. They're like benign tumors—not actively harmful, but taking up space and resources anyway.

Then there are those who join the system because abandoned and unwanted children are exactly what they want. They look for kids who have been neglected, who will take any attention as a sign of love, who will not complain, and who will not be believed when they do.

A child who doesn't speak, as it turns out, is just perfect for them.

That's why I don't talk about my childhood much. It took me too long to find the right words then. It seems like a waste of time to say anything about it now.

BY THE TIME I got to high school, everyone paid to care about me was pretty much done. I was marked first as a poor candidate for adoption, then a problem child, then a recurrent discipline case. All true, I have to admit. Before I got it under control, my talent made it tough to play along with even the most harmless level of social bullshit. I was the kid who said exactly the wrong thing at the wrong time. What's worse, it was always true.

I couldn't help it. When I was stuck in an evaluation session with social workers, their worst qualities would bleed out from behind the smiles and therapeutic language. I could see the hangovers, the frustration, the anger, the dislike, and worst of all, the indifference. I knew instinctively that many of them simply did not care what happened to me. They couldn't afford to care after working for so long in such a broken world and seeing so many young lives abandoned and discarded. They had retreated into a protective shell of apathy. None of them wanted to be reminded that they'd given up.

There were true believers, of course, real champions who still bled for us and did their best to defend us. Those were the ones I turned to when I discovered things that I could not tolerate in one of the houses where I was dumped with the other unwanted. And they did their jobs, just like they were supposed to.

That didn't mean there were no consequences. You expose a guy who's diddling his kids, or a woman who's drinking away the child-support checks, and sure, someone will apologize and move you along to the next house. But the system will remember. There will be lingering suspicion simply because you were there, in a house that had seemed perfect—or at least, adequate to fill the boxes on the government checklist—when it all fell apart. You managed to expose, even if no one knew how, a flaw that everyone else missed, or agreed to overlook. When it all blew up and people lost their jobs, you were there. Again. That makes you somehow culpable, somehow a part of the problem, because it always seems to happen with you. You become that creepy little kid who's always in the places where things go wrong.

In other words, the system will remember that you fucked with it, that you kept it from running smoothly, no matter how good your reasons. You were not quiet, you did not behave, and you were not to be trusted in the future.

That's why, when I was sixteen, I ended up with the Thompsons. They had a reputation for dealing with troubled kids, for meeting rebellion with impenetrable discipline.

Looking back, I can see they deserved better than me. They were decent, if rigid, people: an older, churchgoing couple who thought it was their responsibility to take in troubled youth and turn us into something more like themselves. They didn't love all the kids they took in—they didn't even like most of us—but their motivations were pure. They never raised a hand or even their voices to us. They had their own money and never spent the checks from the state on anything but our food and clothing.

Still, I could sense their underlying revulsion when they looked at me and the other kids in their care. It tasted like a dirty coin in my mouth. They couldn't help seeing us through a lens of hardened pity and contempt. We were inferior specimens, carrying the sins of our failed parents in our morally weakened souls. Every time one of us screwed up, it only confirmed their judgment. They were good people; we were fallen. They'd do their best, but privately, they thought most of us were already lost.

I could see all this like it was under a halogen lamp, and it pissed me off. I didn't think that they were any better than I was, and I didn't want to be like them.

They tried to keep me in line using the same tough-love approach that had worked for them for a couple of decades. It didn't take. We fought. I cheated.

By then, I'd learned to hide what I could do, but that didn't mean I wouldn't use it. Teenagers are borderline psychopaths under the best of circumstances, and I was not raised in anything like the best of circumstances. So I used whatever advantage I had.

If I was in trouble, I'd reveal my foster siblings' secrets to deflect attention away from myself. Or I'd play on my foster parents' fears and vulnerabilities and set them arguing about the mortgage or the electric bill.

Within a month, everyone had learned, at least on a subliminal level, that as long as nobody bothered me, life ran smoothly. But any attempt to get me to follow the rules or to punish me for any infractions, and a black cloud would descend on the house. Vicious arguments broke out, everyone at each other's throat, suspicion curdling over every stray word or look.

Eventually, they all kept their distance from me, and I did the same with them. I would glide into a room just as other people were leaving, and make my escape the instant I felt someone get within range. As much as possible, I was in the house only to sleep or change clothes. I coasted through school when I bothered to show up, reading the answers straight out of teachers' heads. I'd figured out how to use my talent to scam money and whatever else I wanted. I spent the rest of my free time peeling the underwear off lonely girls who couldn't see through my cheap tricks. (Ever think it would be great to have a boyfriend who would just know what you were thinking? It's not.)

I wore a lot of black, in case you haven't guessed already.

As graduation and legal adulthood came barreling toward me, I knew that, very soon, I would be on my own. I signed up for the army for the same reason a lot of kids that age did: I didn't know what else to do, and there was a war on. They were taking almost anyone then.

Mr. Thompson signed the early-enlistment consent form with something like a stadium cheer going off in his head. He did his best to keep from smiling while he drove me to the bus station. His wife found a corner of sympathy somewhere in her heart for me, and gave me a bag filled with sandwiches and cookies before I got on the bus.

I headed off to basic training, clutching a duffel with everything I owned and that paper sack. For some reason, I couldn't bring myself to eat any of the food inside. I just held on to the bag until the end of the ride. Then, feeling like an idiot, I stuffed it into the first trash can I found.

I TESTED HIGH enough for One Station Unit Training, which is the gateway to Special Forces. I'd heard—wrongly—that Special Forces got better pay and better food. And, idiot that I was, I also wanted to get into the fight as quickly as possible.

As it turned out, that wasn't all I was tested for. I just didn't know it at the time. Millions of high school students in America take the ASVAB, the Armed Services Vocational Aptitude Battery. It's designed to discover your talents, to figure out where you'd best fit in the military—whether you'd be a good mechanic or cook or medic.

It's also got a few trip wires hidden, searching for people with certain tendencies. Some of the questions measured the moral flexibility of a new recruit, looking for responses that might be called sociopathic by some psychologists. Those guys were taken aside relatively quickly, and put on a different career path from the rest of us.

But there were also questions designed to find people like me: people with inexplicable ability, people who know stuff they shouldn't be able to know. They'd been added to the tests way back in the 1970s. Almost nobody answered those questions right.

I hit all of them.

[5]

Kelsey and I go through the usual indignities of renting a car and checking into our business-class hotel. She handles everything so I don't have to deal with the mouth-breathers behind the counters. (Customer service: where a blank stare is your umbrella.)

We drop off our suitcases and change. I'm in jeans and my old army boots. Kelsey meets me in the lobby wearing a soft-shell jacket over spandex gym gear. Hopefully that will do for serious play.

We head toward the rental car. I open the passenger side and pop another Vicodin. "You can drive," I tell her. I've been through two airports today and I haven't shot or disabled anyone, and I'm about to go to work. I need to be unconscious for a while to reboot my brain.

"And they say chivalry is dead," Kelsey says as she gets behind the wheel.

"It's not dead," I say. "It's just taking a nap."

The drive to the preserve takes a little more than an hour. Somewhere along the way, the Vicodin and the whiskey catch up to me, and I drop off to sleep. The last thing I feel is a sense of relief from Kelsey. I don't blame her. It's enough work watching what you say to other people. Watching what you think is a much bigger chore.

I wake up to the sound of Kelsey shutting her car door. We've arrived at the game preserve.

I grew up in the Midwest, so I got all my ideas about the East Coast from Marvel Comics and sitcoms. I thought it was nothing but concrete and high-rises. Then I finally got to see it in real life. Get outside the city limits and you'll find lots of forests and open ground.

The game preserve is in the middle of one of those chunks of wilderness on state land. There's a big dirt parking lot right off the highway, filled with luxury buses and a few other rental cars, with a small bridge going over a stream, leading to the main lodge.

Before we can cross over to the lodge, OmniVore has set up a check-in station. A dozen tech geeks are in line, waiting to go through.

The OmniVore employees look as if they had as much trouble deciphering the invite's dress code as we did. They're in the standard geek uniform, novelty T-shirts on top of jeans or shorts or sweatpants. On their feet, they've got sneakers and flip-flops. Which is probably what they wear to the office too.

Kelsey stands at the back of the line, waiting for me to catch up. As soon as I join her in the crowd, the surrounding buzz of thoughts strips the last bit of grogginess out of my skull.

<fucking cold here should have brought my jacket> <whoa who's that is she a hooker are there going to be hookers> <we are way out in the damn boonies> <maybe I can go back to the bus> <are we actually going to shoot animals that sounds pretty awful actually> <oh shit what if we have to pay the hookers I don't have any cash> <hurry up hurry up really gotta use the toilet man> <whoa wait a minute what the hell is that about my phone>

That last thought is from the guy at the head of the line, a tall, skinny dude with CODER written in binary on his shirt.

"Why do you need my phone?" he says out loud. He probably didn't mean for it to come out like a whine.

The pert blond cheerleader type behind the table gives him a smile. "It's no big deal," she says. "Everyone's doing it."

Which is exactly the wrong message from exactly the wrong person for this guy. It causes flashbacks to another blond cheerleader telling him that everyone on the senior-class trip was going skinny-dipping, so he wouldn't need his swimsuit. I don't need to go any deeper into his memories to see how that turned out.

But the cheerleader has backup. Big guys in OmniVore polo shirts and khakis. Corporate security. One of them steps forward. "No phones," he says, and holds out a small metal lockbox. "You won't need them."

Which actually translates to: OmniVore doesn't want any of this being recorded or photographed. Can't blame them. Too many embarrassing pics from other tech parties have shown up in the media later. It's cost more than one company big chunks of venture capital and punitive damages in court. It only makes sense to keep someone from bringing a miniature piece of evidence-gathering hardware into the event.

The coder knows all this intellectually. Emotionally, it's still difficult for him to put the phone into the box, his fingers sticking to it like they're covered in glue. Like everyone else, he's come to rely on that thing more than his own limbs. This is because of a complex conditioning system that's wired down deep in our brains. We pick up our phones and press a button. And every time it responds with a new email or a text or a funny cat video, our brains release a little burst of dopamine. Pretty soon we're pressing the button every couple of seconds, looking for that next hit. We've turned into those monkeys who were given a lever that delivered cocaine every time they wanted it.

It's worse for guys like the tech geek. His phone is a vital organ that just happens to exist outside his body. It carries his whole world and keeps his secrets. It feeds him data and soothes him when he looks into its screen. I can almost see the string of affection linking him and his favorite toy.

But he still gives it up, because he's got to get into the party, and the cheerleader and the football player are both telling him this is the price of admission. With a little mental whimper, he drops his phone into the box, which I'll bet any amount of money is RF-shielded against all transmissions. The coder gets a claim ticket, and the lockbox goes onto a set of IKEA shelves they assembled in the parking lot just for this.

Every single one of the geeks goes through this same little psychodrama, so it takes us a while to get to the front of the line.

Both Kelsey and I drop our phones in without complaint. I don't have any reason to worry about it. Even if anyone here knows who I am—which they don't—they'd get nothing from my phone. It's encrypted against most of the obvious password-cracking and snooping software. I'd be shocked if Sloan didn't equip Kelsey with the same stuff or better.

We walk up the gravel path to the lodge together.

"You sure this is the way you want to do this?" she asks quietly.

"Why wouldn't I be?"

"It doesn't seem very covert."

"Nothing's going to happen here," I reassure her. "This is just to survey the territory. Get a feel for the state of play on the board."

"If you say so." There's a little more skepticism there than I think is necessary, but she shoves it down and smiles brightly as we enter the lodge.

. . . .

THE PLACE IS huge, decorated in early Great White Hunter straight out of Tarzan movies and Hemingway novels. There are enough dead animals on the walls to qualify for a minor extinction event. The website for the preserve boasts that it offers a chance to hunt every exotic species from "Aardvark to Zebra" and they've got the heads to prove it.

There are more than a hundred OmniVore personnel inside the main room, and they're all on edge. The nervous chatter in the air is nothing compared to the anxiety bouncing around in their brains. It's a cage full of white mice right before feeding time in the reptile house.

<shit there's Noah I owe him a status report> <must have picked up a bug on the flight can't believe they put me in coach> <ha ha ha yeah keep smiling dickhead I'll be running your department next year> <twenty minutes with Preston I could totally sell him on this project> <I really thought there'd be hookers>

They cluster around the bar to self-medicate. Which means that it's too crowded for me to do the same thing. (Dammit.)

At the front of the room is a table and a podium set up for a speech. The anticipation gets thick in the air. I snag a few impressions from some of the longtime employees. Once, when the company was starting out, Preston showed up at one of these retreats and fired half of the people in the room. Another time, he walked in and gave everyone a $20,000 bonus.

Exactly fifteen minutes after the hour, Preston appears. He jogs out from a side door like the host of a late-night show. Preston's employees give him a roar of approval normally reserved for a rock star. I do my usual sweep of the minds around me to see what they really think of him.

This is why I didn't waste my time on Kelsey's carefully assembled profile. That's only paper. It holds only what people are willing to say out loud. But people are good at lying. They do it all the time, especially to themselves. If it sounds especially convincing, they write it down.

But when they see someone in person, they're immediately reminded of their true feelings. And I get a straight shot of what they actually believe, unfiltered by any illusions.

There are dozens of competing impressions of Preston bouncing around the room, carried forward on the waves of fear and hope generated by the crowd. I sift through all of it. It's not easy, but I've had practice at this, and I assemble my own portrait of Preston directly from the memories of his people.

I'm surprised: for the most part, they genuinely love him.

One guy recalls how Preston found him utterly stuck with an error in a compiler—whatever the hell that is—and Preston sat down and they hashed it out together, chugging caffeine until their vision blurred, stuck in front of their keyboards for ten hours straight. Another programmer remembers how he once mentioned he got into Radiohead when he was in college. Preston mocked him mercilessly—he called it "music for the funeral for the death of music"—but then the programmer found a custom playlist in his email, all obscure cuts and bootlegs. There's the customer-development guy, no programming experience, just sales and marketing, who never felt like he fit in. Then Preston praised him in front of the entire company for bringing in the cash that bought all the cool geek toys.

There are a few images of Preston as the abusive dad too. One guy can't forget how Preston screamed at him for nearly an hour over some bad coding—just utterly dismantled him, tore him down to the foundations, and left his ego in the rubble. But the guy blames himself. He mainly feels bad for letting Preston down. Preston forgave him the next day and complimented the repair work he'd done. Now he treasures that moment like the memory of a favorite toy at Christmas.

More than anything else, they think he's cool. And he makes them feel cool. They see him drive up to work in a Bugatti Veyron, and they think <*pretty soon that's going to be me*>. There are a dozen memories of Preston in Vegas, taking them to Spearmint Rhino and dropping tens of thousands of dollars on strippers for everyone. Blowing off a crucial deadline so the whole company could go out and get some sun on the first decent day of spring. Sending a charter jet to pick up Five Guys burgers so they could see what all the hype was about.

Most of these guys—and they're all guys, aside from the hired cheerleaders and Kelsey—remember all too well what it was like to be left out, to be excluded and ignored. No matter what the media says about the geek inheriting the earth, these guys all have a hard diamond of pain buried deep somewhere. They stayed inside when everyone else was on the playground. They will always know, deep down, that there was something that made them strange before it made them valuable.

Preston doesn't suffer that the same way they do. His charisma, his charm, his confidence—it all seems to come from another planet. Right now, at this point in time, everyone in the world wants a piece of him. He could sit at the cool kids' table, if he wanted. And he chooses to hang out with them instead. He blows right past the velvet rope and goes into the VIP section, and he takes them along. He makes the headlines, but they bask in his reflected glory. He's their hero.

Just from swimming around in their pool of memories, I'm starting to like Preston myself.

He's smiling and greeting everyone clustered around him. He

dresses like his people, but there's a cosmetic layer of muscle under his vintage T-shirt; nerds can afford personal trainers now. In one hand, he holds a novelty-toy key chain. He presses a button, and a tinny electronic voice from a computer chip spits out an insult: "Fuckyou! Gotohell! Eatme! Eatme!" He clicks it incessantly, even while he's shaking hands.

This is one of his trademark kinks. He usually carries a gag gift like this—a bottle opener that says "It's beer-thirty!" when used, a coffee cup shaped like a toilet, or a pen that reveals a naked woman when it's flipped upside down.

The business reporters love it. It makes him colorful. One magazine profile about Preston went into detail about this little habit. His grandfather owned a novelty shop, and Preston spent a lot of time there after school while his parents were at work. The article made it sound like a cherished memory. Now he carries these toys as a way of remembering the place where he started.

Preston grips and grins his way through a half dozen more people before putting the key chain in his pocket. He takes his place at the front of the room. One of his flunkies places a black case on the table behind him. He raises his hands and gestures for quiet.

"So," he says to the crowd. "I bet you're wondering why I've called you all here. Well, it should be pretty obvious."

Then he turns and theatrically opens the case. He brings out a combat shotgun. It's a Mossberg 500, popular with the police and the military for busting doors and clearing rooms. I'm betting it's the first time most of these guys have seen one outside of a video game.

Discomfort spreads like a stomach flu through the crowd. "Are we going hunting?" one guy near the front asks.

"Hunting? What makes you think that?" Preston says. He looks around the lodge, as if seeing the dead animals for the first time. "What, you think I want to kill cute little fuzzy animals? Hunt helpless, endangered species?"

He looks around. No answer this time.

"Well, where's the fun in that? Stupid things barely know when to get out of the way of a bullet. Evolution left them behind a long time ago. That's survival of the fittest—you're either fast or you're meat."

That gets a big laugh. Then he shifts the Mossberg into ready-to-fire position, the stock braced against his body, aiming it at them. The laughter dies to nervous chuckles.

"No," Preston says. "I'm going to hunt you for sport."

Silence. He lets it stretch for a moment, then busts out laughing.

The OmniVore employees begin laughing too, even though they're not entirely sure why.

"In fact, you're all going to hunt. Each other. Every one of you gets a fine weapon just like this one. Every one of you will get twenty rounds. And then you'll all be released out there, onto the grounds, and the last man standing will be the winner. Hunt and be hunted. The most dangerous game. The toughest, the smartest, and the strongest will survive."

One of the techs in the crowd tentatively raises his hand. "Like paintball?"

"Paintball?" Scorn oozes from Preston. "Paintball is for pussies. Go to Google—hell, go to Facebook—if you want to play games. You might as well be playing Candy Crush or Angry Birds. We deal in real threats and real results. Every day, out there, when we are facing the unknown scumbags who attack our clients, when we engage with our competitors and enemies in the market, we are not playing games. We don't do trust exercises at OmniVore. We don't do drum circles or sharing time or Pictionary. We are free-range capitalists. We use real guns."

There's a long moment of uncomfortable silence. Preston breaks it with another huge, mocking laugh.

"Oh relax, you guys. Human Resources would have a shit fit if I gave you live ammo. This gun is loaded with beanbag rounds. Totally nonlethal."

That same guy in the front row—clearly a favored employee, to be so close to the boss—speaks up. "Don't the cops use those?"

Preston looks at him blankly. "Yeah. What's your point?"

The guy looks around for support and chuckles. "Well," he says, "won't that—won't it hurt?"

Preston shrugs. "You tell me."

Then he shoots him.

The sound is huge, a thunderclap echoing off the walls and ceiling. The employee goes down with a sudden cry of anguish. Some of the OmniVores scream. A couple even dive for cover.

For a moment, nobody moves. There's a murmur through the crowd. Panic and fear and disbelief, straining against one another.

They realize, one after another, that the howling noise is the guy who was shot. He's wailing in pain. But he's still alive.

Preston gestures, and a couple of guys from security haul the guy to his feet. Tears are streaming down his face. He's bent in half, but they keep him upright.

Preston lifts the guy's shirt. There's a pattern of fat red welts all over his torso, standing out vividly against the flabby white skin. But no blood.

"Yeah, that sure looks like it hurts," Preston says. "Better try not to get shot."

He pulls the guy into a bear hug, and the crowd starts laughing and cheering. Preston shoves him away, and the guards take him over to a medic with an EMT's kit. The shooting victim is helped from the room by the musclemen and the medic. He looks like he's aged twenty years, shuffling his feet along the floor as if he's on thin ice.

Nobody's really paying attention to him now, though. Their focus is back on Preston.

"Of course, I wouldn't expect any of you to take a risk without a reward," he says. "That's the whole point of what we do. So the last man standing, when all the smoke has cleared, he gets one hundred thousand dollars. Not in equity. Not in options. I'm talking one hundred K, *cash*, to whoever wins."

He lets that sink in for a beat. Then he smiles.

"Who's ready to start shooting?"

The crowd lets out an animalistic roar. I feel the consensus wash over them like a wave. This is all part of the game, they decide. Only a loser would complain about the rules.

"Weapons and gear are out front," Preston tells the others. "You get a fifteen-minute start, and then it's every man for himself."

The OmniVores knock back their drinks and stampede for the exit. Preston wades into the crowd, gives high fives and fist bumps to his chosen favorites. He takes the key chain out again.

I step back to where Kelsey is waiting, drink in hand, close to the wall. The OmniVore crew streams past us toward the door. The tide of bodies is bringing Preston slowly in our direction.

His eyes lock on to Kelsey and there's a spike of lust as he recognizes her.

"Kelsey," he says happily, voice booming, walking past two other guys to get to her. "So glad you could make it."

She offers her hand, he takes it and pulls her closer, going for a kiss and hug. She manages to deflect both with a turn that's almost like a Krav Maga move.

"Eli," she says. "Thanks for the invite. I know Everett really appreciates it."

"Well, I'd hoped I would get to see him in person." His voice is still way too loud. He looks at me. "You must be the new errand boy, then."

With that, he turns to me and steps just to the edge of my personal space. It's a frat-boy/Business 101 intimidation tactic, and it's all I can do not to laugh.

Now that Preston is close enough, I realize why he's been shouting since he entered. It wasn't just to reach us in the back. He has foam plugs stuffed in his ears, the same kind they hand out on gun ranges to protect your hearing. He was ready to shoot someone before he even stepped into the room.

He puts out his hand. "Eli Preston," he says.

"John Smith," I say, and take it.

He hits the key chain and smiles. "Fuckyou! Gotohell!"

Then I see it. In his memory: A dingy closet of a store in a mall, almost always empty, every surface covered in thick dust, cheap crap on the shelves that no one ever bought. The looming, sullen figure of his grandfather, who rarely smiled. The other kids who didn't have to work for their money, who came into the store and mocked him. The computer in the back office, a lifeline to a whole other world.

Looks like Preston knows a thing or two about being excluded. And resentment.

He hits the button again. "Gotohell! Gotohell!" His bodyguards are at his shoulder the whole time, watching me, making sure I don't get too angry at the joke.

Up close, I notice something off about them. I expected a couple of bored former cops, hanging around to satisfy Preston's ego. Private security is usually nothing more than a status symbol, another way for rich people to keep score. Despite some of the Occupy Wall Street rhetoric, bullet wounds are an occupational hazard for a dealer working a corner, not executives moving credit default swaps.

But Preston's guys are the real thing. They've got a profile I recognize: cold, constant awareness, ready to hurt someone without hesitation or remorse. They're so fresh from the wars that they still have the faint echoes of gunfire in their heads.

Preston didn't hire them from any rent-a-cop shop. They're PMCs—private military contractors, the kind I used to see babysitting Halliburton execs in the Green Zone. Professional killers, wearing company polo shirts.

They regard me with a little wariness. I don't cast the same shadow as the rest of the people here. But they don't have my gift. They don't see me as anything more than an anomaly. If they did, they wouldn't let me get this close to their boss.

I figure this must be the latest thing in personal protection, and another way for Preston to show off: if Sloan hires ex-military like Keith and David, Preston hires former Navy SEALs.

Fortunately for them, I've got no intention of hurting him yet. Like I told Kelsey, this meeting is all recon, a chance to get a look at the opposition and evaluate. Nothing serious is going to happen here.

So I smile and shake his hand like a normal person and let my talent pick his brain.

He's not as smart as Sloan, but still much higher up the IQ scale than I can climb. I catch a couple of coding problems he's fussing over in the back of his head, and it's like an alien language.

But he's easier to read than Sloan. He has none of Sloan's calm or patience. Preston is all jagged edges and wandering attention. His mind is like a strobe, illuminating one thing for an instant, then flickering to the next.

For the first time, I start to think what Sloan asked might actually be possible. I never doubted I'd be able to get the algorithm back, at least in software form. But wiping out a memory is, as I said, something I've done only once, and not exactly with surgical precision.

Looking into Preston's head, however, gives me some hope. He's got almost no inner resources, aside from his intellect. He's obsessive, which is not the same as disciplined, and he's easily distracted. Given a little time, I can probably grab whatever I need from him.

"So you two know each other?" I say, nodding at Kelsey.

He grins hugely. "Oh yeah. We overlapped when I was at Sloan, didn't we?" He puts more saliva than I thought possible into the word "overlap."

Kelsey's smile turns into a mask. <*wishful thinking, creep*> "We didn't work together," she tells me. "Eli left the company a couple of months after I started."

Preston's barely paying attention to me, spending most of his mental energy picturing Kelsey naked. But it's pretty clear they didn't sleep together, no matter how much Preston wishes it were true. I remind myself that it shouldn't matter to me.

"I was hoping we could talk about you doing some work for Mr. Sloan again," I say. "He's been watching your progress, and he thinks you might be able to help him. He'd like to hire OmniVore to root out a few old, buried secrets."

I get a small charge of triumph from Preston, but no guilt or anxiety.

"Well, we're pretty busy. I don't know if we have the room to take on any new clients right now." He turns to Kelsey. "This is all hush-hush, but you know we're prepping for our IPO. It's not too late for you to come over, get in on the ground floor."

"I like my job, Eli," Kelsey says.

"Working for the old man? Come on. That place is a retirement home."

"I don't think Mr. Sloan will let you steal her," I say.

"She's about the only valuable thing Sloan has," Preston says, then remembers I'm supposed to work for Sloan too. "No offense."

"No fear," I say. "But given how much you took away from your time with him, I think you'd want to hear his offer now. He helped make you what you are today, after all."

There's a prickle of self-righteousness at that. Preston's ego throws up automatic defenses to any suggestion that his success isn't his alone. But again, there's no guilt. I'm tossing plenty of key words that should trigger some kind of response: *buried secrets, steal, fear, took away from him*. And I'm getting nothing. If he did steal from Sloan, he's got it covered well, or he managed to justify it to himself long ago.

He teeters on the edge of a decision, and then his curiosity pushes him over the brink. "Sure," he says. "I can't promise to give a shit, but I'll listen to your pitch."

"That's all I ask," I say. "When?"

"Let's get it over with. The lodge has an office I'm using. Give me a few minutes to get this party started, and then we can talk, cool?"

He turns back to Kelsey without waiting for my response. "What about you, Kelsey? You going to help your boy here? I'd rather listen to anything coming out of your mouth. Or at least watch it while it moves."

For a second, I think she's going to lose it and punch him. I can feel the impulse run down toward her fist. I wouldn't blame her.

Then she surprises us both by saying, "Actually, I thought I'd go shoot a few of your nerds."

That wipes the grin right off Preston's face. "Seriously? You want in on this?"

Her smile is something sharp now. "What, your boys can't handle a girl on the field? Are you scared of me, Eli?"

He laughs. "Hey, knock yourself out. You want to try for the cash, you got it. I guess Sloan's not paying you that well these days. Be careful out there." He looks at me as if he's won some kind of point. "Office. Twenty minutes," he tells me, and then his bodyguards escort him away.

Kelsey finishes her drink and sets the glass down carefully on a nearby table made from the foot of an elephant. She turns to go as well.

I stand in her way. "This is a bad idea," I tell her. "I've had people shoot at me before. Trust me, the novelty wears off pretty fast."

"I can handle myself," she says. "Why shouldn't I take a shot—yes, I know, terrible pun—at a hundred thousand dollars?"

"Because it's idiotic. You could get badly hurt. Take one of those rounds in the face and you might not get back up."

She smiles brightly. "That's assuming they get me before I get them."

I can see she's completely serious, completely unafraid. And the more I argue with her, the deeper she's going to dig.

I step back. "Do what you want," I say. "I'll be here when I'm done with Preston."

"Try not to melt his brain before I get back," she says.

"I told you. Nothing's going to happen."

She walks away, and I watch her go.

All right. Let her have her version of fun. She'll be fine. And besides, protecting her is not part of my job.

I KNOW WHY Preston wanted time before he met me. He needs to run me through his databases. He'd be an idiot if he didn't.

I felt one of his goons snap a picture of me with his phone earlier. It's the same tingle I get when someone looks at me through a gunsight. I could have spoiled it easily, but I want him to have my photo.

With Kelsey's help, I've already got a full cover ID. My fake credit report lists me as an employee of Sloan's firm, and I've got a fake address with a fake mortgage. My fake credit-card numbers lead to a full purchase history—copied and pasted from another guy's account—so that even if Preston uses his data-mining software, he'll find a complete record. I checked it out on Kelsey's laptop on the plane. Apparently I spend a lot of money on dog food.

It's enough to stand up to whatever Preston can throw in twenty minutes. I don't think he's going to look at me too closely, because he wants to believe that Sloan would come to him for help. It's a chance for him to be smarter than his old boss, to show that he was always the bigger brain.

I'm counting on that. I want Preston to treat me like any other prospective client. The full sales pitch, complete with a tour of his operation and expense-account dinners. That should be plenty of time for me to figure out a way inside his computers and his head.

In the meantime, I get a drink from the lodge's bar—which is finally empty of brogrammers and the math club—and then go out to the porch to watch the games begin.

The air is already filled with flat, hollow booming and shouts of surprise and pain; the music of idiots with shotguns.

Most of the OmniVore employees have scurried into the forest like overfed squirrels, but there are still a few stragglers. There's a rack of guns, mostly empty now, next to a big table of boxed beanbag ammo. Some of the employees are still struggling to load their weapons, which makes them easy targets for the guys who figured it out first.

One tech in a classic Atari T-shirt fumbles with his shells, spilling them all over the ground. Another guy wearing a Doom shirt comes up behind him and aims from about ten feet away.

"Ah come on, man," Atari Man shouts. "No fair! No camping!"

Doom Boy pulls the trigger anyway. The recoil catches him by surprise, and his first shot goes wide. The beanbag round knocks a bunch of boxes off the table. Atari still can't get his gun loaded. Doom Boy walks about five steps closer, aims more carefully, then fires again.

Atari starts running, but he gets hit anyway. He screams in pain, then starts cursing Doom Boy.

Doom Boy sees me on the porch and considers raising his shotgun.

"I'm not playing," I tell him.

He smiles as if that's a joke. "Everyone's playing, dude," he says, and starts to aim.

I don't even put my drink down. I give him a hard stare, with a small sense of some of the things I've seen behind it.

"Don't make me tell you again," I say.

He blanches, not sure why he's suddenly got a picture of a sucking chest wound and the screams of wounded men stuck in his brain. He lowers the gun and shudders, backing away from me slowly. Then he jogs into the woods surrounding the lodge, looking for easier targets.

Behind me, I sense Preston's bodyguard before the man politely clears his throat.

"Mr. Preston will see you now," he says. I turn to follow.

Meanwhile, Atari hauls himself to his feet and limps to the medical tent, which Preston thoughtfully set up on one side of the lodge. I hope he brought lots of paramedics. Somebody's going to get hurt.

I'm glad I'm going inside, where it's safe.

. . . .

THE SECURITY GUY walks in front of me, his mind stuck in neutral. *<hotel better have a decent bar is all> <wonder what the local situation is like> <got the morning shift for a change thank God> <maybe I can finally get laid>*

He opens the door for me, and I get a jumble of impressions. The office is decorated the same way as the lodge, only with photos of dead animals instead of their actual corpses. Which is fortunate, or there wouldn't be enough room for Preston and the five large men inside.

The bodyguards have a kind of relaxed vigilance. They're not expecting any problems from me, but their training won't let them slack off completely. They run through the motions. One is behind me, next to the door, and my escort takes a position opposite him. Two more on either side of me and one guy behind Preston at the desk. They check my posture and my attitude and box me in neatly without being obvious about it.

Preston doesn't look at me. He's got three different laptops up and running. I can't see any of the screens, but through his eyes, I see my profile picture and my fake LinkedIn page on the first computer. He's got queries running on the other two.

He says, "Have a seat," and points to the empty chair in front of the desk.

It's upholstered in zebra. I wonder if I can remain standing without seeming rude. He finally turns and stares at me, waiting. I sit down.

"So, do you know what we do at OmniVore?" he asks.

Ah. So this is where he proves how smart he is. "Data mining."

A snort of contempt. "Yeah. But what does that mean?"

When I hesitate, he smirks. *<I knew it> <moron>* "Let me explain it to you, then. We've got a proprietary algorithm—" He pauses when he sees the blank look on my face. "That means we have a piece of software called Cutter. Does that make it easier for you?"

I nod.

<*Christ, what a retard*> Preston thinks, and then continues. "What Cutter does is search through any big collection of data and find the patterns. Like, let's take you for example. John Smith."

He punches a few more keys on one of the laptops. "Very common name. But by cross-referencing that with what we already know, your age, your occupation, we can get more detail. We can find your address. We can find how much you owe on your mortgage."

He's typing faster now. This is where we see how well the cover ID holds up.

"We can even take your biometric information—that's the photo we snapped of you earlier, hope you don't mind—and run it through law enforcement databases, in case you're using a false name. We can learn stuff about you that even you don't know. I can tell if you had a bad piece of fish by checking your restaurant bills against your purchases of Imodium and toilet paper—"

He stops again. Then there's a sudden, tectonic shift in his mental landscape.

A window just popped open on his third laptop. He scans the information—I can't get all of it, because *damn* he reads fast—but suddenly he's on high alert, adrenaline spiking through his veins.

He leaps up from his chair so quickly he knocks it over. The bodyguards are confused, but they snap to attention.

"Get him the fuck away from me! Get him out of here! Now!" The smirk is gone. He's genuinely afraid of me. His mind is jumping all over the place. He's on the verge of panic.

I'm caught flat-footed, trying to sort through his racing thoughts.

I get only a glimpse of what he saw on the screen before it vanishes in the rush: TWEP TWEP TWEP.

It's a phrase I recognize from my CIA days: Terminate With Extreme Prejudice.

And Preston knows it too. I can see the thought form, without hesitation.

He's going to have them kill me.

The bodyguards move in on me, all at once.

CONFESSION TIME: I'M not a great fighter. This isn't false modesty. My instructors in hand-to-hand combat would have given me a B-minus on my best day.

These guys have had the same training, and they're better than me. They know how to use their muscle. They know to get close and throw quick, devastating blows. They will aim for nerve clusters, masses of blood vessels, the fragile edges of bones, the tender spots in the neck and gut and face.

Their minds suddenly sharpen, and deadly intent forms. I'm a threat now, and they're going to remove me. They're not out to win. They're out to disable.

Fortunately for me, it's almost impossible to hit a guy who can see a punch when it's still just a bad idea. I know every move an opponent is going to make before the nerve impulse reaches his muscles.

The guy on my right is closest and steps forward. My escort moves away from the door to back him up. The guy on my left pulls a pistol from a concealed-carry holster under his polo shirt.

This might seem like an odd time for a fashion note, but I wear a Baume & Mercier Capeland on a steel band around my wrist. A lot of guys in my profession prefer something made of black impact-resistant plastic because they think it looks cooler. They like the dials and timers and pulse counters and pedometers or whatever else can be crammed under the Nike logo. I did too, when I first joined the service. Then I noticed that Cantrell and all the other old-school operators wore something high-dollar and metal around their wrists, usually a Rolex. I asked him why.

That was the first time I ever made him proud. I could feel it. It was the right question.

"First place," he told me, "it looks better."

Then he got into the other reasons.

Like Cantrell's Rolex, my Baume & Mercier is powered by the movement of my wrist, so there's no battery to go dead. It has luminous hands, rather than an LED that lights up at the accidental press of a button, so it will never reveal my position in the dark and make me a target. And it's worth money. You can pawn it if you're out of cash, use it as a bribe, or trade it if you don't have any of the local currency.

But best of all, it weighs about a third of a pound, which is the same as the head of a hammer. With practice, I've learned to pop the clasp and let the watch drop around my fingers one-handed.

I turn into the guy on my right and swing as hard as I can with my left fist, which now has the watch wrapped around it like a set of brass knuckles.

He runs right into the punch. His head snaps back, his eyes roll up into his head, and his knees buckle.

The crystal on my watch doesn't even break. Swiss engineering at its finest.

I duck the arm of my escort as he tries to grab me around the neck, then fire a kick into his midsection that bends him double and knocks the wind right out of him. His body becomes an obstacle for the other two on that side of the room.

The guy on the left has his gun out now. I send him a message, as hard as I can:

<Safety's on.>

He's a professional, so some part of him knows he didn't do anything that stupid. But his eyes dart down by reflex, just to make sure.

The instant he looks, I get my foot under the zebra-skin chair and kick it at him. It hits him dead center, tangles with his legs, and he goes down.

With the gun off me, I've got enough time to focus my thoughts, which is bad news for everybody else in the room.

I don't have to touch my forehead or gesture dramatically like psychics or magicians. I just have to think hard.

No time for anything cute, so I light up the amygdala region of their brains, which, among other things, regulates fear and emotion.

And suddenly everyone except me is on their knees or their backs, gasping for air. It's like a needle of adrenaline, plunged right into the carotid artery. You choke on your own breath. Your blood pressure shoots so high you can hear your own pulse behind your ears. Your arms and legs turn to jelly. Your gut clenches and you taste stomach acid at the back of your throat. Your skin feels like it's on fire. You're drowning in your own sweat, and for a few moments, all you know is that you are going to die.

I get a percentage back, as always, but I'm ready for it. It only makes me breathe a little harder. It's a neat trick. I'd pull it more often, but an army cardiologist once told me it does bad things to my EKG. I don't want to drop dead of a real heart attack while giving someone else a fake one.

While they're down, I need to get out of this room. But first, I want to know why this went pear-shaped in less than five seconds.

I reach for the third laptop, the one with the message. My fingers are on the edge of the screen when Preston's hand comes up and slams it closed.

He's looking at me with pure terror etched on his face, but he still wants to protect that information. Something on that computer scares him more than I do.

So I get scarier. I reach under my shirt and take the Walther P99 from my waistband. The people at the check-in were so concerned about our phones they didn't think about weapons.

I aim the gun at Preston's face. I have time for one question: "Why? Is this because you stole from Sloan?"

He just stares. I didn't expect a verbal answer. I want the involuntary response, the reason delivered bright and clean from his head.

Then his closest bodyguard shakes off his fear faster than I thought possible—stupid of me, guy's been in a war zone, of course he does—and tackles me.

He's still not 100 percent, so I keep him from getting a decent grip anywhere, but he won't let go.

Preston watches while we struggle, a stream of thoughts pissing out of his brain and splashing all over, none of it making much sense. I download it from him as fast as I can, and hope I get a chance to sort it out later.

I'm out of time. I've got maybe twenty more seconds before the others regroup. Worse, they're all between me and the door.

But there is a window behind the desk.

I plant my feet, bend my knees, lift, and throw—and send the bodyguard flying right through the glass.

It's only in the movies that the hero crashes through a window without major blood loss. Double-paned glass cuts deeper than knives.

The guy gets chopped up bad. I feel the shards slice cleanly through skin and muscle, all the way to the bone.

But thanks to him clearing a path, I'm able to dive through with only a few scratches.

I hit the porch outside and roll and come up running.

Behind me, I hear Preston shout, "Shoot him! Kill that son of a bitch!" He's not being careful now. He doesn't care who hears him.

Neither do the guards.

There's almost no pause between the order and the shot. A bullet splits the wood of the lodge's outer wall a couple of feet from my head.

Rather than run toward the parking lot, where we left the car, I sprint into the woods. It only looks like I don't know what I'm doing. Even as I'm running I am thinking hard, putting it together as fast as I can. Out of that tangled, crazy mess of thoughts behind Preston's eyes, I was able to get two things clearly.

First, he wants me dead, and he's got men who will carry out his orders. There are a lot of sociopaths in corporate America, but even if they want to, they can't kill everyone who annoys them. Your average CEO usually doesn't have trained soldiers on his payroll.

Preston does. Worse, he went from zero to murder in nothing flat. As soon as he got that message on his screen, he made the decision to kill me without hesitation.

And not just me.

That's the second thing I picked up: he's going to kill Kelsey too. Because she's the only witness who can connect us.

Whatever is going on here, Preston is hiding much bigger secrets than stealing an algorithm.

I seriously underestimated this guy.

Now I have to make sure that Kelsey doesn't pay the price for that.

. . . .

It's easy enough to avoid the OmniVore people as I search for Kelsey. Their minds wail like sirens in the distance, broadcasting excitement and fear and greed. Whenever they get close, I step behind a tree and wait as they huff and puff away.

Kelsey is a little harder to track than I expected. Her mind is quieter. She's actually stalking the others out here, her attention focused, her guard up. She's a lot better at this than I would have thought.

I catch up to her on the edge of a clearing in the woods. Bright sunlight with deep shadow on either side. The clearing is exposed, but the way around it could hide any number of people.

So Kelsey heads out into the open, moving as fast as she can across the ground. She'd rather force someone to take a shot at her from cover than stumble across them in the woods. She's minimizing her risk. Pretty smart.

The problem is, I'm not the only one tracking her, and she's running right into an ambush.

Two guys wait for her on the other side of the clearing. One I recognize from the office. He pulled the gun and took the shot at me. Long hair, wearing Oakley sunglasses now that he's out in the sun. The other is new to me. He's wearing the same OmniVore polo and khaki combo, like he's out for a round of golf. But the polo doesn't quite cover the ugly tattoo creeping up his neck.

He had to have gotten that after he was discharged. No way they would have allowed something that distinctive on someone in covert ops.

They're maybe thirty feet from my position, partially obscured by all the leaves and branches. Then they move deeper into the brush, disappearing from sight. They're both carrying Mossbergs, like everyone else in the woods. But theirs have live ammo.

Their plan is right up in the forefront of their minds. Sneak up on Kelsey and me, unload their rounds, and then split and wait for someone else to find the bodies. The aftermath handles itself: a tragic accident, a mix-up with the shotgun shells. With the blame spread out over a hundred suspects, no one would ever expect this to be solved.

They're going to wait until Kelsey is right in front of them, and then they'll start shooting. Even if she does shoot back, her shells are nonlethal. They think they're safe.

Unfortunately for them, they're not the only ones with real bullets.

I feel their thoughts ping back from the trees. I close my eyes and focus like I'm getting an image from radar.

Then I fire.

Three-shot burst.

A sudden flare of pain, an instant before a scream. The first one is down.

Second man running now. Neck Tattoo emerges from the trees. Determined to close the gap between him and Kelsey, get on top of her, finish the job.

I don't need my talent this time. Just fire. Three-shot burst.

Neck Tattoo pitches forward from the brush and lands facedown, right in front of Kelsey.

I emerge from the tree line a dozen feet away. She's frozen in place, her mouth open.

I cross the distance between us quickly. "You all right?" I ask.

She doesn't reply, just gapes at the gun in my hand. Then she looks down at the guy with the neck tattoo, on the ground, unmoving. His polo shirt is open enough to see the details of the ink work on his skin. It's an old-fashioned Vietnam tat, something from way before his time. A snake winding from the mouth of a skull wearing a green beret. Snake Eater. He must have had a relative in Special Forces way back when. Or he likes old movies.

I'm getting a screech of panic from her. She doesn't know that these men were carrying live rounds. She thinks I just killed an OmniVore employee in cold blood.

She stands there, staring at me in shock and horror.

"No, wait—" I say.

Then the long-haired guy emerges from the woods, Oakleys gone. I see three holes in his polo shirt, and deformed Kevlar underneath. He shines with pain like a spotlight. I cracked a couple of ribs, but the vest saved his life.

I knew both of the guys were wearing body armor. I could feel it chafe. So I aimed for center mass to put them down without killing them. I just didn't think either of them would recover this fast.

He raises his shotgun.

I aim past Kelsey, at him. She turns and sees, and my mental download of information hits her.

It's mostly just images and feelings, but it gets the point across: *<They're trying to kill us both.>*

She lifts her shotgun. We fire almost simultaneously.

Her shot catches him in the chest. Mine takes him in the neck.

He doesn't get up this time.

Kelsey drops her gun. I can see the realization begin to blossom in her mind. People are trying to kill her. That's a good reason for anyone to curl into a nice little ball of panic.

But Snake Eater is still breathing, and I don't want to be around if any more of Preston's goons find us.

So I grab her and pull her along until we're both running as fast as we can on the uneven ground.

We've got to get out of here.

[6]

There's always been a fundamental divide in military thinking. One side believes that wars are won by the army with better soldiers. The other side believes wars are decided with better weapons.

The better-weapons side has been winning the argument for the past hundred years or so. In World War I, the Germans had the best-trained soldiers in the world, the product of years of tradition and schooling, thousands of young men raised for nothing but combat. And they were wiped out, wave after wave, by machine guns and poison gas, as if they were mere mortals like anyone else. After that, World War II showed that you could erase whole cities with one bomb. Soldiers, to these people, have been reduced to the meat left on the battlefield as a way of keeping score. They believe our defense budget is best spent on cruise missiles, drone strikes, and orbital lasers.

But the better-soldiers side points to conflicts like Vietnam, where it didn't matter how many tons of bombs and napalm we dropped on the enemy. They put their money on Special Forces, and turncoats buried deep in the enemy's headquarters, and highly trained covert operatives. They believe that the right man in the right place can change the course of a war.

That group is the reason, more or less, that I exist. Along with a man named Wolf Messing.

Messing was a Russian psychic and showman who lived in Moscow in the 1950s. There are a lot of people who will tell you now that he was a fraud. Maybe he was. But if that's the case, he was a fraud who managed to fool Sigmund Freud, Albert Einstein, the Gestapo, and most important, Josef Stalin.

Stalin, for you illiterates who can't remember anything before Kim met Kanye, was the absolute ruler of the Soviet Union and one of the great butchers of the twentieth century. His body count has been estimated as high as ten million, and that's not including the people who died in famines or in the massive prison system he created during his rule. People whispered his name, as if he would appear like Satan and drag them off to the gulags personally. He could not have been more terrifying if he slept on a bed of skulls and drank blood for breakfast.

And even he was scared shitless of Wolf Messing.

Messing was performing every night for the Russian elite then, and Stalin had heard stories about his psychic abilities: how he'd escaped the Nazis in Berlin by convincing his jailers to open the cell door and lock themselves inside; how, as part of his act, he walked into the state bank of Moscow and convinced the manager to hand over 100,000 rubles, no questions asked; how he knew your deepest, darkest secret the moment he met you.

Stalin decided to test Messing. A couple of men in dark suits from the KGB showed up at Messing's theater one night and told him that the glorious leader wanted to see him at 1:00 P.M. the next day. The only catch: Messing had to get past the guards first. He was ordered to use his abilities to try to get into the Kremlin without the proper authorization. No big deal: just walk into one of the most heavily guarded buildings on the planet without papers or an escort.

To make it even more interesting, Stalin gave his men photos of Messing and ordered them to shoot any intruder on sight. If Messing failed the test, he'd be dead.

But the next day, at 1:00 P.M. sharp, Stalin looked up from his desk—and Messing was standing there. Close enough to touch Stalin—or put a bullet into him, if he wanted.

Stalin demanded to know how Messing pulled it off. Messing said he projected the words "I am Beria" into the minds of everyone who saw him. When they looked at him, walking past the guards, down the halls, they didn't see the unassuming little Jewish man. Instead, they believed they were seeing the head of the Russian secret police, possibly the only man in Russia more frightening than Stalin.

Stalin never let Messing get that close again. But he began pouring a lot of money into psychic research. The Soviets reportedly came up with agents who could make themselves invisible, who could implant ideas into the minds of other people, who could pinpoint the positions of America's top-secret missile silos just by looking at a map. They had one woman, Nina Kulagina, who was supposed to be able to move small objects, coins and dice, with the power of her mind alone. That doesn't sound like much, until you think about all the tiny, vital things inside the human body—like, say, a blood vessel inside the brain, being squeezed like a balloon until it pops.

Once the CIA and the army heard about Messing and the other Soviet psychics, they panicked. This was back when the Soviet Union was still something to be feared. There was only one satellite in the sky then, and it had a red star painted on its side. American kids hid under their desks during H-bomb drills, ready for atomic war to break out at any moment. The best and brightest in the government were not about to let the United States fall behind in any race with the Russians. In 1953, Allen Dulles, the head of the CIA, told a group at Princeton that "mind warfare is the great battlefield of the Cold War, and we must do whatever it takes to win."

So, in the grand tradition of the CIA, they began throwing millions of dollars at the problem. They sent recruiters out to séances and carnivals all over America, looking for psychics who could match the ones at the Soviets' Brain Research Institute. They started Project MK-ULTRA, which dosed unwilling subjects with LSD in an attempt to control their minds or awaken paranormal abilities. They created Project Star Gate, which was supposed to use remote viewers to pinpoint hidden Soviet military installations through ESP.

None of it worked. At least, as far as the public ever knew.

There's a reason you hear only about the CIA's failures. By definition, if a covert operation is successful, no one will ever know about it. But for decades, we've learned in painful detail all the ways the CIA has stepped on its own dick: the failed Cuban invasion at the Bay of Pigs; attempts to kill Castro with exploding cigars; smuggling cocaine to pay for weapons for anticommunist rebels in South America; "slam-dunk" intel on Iraq's WMDs.

And things like Star Gate and Project Jedi and the First Earth Battalion. High-ranking officers were told they could walk through walls if they concentrated properly. Special Forces soldiers were told to focus their inner chi until they could kill a goat by staring at it. Others sat in a run-down building on the grounds of Fort Meade, racking their brains for visions of Russian submarines. They didn't even have the budget for coffee; they had to bring their own.

Things like this make the CIA look like Chris Farley in an old *SNL* rerun, stumbling through the living room and smashing all the furniture; a bumbling, barely functional, mostly harmless clown.

Nobody sees the men and women behind the dictator who has a fatal heart attack, or the coup right before the crucial election, or the bigmouthed union leader who vanishes from his bed in the middle of the night. Nobody suspects the clown.

John Wayne Gacy used the same trick, until they found all the bodies in his basement.

There's the cover, and then there's the real work. In my case, Star Gate was the cover, the exploding cigar designed to make a lot of noise and smoke.

My group did the real work.

I THINK IT must have surprised them, when my test results showed up. Maybe it had been so long since they'd found someone like me through the exams that they had to get orders from higher up in the chain of command. It certainly took them long enough to come find me.

Or maybe they only went back and looked at my tests after what happened with my drill sergeant.

SERGEANT LEARY WAS a throwback, a draftee during Vietnam who opted to become a lifer. He was something prehistoric compared to the kids who'd seen the towers fall and then signed up for revenge and college tuition. There he was, quietly grinding out his time at Fort Benning, and then, suddenly, he was expected to teach a bunch of children raised on Nintendo how to fight in the real world.

I did my best to avoid him. I was arrogant, but I wasn't completely stupid. I knew that the army wasn't the place to test authority. It wasn't high school anymore. So I wrapped my usual attitude tight and kept my head down. I was determined not to be noticed. I wanted a fresh start, without my talent separating me from everyone else. I wanted to be human.

It didn't matter.

Leary made me the squad's official scapegoat. If we had to do extra miles on a run, it was because I was dogging it. If we failed inspection, it was because I was sloppy. Or I looked at him the wrong way during lineup. That sort of thing. At first I told myself it wasn't personal. Get a group of humans together and basic primate politics take over: someone will be the class clown, someone else will be the teacher's pet. I got to be the designated punching bag. A big silverback gorilla like Leary would shove people into these roles if nobody took them. It's a quick and dirty way to get a bunch of strangers to think of themselves as a unit. Even I knew that.

Then it turned into something uglier. For me, Leary tapped into a reservoir of cruelty that probably surprised even him.

He singled me out for every humiliation. I was the practice dummy during hand-to-hand combat for the entire squad. I ran extra miles. I did push-ups until I was facedown in the mud. I hit my bunk bruised and bleeding every night, long after lights-out, usually because I was finishing some punishment detail, and then woke before reveille to see Leary's face as he shook me out of bed to start the cycle again.

Before long, everyone else in my unit picked up on this hostility, and they reflected it back. I didn't blame them. Anyone who made even a small gesture of friendship in my direction found himself punished along with me.

I'd seen this sort of reaction before. There are people who respond to my talent instinctively and violently. It sets off some primitive warning system, deep down in their brain, that lets them know I'm invading their privacy just by existing. Leary wasn't anything close to sensitive, but he'd spent time in combat, and he had a pretty well-honed sense of survival. It was like he smelled something on me. Maybe he had some kind of evolutionary defense against people like me, a built-in alarm that went off when it detected someone who could intrude into all his dark places.

Whatever the reason, he knew right away there was something different about me. And he hated it.

I tried my best to stay out of his head. I figured I could survive whatever he threw at me, then I would be out of his life after ten weeks. Getting inside his thoughts would only make things worse.

That was the plan, anyway.

Then, near the end of Blue Phase, the section right before graduation, Leary pulled me aside one night after dinner. He took me into a nearby restroom, which is what he called his conference area. This wasn't unusual. He'd scream at me for a while and order me to clean toilets or pick up litter on the parade grounds in the dark. I could handle it. I thought the end was in sight.

This time, he was quiet. No screaming. With a grim, clipped satisfaction, he told me that my scores were inadequate for advancement. I wasn't ready to move on to individual training. I'd have to repeat basic. With him.

My self-control crumbled. Rage shot right through me, along with disbelief and, I admit, a strong need to wail like a toddler. I wanted to know why he just kept picking on me. I let my guard down in that moment, and peered inside his head.

I saw it all clearly. He'd falsified my scores to keep me in basic. He'd do it again, and again, and again, if he had to, until I dropped dead on the parade ground. He wanted to grind me down into nothing. He wanted to break me, reduce me to a beaten animal. It had to be him, personally. And he didn't even know why.

But I did. I blew past all of his thoughts about me, and saw the reason that he feared me, that he feared any kind of exposure.

I got only glimpses. I didn't have the kind of control I do now.

He was nineteen. A private in Vietnam. A smell of burning flesh, mingled with *nuoc mam*. A young woman, almost childlike, a black wing of hair over half her face, bright red blood covering the rest. Leary's hands, shaking, spattered with the same bright red. A burst of sudden dark shame, mingled with an unhinged joy. For a brief moment, he and his friends had become animals—worse, they had become monsters.

The massacre was never officially recorded. His superiors buried the bodies, and Leary began to bury the memories. But they always lurked, in the back of his head with the real secret, the one he'd barely admit, even in his darkest moments: He felt no guilt. He liked it.

I saw that was why he had stayed in the army for life. Jesus might have required some kind of repentance to forgive him, but the army didn't. It took his greatest sin—every horrific, vicious second of it—and embraced him for it, drawing him closer than ever. From that moment on, the army was his god.

I came back out of his head, reeling, and we locked eyes for a moment.

Until that point, I had never consciously projected into another person's mind. I didn't know how. There were probably times when my thoughts radiated out to anyone nearby, but it was a weak signal, like the sound of two calls overlapping on a cheap phone.

At that moment, however, I was linked with Leary. I peered right into his mind, and then I sent back all the fear and disgust and contempt at what I found there. For that split second, my thoughts washed into his, crashing into that small place he thought was his and his alone—and he knew. He knew that I'd seen.

Without another thought, he tried to kill me.

I'd been beaten before. As a kid. On the playground. By foster parents. That was amateur hour. This was the dedicated work of a professional.

He grabbed my ears and dented the steel mirror above the sink with my head. He punched something below my sternum and I stopped breathing. I lifted an arm to defend myself and he twisted it into a spiral, breaking it so fast I heard the snap before I felt the pain. In a moment, I was on the floor, feeling my ribs crack as he kicked me.

I cast out desperately with my mind, hoping to find someone on their way to help, or even someone on their way to take a leak. All I got from the small crowd outside the door was fear. Nobody wanted to interrupt. No one was even sure if they should. There might have been an urge, in one or two of the people listening to him beat me, to find someone of higher rank to break it up.

But by the time one of them managed to overcome his indecision, I'd be dead. Leary meant to murder me. I could feel his hatred, burning like the heat from an oven. And I felt something I'd only seen in his memory before: that same unhinged joy he felt in Vietnam, his pure unalloyed delight that he was about to kill something with his bare hands—again—and no one would be able to stop him.

I don't know exactly what happened next. Only that I've never done anything remotely similar since.

The last thing I remember clearly is one of Leary's big leather boots coming for my face, blotting out the light from the lamp. He was old-school, so he laughed at what he called our "tenny-runners," the lightweight desert BDU footwear. He still wore steel-toed combat boots.

I fixed on that boot. If it hit me in the face, I was done. I knew it. My skull would crack, and my brain would bleed, and everything I was, or ever could be, would die right there.

It was nothing conscious. It was, I think now, the only attack I had left. My final defense.

I lashed out with everything I had inside, everything I'd ever contained, every wound I'd ever suffered in silence. The abandonment I'd felt before I could form words. The abuse at the hands of people meant to care for me. The paranoia and suspicion from the other kids forced into proximity with me. I gathered all those years of fear and rage and pain and hate from the place they burned in my mind, and unleashed them in one primal, silent scream.

The boot never connected. I heard Leary sink to the floor, like he was sitting down for a rest, but I couldn't see him. One eye had already shut, and I couldn't move my neck. I lay there, curled in a ball for what seemed like a long time. It was very quiet.

Someone finally opened the door to check on us. I heard a voice say, "Holy shit."

I slid into unconsciousness.

WHEN I WOKE up in the infirmary, I was handcuffed to the railing on my bed. Not strictly necessary. My head felt like a cracked egg, with the yolk dangerously close to slopping out. One eye was still swollen shut, and I could barely move without pain lancing through every part of me.

There was someone waiting for me. A young guy, in anonymous BDUs, no name tape, no rank. He noticed I was up, and left the room without speaking to me.

I might have blacked out for a little while again. The next thing I knew, there was another man sitting next to me, older and heavier.

"You back among the living, son?" he asked.

I blinked and focused on him as best I could. He was wearing the same black BDUs as the other guy, and his hair was sloppy and slicked back. But there was no question he carried some kind of rank. It was like a soft cushion of authority all around him.

It wasn't just hard for me to see. It was hard to read anything. The man was basically a blank to me. That was a little frightening.

It took me a moment to realize that it wasn't just him. I couldn't hear any of the usual mental babble from anyone.

I found out later I had a concussion from where Leary used my head to dent the mirror. The pain made it hard to think too. The medical staff had decided to ignore the doctors' orders for painkillers. The pain and the head injury had shut my talent down. It was both amazing and terrifying. I suddenly knew what it must be like to wake up blind or deaf.

I wanted to lie back and enjoy the silence for a while, but the man in black kept staring at me, waiting for me to respond. I didn't know what to say. Without my talent, I had to rely on the same clues as normal people. I looked him in the face. He had the kind of regular-guy good looks that instantly inspired trust. I could see him behind a desk in a bank in Iowa, telling some elderly couple not to worry about the mortgage payment. You could fool a lot of people with a face like that.

"Who are you?" I asked. Not exactly brilliant, but it seemed like a pretty safe question.

"You want to tag a 'sir' on the end of that question, Private?" he shot back. There was a gunslinger drawl tingeing his voice like the smell of BBQ and horse manure.

I used my one good eye to take a long scan over his no-name, no-rank uniform. "Why should I?"

The stern look on his face vanished as he broke into a grin. "Well. Good to see you didn't have the shit completely beaten out of you."

I rattled the cuff against the railing. "Am I under arrest?"

"Not at all, son." He snapped his fingers and an MP, waiting in the hallway, came running to unlock my wrist.

"Think you're up for taking a walk?" he asked.

It didn't really sound like a request. And I was curious. Most of the time, I knew what was coming because I could see inside the minds of everyone who got close to me. For the first time in my life, I didn't know where this conversation was going or where it would end. This was like being a visitor to an entirely new country. I figured I should see the sights while I could.

So I lifted myself cautiously, waiting for something to rupture or pop. There was pain everywhere, but I managed to swing my legs out of the bed and stand without falling over.

"That's good. On your feet, soldier," the older man said.

"Who are you?" I asked again.

"You can call me Cantrell," he said, and offered his hand. I took it, and he hauled me the rest of the way up. "Come on. Want to show you something."

The MP offered to accompany us, but Cantrell waved him away. I was no threat. I dragged myself along like an old man, leaning on my IV for support. Cantrell walked confidently down the halls, and I quickly got lost.

He talked the whole time. He began lecturing me, as if we were just picking up a lesson from an earlier conversation, right where we'd left off.

"You know, a lot of people think the military is where you send your subnormal sons and high school dropouts," he said. "And sure, we got our share. Smart people don't usually volunteer to dodge bullets on a regular basis. But the military is actually highly invested in intelligence. I mean both kinds: what you know and what you learn. Some of the greatest innovations in history have come from the military.

Because any army that doesn't think ahead is going to be nothing but a bunch of corpses in uniform before you know it. Which, unfortunately, is where we happen to be right now. See, we thought we won the only war that mattered. The commies folded up and left the table. Boy, let me tell you, we thought we had it all figured out. One world under America, with our only rival finally put down for the count. We were busy taking a victory lap. Then those Arabs"—he pronounced it *Ay-rabs*—"crawl out of the sand and fly a plane into the Pentagon. We didn't expect our next big threat to be a medieval religion that promises a virgin to every dipshit willing to strap on a suicide vest. We never saw it coming."

He paused to open a set of double doors to the intensive care unit.

"You have no idea the shit that hit the fan on September twelfth. For years, we thought we understood hijacking and terrorism. We thought there were rules, even though we called it unconventional warfare. Point is, war changes all the time, and we have to change with it."

He stopped outside a room with a glass wall. Inside was a bed and a bunch of machinery dedicated to keeping a dead man alive. Monitors for heart rate and breathing and oxygen, all beeping and pinging softly, all hooked up to the still figure under the bedsheets.

Leary. His eyes were open, staring at nothing. Tubes ran into his mouth and nose. There wasn't a mark on him, but he still looked like a body ready for viewing at a funeral.

Cantrell paused his speech to let me get a good, long look.

"What happened to him?" I asked.

"Now that is an excellent question," Cantrell said. "The short answer is, nobody can tell. The doctors say there's no trauma or injury. He doesn't have any wounds. You didn't land a single punch, son—which is nothing to be ashamed of, you were totally out of your league here. I read this guy's service record. He's been winning Advanced Combatives competitions for longer than you've been alive, against guys with a lot more training than you. But you're up and walking around, and he's the one sucking his meals through a straw."

I kept staring. For a moment, there was only the sound of the machines.

"See that little screen over there, to the left?" Cantrell stood very close and pointed. My eyes followed his finger. I saw. It was another monitor, a green screen with a steady line scrolling past. "That's his EEG. Measures brain activity."

"I know what an EEG is."

"Good for you. See how flat it is? All those other screens have squiggly lines, going up and down. But that one ain't moving. Doctors say his brain activity has ceased, except for the basic functions—breathing, pissing, and shitting. Other than that, nothing. He can't even remember how to swallow. He's a vegetable. They don't know if he's ever going to recover. They don't know what caused it."

Cantrell paused to let that sink in. He remained right next to me, speaking practically into my ear.

"But I think you and I both have a pretty good guess," he said.

I was too shocked by what I saw to wonder how Cantrell knew what I'd done. I looked at Leary's dead eyes and knew he was gone. That somehow I'd extinguished everything in him, every thought, every idea, every memory. Like bricking an iPhone. Erasing a hard drive.

Only this was a human being, and I'd simply wiped his mind clean.

"I didn't mean to do it."

"Oh hell, I know that," Cantrell said. "You think I'm angry at you? You think anyone blames you for this? I could give a damn if he spends the rest of his life shitting into a diaper."

I was tired and in pain. I couldn't read Cantrell's actual intentions.

I was stumbling around in a dark room, hitting my shins on chairs and tables. It was unsettling and irritating. So I just asked him straight-out. "Then what do you want?"

Cantrell grinned like this whole world was a joke and only he knew the punch line. "I want to know if you can do it again."

HE TOOK ME to the hospital's cafeteria. It was empty. One guy in scrubs came inside while we got coffee. He saw Cantrell's black uniform and immediately turned around and left. Didn't even break stride, just spun completely on one heel and back out the door before it closed.

We sat down at a table. "Something not a lot of people know about 9/11," Cantrell said, picking up where he'd left off. "We knew who the hijackers were."

That was still news at the time. "You're kidding me."

Cantrell shrugged. "Classified right now, but you'll start hearing it in the press soon. We knew their names. Where they were. We had the plane tickets. We had reports of these guys at al-Qaeda training camps. Hell, we even had reports from the flight schools that they attended. They didn't want to learn any of the parts about landing."

"Why didn't anyone stop them?"

"That's what I'm trying to tell you. Intelligence is the kind of stuff that only looks obvious in hindsight. Our last war was H-bombs and stealth bombers and spy satellites, and then these camel jockeys come along with box cutters and turn three planes into guided missiles. We never saw it coming, because we don't think like they do. We can't, because we live in the twenty-first century, and they're still stoning people to death. We can look right at what they're doing and not see the patterns. We had the data. We had reams of it. But nobody saw the future the way these boys did, because nobody could get inside their heads."

"Why are you telling me this?"

He scowled at me. "I'm going to write that off to the concussion. Your whole life, you've known what people are thinking. You've been able to figure out what they're going to do before they do it. You've always known when someone is lying to you. You've always known if someone was going to try to hurt you. And you've always known just where somebody else will hurt the most too."

"How do you know all this about me?"

"Like I said. Facts are easy, once we find you. Besides. You're not the first one I've seen."

"First what?"

"A reader. Someone who can flip through other people's thoughts like a book. This is why we need you. We can listen in on every phone call made in the United States. We can track money from the Swiss bank accounts of every terrorist organization in the world. Our satellites can look at the exact spot where Osama was hiding two weeks ago. Hell, I can tell you what Saddam Hussein had for breakfast. And it still don't mean shit. Because all that data is nothing without context. Without human emotion or motives or thought, all you have is facts. We don't need to know what people are *doing* anymore. We have machines for that. We need to know what they're *thinking*. That's where you come in."

That was the first time I'd heard a name for what I was. Or that there might be more people like me outside of comics and movies. Still. It was a lot to take in. I was nothing but tired. My head throbbed.

"I'm not sure I can do what you want," I said.

"Oh, I think you can do more than you know. Sergeant Leary up there is the proof."

I thought about Leary's dead stare and immediately shoved it away.

"Let me ask you something," Cantrell said. "You ever tried making someone do something? Just by thinking about it?"

I probably just looked stupidly at him. Up to that point, I'd only read other people. Or at least, that's what I thought at the time.

"Give it a try. See what happens."

"You think I can control people's minds? That's insane."

"I admit, it sounds that way. But if anyone could do that, we wouldn't have wars anymore. So you can understand why I'd be interested."

"Aren't you afraid that would put you out of business?"

He smiled. "Everything I do is to keep people from dying. Everything. If there was a way to stop wars altogether, then I'd happily find another line of work. You join up with us, and you'll see that for yourself. That's what I'm offering. We'll train you. Put your talent to use. Save some lives and keep another 9/11 from ever happening."

I have to give Cantrell credit. He was a hell of a salesman. He was offering a chance to work for the good guys. To finally understand a little bit more about the weird echoes I'd always had in my head. To be valuable. To be needed.

And there was the stick too, just in case I wasn't smart enough to see it on my own.

"What happens if I say no?"

Cantrell yawned and stretched, as if that was the least interesting question he'd ever heard. "You can always go back and finish your time in the regular army," he said. "'Course, I'm not sure how much of a future there is for a guy who crippled his drill sergeant."

I hesitated. Cantrell knew when to back off. "You still got some healing to do," he said, pushing his chair from the table. "Sleep on it. I'll be back in the morning."

. . . .

I WANTED TO sleep that night. I wanted to rest. But once I was awake, the pain wouldn't let me.

I hit the buzzer for the nurse once, then waited. Nothing. Hit it again. Still nothing. After a while, I just kept my thumb down on the button.

The nurse came in, looking pissed. "What is it?" she said. "We're busy with other patients."

"Hey," I said. "I could use something for the pain."

She gave me a cold look. "Sorry," she said. "You already had your shot."

<Boo-hoo, you bastard> she thought. *<feeling some pain> <tough shit> <exactly what you deserve>*

That's when I realized my talent was functional again. I could read her. And I saw clearly what was going on.

The medical staff didn't know why I was there. They'd seen the handcuffs and the MP, and they'd seen Leary brought in at the same time. Nobody could figure out what had happened to him. Rumors started, and I became the villain in all of them. I'd been beaten bloody, but I could still talk and walk and wipe myself. Leary was simply gone, AWOL from his own body, and that was deeply frightening to all of them.

Just like Cantrell said, they decided I'd permanently damaged a superior officer, and they took it out on me in the only way they could. They wouldn't compromise my actual medical care, since they took pride in their work. But they were happy to skip any extras that might make me comfortable. That included withholding my pain meds.

I wondered if Cantrell was right. If I might be able to change that.

The nurse turned to leave the room. "Hey," I said sharply. "Give me my painkillers," I told her.

And as Cantrell had suggested, I *pushed*. For the first time, I tried transmitting instead of just receiving. It felt like moving through syrup rather than air. But I felt something. I got something back, instead of an echo.

She wavered. There was a little resistance, a nagging thought somewhere in her head that told her this might be a bad idea. Even though I was pushing as hard as I could, she still had to make the final decision.

What the hell, I figured. Might as well be polite. "Please," I added.

That did it.

She turned and opened a drawer, moving automatically, just like she did for every other patient. She took a syringe and injected a clear liquid into my IV.

Then she went through the ordinary steps of disposing of the syringe and marking the shot and the time on my chart. The warmth of the military-grade morphine was already making the pain a distant memory.

It wasn't a huge victory. I'd really only convinced her to be a nurse, to do her job.

Still, that was how I learned I could push people. Not into doing something they didn't want to do, but into doing the things they would ordinarily do. I could nudge them into following their regular habits, the tasks they'd done so often they were almost unconscious. To break someone out of that kind of habit, to actively fight them, that woke up all kinds of defenses, convinced them to dig in and get stubborn.

But there are a lot of things people will do without thinking.

[7]

Two hours later, Kelsey and I are at a truck stop about forty miles from the game preserve.

We hit the highway on foot, after running for about thirty minutes as fast as we could over the uneven ground. We got lucky. We didn't meet any more of Preston's security detail, and I was able to steer us around the OmniVore guys still playing their live-action first-person shooter game.

We walked for nearly an hour before we flagged down a trucker. He was friendly enough when he heard that our car broke down and gave us a lift here.

I'm on full alert, scanning everyone in range. There are families out for the day, truckers, and long-haul salesmen of the kind I didn't really think existed anymore.

But no sign of OmniVore security.

Kelsey hasn't said much to me since the game preserve. She wanted to go back, to get our car and our phones, but I helped her do the math. Bad guys plus guns equals bullets in brain. She didn't need a lot of convincing.

We didn't talk much around the trucker, but I know she's still having a hard time believing that Preston suddenly went batshit crazy. She wants to know why. I don't have a good answer for her yet.

We get a table in the truck stop's diner and take a minute to regroup. Kelsey talks first.

"Jesus Christ, I'm starving," she says. "How is that possible?"

"Adrenaline," I tell her. "Your body just used a lot of energy. You need to refuel."

She rubs her eyes, and for a split second, I see what she's seeing in her brain. A man falling, blood at his throat. She didn't get a lot of detail. Which is good, because I suspect it's going to be with her for a long time.

"Not what I meant," she says.

"I know what you meant," I say quietly.

She makes a small noise, not quite like laughter. "Of course you do."

"I'm sorry. I know this has to be hard."

She looks up at me again. "What's happening?"

"Honestly? No idea."

The package of memories and thoughts I scraped out of Preston's mind is a big, gnarled mess, and it's deteriorating rapidly. As I've said, what I do is not an exact science. Usually, I try to tailor an interrogation, to ask questions to guide people to the topics that I want to explore so I can get specific memories and knowledge. But if I have to, I'll just take whatever's available.

This leads to holding on to a bunch of stuff from someone else's mind that can be completely irrelevant, because there's a lot going on in there. People's brains are rarely tidy places. They jump from childhood experiences to sex fantasies to Hollywood gossip to concerns about random body functions, all in the space of a few seconds. When I do a quick smash-and-grab, like I did with Preston, I can get almost anything. It takes time to unpack it all. Time and quiet and space. None of which we've had.

Still, there's one thing I know for certain: he didn't know me, and he didn't know why I was there. And yet he got a message from someone telling him to kill me. It doesn't make any sense.

I try to zoom in on that moment. That message on the computer screen. Who was it from? I pick at the memory carefully, keeping as much of myself out of it as possible. I don't want to contaminate Preston's thoughts with my own. I'm almost there, almost able to see it like he did.

And then Kelsey starts talking again. "Hey. Hello? Anyone home?"

"What?"

It comes out sharper than I intended. She snaps back at me. "You were just staring into space. I asked you what we're going to do now."

She's scared, I remind myself. She's out of her depth. And it's not a bad question.

"Tell you what. I saw a rack of pay-as-you-go phones over by the entrance. Buy one and get some time on it, then call your boss."

"I can't."

Right. He's out of reach. Convenient.

"Fine, you can't reach Sloan. Who are you supposed to contact if he's not around?"

"You don't have to talk to me like I'm a toddler. I didn't mean I couldn't talk to Everett. I meant I can't buy a phone. I don't have any money."

Of course. She left her purse in the car.

I've got about a thousand dollars in my wallet. I carry a lot of cash. Mainly for situations just like this.

I hand her a hundred.

"I'll call Lawrence Gaines," she said. Sloan's right-hand man. This ought to delight him. "He'll arrange for some transportation for us. Then we'll get someplace safe."

For a moment, I'm not sure what I'm feeling from her. Then I get it, but I still don't understand. She feels responsible. It's her job to manage the situation, and it's gone spiraling out of her control. Other people might dissolve into a puddle at this point. She's trying to solve the problem.

I nod, and she goes off to buy a cheap phone.

I spend the next few minutes trying to tease something else out of Preston's ball of memories, but it's like a string of old Christmas lights: just one knot leading into another.

This isn't the best place to concentrate either. Kids are wailing for ice cream, the exhaustion of the truckers fills the air like paint fumes, and the waitress's feet hurt.

On the edge of all of that, the death of the OmniVore security guy—the one with the long hair—hovers over me, waiting for my defenses to get weak so it can come in and tear out my liver.

I shove it back again, but it will land eventually. The question is when.

I realize the waitress is standing by the table, waiting for my order. I ask for a drink. The truck stop doesn't serve liquor.

This day just keeps getting better.

I order what passes for a steak here and a chocolate milkshake—I need to refuel too—as Kelsey returns to the table.

She's already activating the phone. She puts the change on the table next to me, along with the plastic packaging. She makes a show of folding the receipt and putting it into her jacket pocket. "You'll be reimbursed," she promises.

After the insanity of the morning, she's finding comfort in assuming the familiar role of the hypercompetent handler, the gal who takes care of everything. I'm impressed, and a little surprised. I thought I'd have to be the one comforting her.

"Shauna? It's Kelsey. I need to talk to Lawrence."

Brief pause. "What? I don't care. I need to speak to him, right now." Another pause. "This is more important than any meeting, Shauna," Kelsey says. The calm is starting to come off her voice in strips. "I don't care. You get your ass into that room and you get him."

This is not a good sign. I have a bad feeling about the reason Gaines won't answer Kelsey's call.

I reach over and gently take the phone from her. She looks exasperated. *<seriously everything I've been through today, and now this?>* I don't blame her.

"Shauna?" I say.

"Yes?" A female voice, younger than Kelsey's. Snottier and more officious too.

"My name is John Smith."

"I'm sorry, Mr. Smith, but I told Miss Foster that Mr. Gaines is not available."

Miss Foster. Not Kelsey. Another bad sign. I'd bet serious money that if Kelsey called from her usual number, nobody would have picked up. It would have been blocked.

My talent doesn't work over electronics, like phones or computers. So for this, I just have to rely on the people skills I learned in the CIA.

"Shauna," I say again. "You're going to put Mr. Gaines on the phone. Right now."

A little snort of contempt. "Oh really? And why would I do that?"

As I've said, my abilities don't work over the phone. But fortunately, I learned a lot of other tricks while I was in special ops. One of those was how to threaten people properly.

The essence of any good threat—especially when you are away

from the other person and unable to carry out any actual physical violence—is making yourself believed. That you mean every word you say. That you are not joking or threatening, but simply describing what will happen if you do not get what you want.

So I don't foam at the mouth. I don't use obscenities or raise my voice. Quietly, in simple words, with a minimum of drama, I spend about twenty seconds explaining to Shauna what will happen to her if she does not get Gaines on the line.

And I make sure she knows I am not joking.

There's a sudden silence. Kelsey looks at me with revulsion, because she heard what I said.

But a second later, Gaines is on the phone.

"You sick bastard," he says. "What the hell did you say to my assistant? She's crying and shaking."

I ignore that. "What's going on, Lawrence?"

Pause. He's stalling for time. "I should ask you that same question."

"We've had a setback."

"Yeah, I should say fucking so. I heard from Eli. Personally. What the hell were you thinking?"

"What? What did he tell you?"

"It's not something we can talk about on an unsecured line."

Jesus Christ. "You're not a spy, Lawrence. Please don't try to talk like one. Nobody else is listening. What did he tell you?"

"He told me enough. You tried to shake him down, and then you hurt people."

"That's an interesting version of events. Not at all true, but interesting."

Kelsey is growing more agitated on her side of the table. *<what's going on?>*

I send back to her, *<hell if I know>*.

"Yeah, well, you would say that," Gaines says. "But I had a call from the FBI. They told me the truth about you. We're going to be damn lucky to get out of this without an indictment. I told Everett this was a mistake."

The FBI? There's no way they'd be involved this fast, not even if Preston had them on speed dial. He must have had his people impersonate the feds.

But that's irrelevant right now. We need to get out of town. Fast.

To Gaines, I say, "Listen. Kelsey and I can tell you what actually happened in person. But right now we're stranded. We need you to send a car to us, and some cash. We'll get on the next flight and meet with you to discuss our next move."

He laughs at that. "What do you mean 'our next move'? There is no next move. You're fired."

"I don't work for you. I work for Sloan. He's the only one who can cancel my contract."

"You canceled it yourself. The only reason I'm not calling the FBI on you right now is because it would mean a world of hurt for the company and Mr. Sloan."

"You are making a mistake. And if you won't see that, at least you can contact your boss and let him know that we need him."

Another laugh. "Not a chance. You are not going to bring us down with you."

Kelsey has had enough waiting. She grabs the phone from me.

"Lawrence, it's Kelsey. I don't know what you think is happening, but I can tell you, we need help. Right now. I know Everett would never leave me hanging here like this."

The sound from the phone's speaker is weak, but I can hear Gaines pretty well. "They told me you'd say that, Kelsey. I didn't think you'd really help a guy like Smith. Guess I was wrong."

Kelsey is shocked. "What? What are you talking about? Lawrence, they shot at us. They tried to kill us."

A couple of people at the other tables look around when they hear Kelsey.

I smile at them. <*fuck off*> They look away.

Kelsey lowers her voice. "Lawrence. They tried to kill me."

There's a moment of silence that stretches so long that I think Gaines hung up. Then the weak little voice comes out of the cheap phone again:

"I'm sorry, Kel. I really am."

He hangs up.

She looks at the phone in disbelief, then redials. <*son of a bitch hung up on me*>

I can hear the phone ringing. Nobody answers.

"It won't do any good," I tell her. "They'll block the number."

She glares, disconnects, and dials again.

Let her. Gives her something to do.

I take stock of the situation: trapped at a truck stop in Pennsylvania after dodging bullets and killing a guy, unable to reach my client because his manservant won't forward his calls.

I'm sure I've had worse jobs. There was that whole period of my career where armed religious fanatics were trying to kill me in the desert. But this is still pretty high on the list.

As much as I wanted my own island, it's time to face reality.

"That's it," I tell Kelsey. "I'm going home."

She puts the phone down and looks at me like I've just spontaneously grown another head. "What?"

"I'm out. This job is screwed. Your boss has burned me—"

"—Lawrence is not my boss—"

"Oh please. You think Gaines isn't acting on Sloan's orders right now? He knows this has been blown to shit. He's cutting us off to avoid getting any on him."

"Lawrence might think he's doing the right thing, but Everett doesn't know about this, I guarantee you. You don't know the protocols at Geneva. It's no cell phones, no emails, no outside contact. They're incredibly serious about it. They kicked Murdoch's son out a couple years ago for sneaking his BlackBerry into his hotel room. The whole idea is complete silence so they can think big thoughts."

She believes she's telling the truth. And she's got a powerful sense of loyalty to Everett. I could, if I wanted, drill down and find that it's connected to the disappointment she feels in her own father, that she sees in him a better dad than the one fate and biology dealt her. I sympathize. I know the feeling.

But there's no reason for me to unpack all that baggage. I don't want to convince her or even waste time arguing with her. As far as I'm concerned, this job is over.

"Fine. Whatever. Believe what you want. I'm sure you'll be safe if you make it back to Gaines. I don't think Preston is dumb enough to come after you. But it's clear that I'm not going to be able to do what I was hired to do. So I'm done here. We all go back to our lives. I keep the deposit."

"You're just going to walk away?"

"Until I can find a car."

I don't need to be psychic to see she doesn't think that's funny. The blast of anger coming from her nearly blows my hair back. "He tried to kill you."

"It happens."

"To you? I can see why. But he tried to kill me too, and surprisingly, I'm not okay with that."

"He wanted to scare us off," I say.

"And I guess it worked on you, didn't it?" *<coward>*

I have to restrain a smile. She's loaded for bear, ready to kick ass and take revenge. She's got no idea what it actually means, but she's brave. Not thinking very clearly, operating on rage instead of brains, but still brave.

I explain it to her in very patient tones. "Preston is the CEO of a company that's going to go public soon. Whatever he thought I was doing there, he was willing to take the chance on killing us to protect himself. But he's not dumb enough to carry it any further. He can't be. There are too many risks. From a business perspective, it just doesn't make sense."

She's skeptical, but at least she tamps down her anger.

"Then I'm calling the police. Maybe the FBI."

"No, you won't."

"Oh, I won't? Really? Why not?"

"Because as soon as the police are involved, your boss's name will be mentioned. And that means, sooner or later, this gets into the media. He doesn't want that, and neither do you."

Then I lower my voice so the other customers don't hear any more than they already have. "And finally, you're not going to call the police because I shot a man back there."

She recoils, both at the words and the memory of what I did. The image plays back in her head: body dropping, blood in the air. It takes her a second to regroup.

"If you know so much, then what am I supposed to do now? I don't have any cash or my credit cards. I don't even have my phone, for God's sake."

I've already considered this. I could just leave her here. I don't have any obligation, contractual or otherwise, to her. But that seems like a real dick move. It's not her fault this went Charlie Foxtrot, or that her boss has abandoned us both. Besides, maybe she'll be in a position to hire me again someday.

"I'll get you back to the hotel. You can pick up your stuff, and then I'll even escort you to the airport."

She's instantly skeptical. "Why would you do that? You just said you don't think Preston will take this any further."

"I'm trying to be a gentleman."

She makes a face. "Chivalry's not dead yet, huh?"

"Recovering after a long illness, maybe."

She thinks it over for another second or two, her suspicion fighting her basic desire to go home and forget all of this ever happened.

Suspicion loses. She makes her choice. She trusts me.

I hope, for both our sakes, that's the right move.

[8]

We get a ride with a salesman driving back toward Philadelphia. He's a middle-aged guy who gladly takes a hundred bucks for the trouble. He would have done it for free just to be in the same car as Kelsey. His mind's like a swim in a sewer for the whole drive.

<oh my God what I'd do to you just twenty minutes in a hotel room Jesus look at that spandex bet you could bounce a quarter off those tits first I'd get her on her stomach get a look at that ass and then I'd—>

I sit in the front seat and try to block out the worst of it. I have to give him some credit; at least he makes the effort to picture Kelsey naked instead of using a placeholder image from some porn clip he downloaded. You'd be amazed how many guys have subcontracted their fantasy lives completely to the Internet. They don't even bother to look at real women anymore. Still, I'd prefer he'd pay more attention to the road. He spends most of the trip watching her in the rearview mirror.

Kelsey watches the scenery go by. She's not sure if she can believe what I told her about Preston. Which is smart, because I wouldn't believe a word I said either.

It's true that it would make sense for Preston to cut his losses and leave us alone. It's true that a rational man in his position would try to hush the whole thing up and move on. He'd try to forget it, like a bad nightmare.

And Preston is a rational man. Nothing in the ball of impressions and memories and ideas I took from him suggests he has any psychotic tendencies. A little grandiose, a lot of narcissism, but nothing out of line for most people who get their face on the cover of *Bloomberg Businessweek* before they're twenty-five. There are no treasured thoughts of torturing puppies or the disturbing blank spaces a sociopath has in place of authentic emotions.

That's what worries me. If he's not a sociopath, he needs a hell of a good reason to order two people killed.

I spend the next hour in the passenger seat unkinking his memories, trying to figure out what it is.

It's not easy. Everything I took from Preston's mind is disorganized and hazy. It all got confusing when he went into full-tilt panic mode.

But by the time we arrive at the hotel where we dropped our bags, I'm pretty sure I know what's happening.

Now I just have to test my theory. And hope we survive the result.

KELSEY WANTS TO go up to her room to get her luggage, but I ask her to stay with me while I take care of a few things at the business center.

I use one of the hotel's computers to make reservations. Next flight out of Philadelphia. Boston for her, back to L.A. for me. Then I arrange a wire transfer from my bank account to the nearest Western Union. Ten grand. I tell Kelsey that it's to pay for any incidentals until she can get in touch with Sloan. She protests. She doesn't think she needs anything close to that much. I remind her that she doesn't have credit cards or anything else that was in her wallet, and it might take a while to get the whole mess resolved with her bank.

I click through the transfer. It's not really for her, anyway.

Then I call for a car service to come pick us up. We'll get the cash, ride to the airport, and hopefully put the whole thing behind us.

We get a drink in the hotel bar. I have whiskey. Kelsey has a Diet Coke. She's tense and nervous, teetering on the edge of the barstool, but I take my time. After my last sip, she decides she's waited long enough.

"Now can I go to my room and get my stuff? Please?" she asks.

I've been watching the lobby. I check my watch. The car service is maybe five minutes away.

The ice rattles against the glass as I put my drink down. "All right," I say. "Let's go."

KELSEY HAS HER replacement key from the hotel's front desk out and ready before the elevator doors open. My room is right next to hers. She steps into the hallway quickly, but I still get in front of her.

Her room number is 2312. It's made to look like an address plate on an actual home. One of those small touches recommended by some industrial designer employed by the hotel chain.

As soon as we're in range, I know I'm right.

<come on come on> <he's almost at the door> <showtime> <come on asshole> <see how tough you are now>

Two men. Waiting inside. Another two, inside my room.

Sometimes I hate being right.

I grab Kelsey's arm and reverse course, pulling her along with me.

"Hey!" she snaps. But then, because she hasn't been asleep all day, she realizes what's going on.

<Oh no> <oh Christ> goes through her head. Then she snaps into formation, moving right alongside me.

I don't want to stand around exposed or get stuck in a confined space, so I hustle Kelsey away from the elevators and toward the fire stairs. We're halfway there when I hear the door open behind us.

I don't have to turn my head to know they're following, but I take a quick glance anyway. They're dressed in the TV-standard costume for federal agents: black suits, sunglasses, wires leading to earpieces, which is a nice touch. That's how they got into the room; they badged the desk clerk and got a key.

OmniVore security again.

They quicken their pace. They don't want witnesses. The stairwell is perfect for them.

"Run," I tell Kelsey quietly as soon as the heavy door slams behind us. "Get to the lobby. Stay there."

She doesn't argue, doesn't question. She runs.

I wait by the door. I feel them coming fast. They're confident and secure in the knowledge that we're both fleeing. It only makes sense. We're outnumbered and in danger. They're professional soldiers, highly trained mercenaries. They're the predators. We're the prey. We're supposed to run.

The limits of that kind of thinking are about to become painfully obvious. This isn't like the office at the hunting lodge. I'm ready for them. Their quick jog down the hallway gives me all the time I need to get inside their heads.

They might have training. They might be tough. They might have the numbers.

But honestly, they don't stand a chance.

The first guy charging down the hall has three tours in Iraq behind him and incipient PTSD. He opens the stairwell door and I've got a nice warm memory waiting for him of the time he walked into a room in Mosul and it exploded with gunfire. For a moment, it's so real it's like he's there. He knows it's impossible, but he immediately drops to the floor, just like he did in Iraq, reflexes taking over.

That turns him into a speed bump for the three guys behind him. The first guy stumbles and trips and pitches forward. I grab his collar and his belt in a modified judo throw and he achieves takeoff. For a second, he thinks he's falling from an airplane, like he did back in Airborne training, only this time he knows he has no chute. His arms pinwheel out and he flails wildly. He lands badly on the concrete stairs and I feel something break in one leg and one arm.

I bite down on the pain, remind myself it's worse for him, and move on to the next guy. He can't understand why he's looking at a brick wall where the open door of the stairwell was a second before. It stops him cold as he desperately tries to process it.

I hit him hard, side of my palm to his left temple, just above his eye.

He collapses on top of the speed bump just as that guy begins to rise, and then they're tangled together in a mess of arms and legs.

The fourth guy doesn't know what's happening. To him, his fellow goons have suddenly turned crazy or stupid. It makes no sense. He's scared and confused, and that makes him angry.

So he pulls his gun.

But when he lifts it to aim at me, I'm not there anymore. He's looking at his mother.

There are some cold-blooded bastards who would fire anyway, but thankfully, he's not one of them.

He stops and says, "Mom?"

And then, unfortunately, his mother lays him out with a hard right cross.

The speed bump has almost gotten up again. I kick him twice: once in the gut to double him over, and once in the head to put him down for the count.

All four of them are safely off the board, and I'm already on my way down the stairs, vaulting over the guy with the broken bones on the landing. I need to catch up to Kelsey. Those four were out of the room way too fast. They knew when we were coming, and they knew when we walked away.

That means there's at least one observer, probably in a room across the courtyard, too far away for me to get a lock on him. And probably on his way to cover the lobby.

Sure enough, there he is, just as I open the stairway door. He's confronting Kelsey.

He wears the same kind of suit as the others, and he's showing her his fake badge. She's at war with herself. She was raised a polite, law-abiding young woman. In grade school, they told her to wave at the police cars as they passed. *<Hi, Officer Friendly!>* And that's only been reinforced since 9/11. She trusts the government.

But she also knows that this guy is probably going to kill her, and she can clearly see his hand on the Glock in the holster attached to his waistband.

I recognize him. I would know his mind even if I didn't see the top of that tattoo under the collar of his white no-iron shirt. He's moving pretty well for taking three rounds to a Kevlar vest less than two hours ago. Snake Eater.

I want him down and I want him quiet and I especially do not want him to pull that Glock. So I load an old, bad dream I still remember from childhood. That might not sound like much, but the kind of upbringing I had means we're talking about something a little more frightening than a rerun of Scooby-Doo. This is like seeing your parents help the bogeyman tie you down on an altar made of children's bones.

I throw it at him and it hits his mind like a brick through a window. Snake Eater is suddenly so terrified that he can't breathe, let alone scream.

He's frozen in place and stuttering when I reach him and Kelsey. Behind the sunglasses, his face is etched with pure horror. He's trying desperately to shake it off, but it's not working.

My nightmares have teeth.

I smile and laugh as if he's just told us that we're free to go—<*all a big misunderstanding, folks!*>—and I project such cheerful belief in this reality that it spreads to everyone around us. The people at the front desk, who were watching, waiting for some kind of real-life shootout in their lobby, are equal parts disappointed and relieved.

Everything is normal. Everything is all right now.

Snake Eater stands there, still trembling, struggling not to piss himself.

Kelsey walks alongside me as the automatic lobby doors slide open and we step out.

A little ahead of schedule, the car service pulls up, a big black Ford Escalade.

The driver is more than willing to go inside and get our bags.

And while he's doing that, I put Kelsey in the passenger seat, get behind the wheel, and we drive away.

The great advantage a psychic has against a rational man: the rational man doesn't really believe the psychic can do what he says.

But *I can*. Preston either doesn't know what I am or doesn't believe it yet. He tried to ambush me. It doesn't work. No matter what strategy, what double cross he and his hired guns plan, I will know it as soon as they are in range. There is no way to surprise me.

Nice try, Eli.

. . . .

As we drive away, Kelsey is a small black cloud of worry and fear in the passenger seat next to me.

She finds the words eventually.

"You said Preston was going to give up."

"Yes, I did."

"And?"

"He didn't."

She looks out the window again, struggling to contain her anger. *<fucking comedian> <liar> <you think this is funny?> <hand on his gun> <what the hell are we supposed to do now?>*

I'm not sure what to tell her. Our situation is worse than she thinks. I gave Preston every chance to end this before it went any further. I made the airline reservations with my own credit card, because of course he would be monitoring that. That was practically telling him I was giving up, taking my ball and going home. Kelsey would go back to her job, I'd move on to another client, and we could all live our lives in peace.

But it didn't work. He came after us.

"Listen," I say, projecting as much calm as I can manage. "I wasn't lying. I hoped Preston would back down. It does not make sense for him to seek revenge."

"But you thought he would."

"I had my suspicions."

"Clearly. You ever stop to think that you were using me as bait too?"

"I hoped it wouldn't come to that."

"Yeah, I can see how well that worked out."

"Preston would have to have a very good reason to suddenly attempt to murder two people. Think about it. It's not a smart move for a guy like him. He needs a reason."

"How about the fact that his whole business is based on the theft of intellectual property?" Kelsey asks. "That's not enough of a threat?"

"He didn't know who I was," I remind her. "Even when he found out, he had no idea what I could do. He'd have no reason to assume I was there to bring him down. His response was completely insane. It doesn't make any sense, even if he had stolen anything from your boss. Which he didn't."

That snaps her out of her anger. "What?"

"He didn't take the algorithm."

<what?> <bullshit> <that can't be right> Out loud, she's more polite. "You barely even spoke to him. How do you know?"

"I grabbed a bunch of stuff from his head when I saw him. It's all a jumble, but there's one thing that came through. I asked him directly about stealing from Sloan. He didn't know what the hell I was talking about."

"You're wrong," she says. "You've got to be wrong."

"I wish I was," I tell her.

Preston wasn't prepared for me. He wasn't ready to lie. He had no defenses. He couldn't fake it or fool me. I caught him by surprise, and got an honest look inside his head.

He was genuinely baffled when I asked him about Sloan. There was no guilt, no inside knowledge. He didn't steal anything.

That should have been good news for us. No guilt means no reason to track us down. No reason to keep going with this, if he was just a tech mogul, or even if he was involved in some form of industrial espionage. There are limits to what's good for the bottom line. Armed hit squads are not only wildly expensive, they're a huge legal liability.

Attempted murder without a motive is, by definition, psychotic. And as I know from my time inside his head, Preston is not crazy. I explain all this to Kelsey.

"So why is he still coming after us?" Kelsey asks.

"Because he's got no choice," I say.

"What does that mean?"

"Someone told him to get rid of me. And you."

"Who?"

I sigh and close my eyes, just for a second, a long blink. Just long enough to remember the laptop's monitor, as I saw it through Preston's eyes.

There, in flashing letters, the instant message: TWEP TWEP TWEP.

It took a little while, but I finally recognized the source of that TWEP order. I'd seen plenty like it while I worked for the government.

It was an encrypted message from a secure server used only by intelligence agencies. Preston ran my name and picture through it. He got a message back, from very high up, telling him who I was, and then telling him to kill me.

There are only a few entities that use that kind of language, that have that kind of secure communications channel, and that can actually expect to get away with murder.

Preston is working with someone in the CIA. And they'd rather see me dead than interfere with whatever he's doing for them.

[9]

We stop at a strip club not far off the interstate.

"Is this really the best time for a lap dance?" Kelsey asks as we turn into the parking lot behind the building.

I don't bother to reply, just get out of the car. Nobody's around. I check the Escalade for a LoJack device; it doesn't have one. Nobody's tracking us.

There are two other Escalades in the lot, both with livery registrations as well. That's why I stopped here. Guys like pulling up to the club in big black SUVs. It makes them feel like Suge Knight. Probably a bachelor party or a group of middle managers inside, out for a little male bonding.

I tear off our Escalade's livery stickers, then swap out its plates with another one. With any luck, whoever drives the other SUV will be too high on stripper-glitter to notice the change. Meanwhile, if anyone runs these plates, they'll come back clean.

That buys us a little time to refuel and to pick up the cash I transferred earlier. From the club, it's a quick ride to a convenience store that has a Western Union terminal. We can get a little breathing space.

At this point, I'm still not too worried. Preston's got some spooks working for him, but I was trained by the same people who trained them. And I've already beaten them twice.

Of course, Preston has his data-mining software. But I can't see how it helps him. I don't do social networking. He can't embarrass me with old status updates from Facebook or any naked pictures from Snapchat. We should be safe as long as I don't go on Twitter and tell people where we're eating lunch.

At least, that's what I think. Then the wheels start to come off.

The clerk behind the gas-station counter tells me several times that my cash transfer was canceled by the sender. I tell him several times that's impossible, since I was the sender. He shrugs, his indifference thick enough to deflect bullets.

We pay cash to refuel the behemoth and I pick up another burner phone by the counter. This one is a smartphone, with full Internet access. Okay, I admit it, I'm a monkey with a lever like anyone else.

I load it up with prepaid minutes. That brings our money supply down to $500, but my intuition tells me what we need to know is only going to be accessible on the Net.

I turn on the phone. First thing, I check to see what happened to the transfer. I log into my bank's website and look at my account. It's gone. I don't mean the money is gone. I mean the entire account is gone. Emptied out. There's a notation that says ACCOUNT CLOSED. The entire balance was transferred.

I have a sinking feeling in my gut. I log into my email. I keep a public address for civilian stuff. Filling out forms, a line on the business cards. Things like that.

Most of my inbox is filled with spam, as usual. Offers for Nigerian fortunes and a bigger penis.

But the message at the top of the box is different:

TO: johnsmith4842956@gmail.com

FROM: eli@omnivoretech.com

SUBJECT: I can't believe you have a gmail account . . .

You know, I thought it would be harder to find you.

Oh, sure, in the real world, you're still out there. I'm sure they taught you all kinds of tricky shit in spy school. But let me tell you something. You're not safe. And what you think of as the real world, that doesn't even matter anymore.

I can touch you without ever laying a hand on you. I don't need my guys to catch you. I can destroy you from right here.

In case you think this is just me talking big, check your bank accounts. All of them. Even that one at the Royal Bank of the Caribbean in Eleuthera.

I would have expected a big-time superspy like yourself to have a little more in the bank. I mean, $675,233? Total? How the hell were you ever going to retire on that?

Well, you've got a bigger problem now. Because it's all gone. Yeah. I did that. Thanks for contributing to OmniVore's bottom line. That should just about cover what we spend on snacks.

But wait, there's more! Your condo in L.A.? Check out this link.

I click on the website, even though I know it could be a virus or some kind of IP address tracker. Because I want to see it for myself.

The link takes me to a real-estate site. With a brand-new listing, "just on the market." It's my address. The pictures show a place that's been professionally cleaned out.

I go back to the email.

See what I did there? Pretty easy, actually, when you've got the right tools. Your mortgage holder suddenly found out you owe about a year of payments. Then a brokerage in L.A. got an alert about your foreclosure—you didn't fight it, which was gracious of you. Your digital signature is all over the surrender documents. Prime condo like that, good location, I'll bet it's in escrow before the end of the week.

I could go on, but I'm sure you get the point by now.

I was able to erase your life. All of it, and it took me about twenty minutes.

That's reality now. You've got nothing. No money, no home, no credit cards, nothing. Try renting a car or a hotel room or getting on a plane, see how far you get. You don't even exist anymore.

The rest of you, running around out there, is like a ghost in reverse. You're just the body. You're meat. I've already taken everything that counts.

But don't worry. I'm going to get the rest of you pretty soon.

I could put you on the sex offenders registry, or the FBI's most wanted, or the terrorist no-fly list, and you'd have every cop in America looking for your carcass too.

But frankly, I don't need the help. I'll find you.

Right now, I have a bot running your picture against every image connected to the Net in the world. I put Kelsey in there too. If you show up in the crowd in somebody's selfie, I'm going to know. I've got another little monitoring program hidden in the bank networks that's sifting through every cash-only purchase within a hundred-mile radius of your last known location. I've got software agents gathering every phone number you've ever used, collecting every address where you've ever slept for a night.

You try to hop on a plane, I'll know. You try to buy a car, I'll know. You want to run, have a blast. I'll find you.

You can go to some cheap hourly motel, sleep under stinking unlaundered sheets on a bedbug-infested mattress. You might even think you're safe.

And then someone will put a fucking bullet into your brain.

You're done, Mr. Smith. You took the wrong job. Your life is over. And you're never even going to know why.

I know that sounds melodramatic. What can I say? It's not every day I get to be a supervillain. I'm enjoying this. It's pretty fun to completely obliterate someone's life and know they'll never be able to do a goddamned thing about it. I've got to admit. I'm having a blast.

Sorry if it's not as much fun for you.

You really shouldn't have fucked with me.

Sleep tight. Don't let the bedbugs bite.

PS—If that bitch Kelsey is still with you, tell her I might find a position (or three) for her when this is all over. But only if she asks nicely.

So that's what data mining can do. Looks like Eli is capable of a few surprises after all.

"What?" Kelsey asks. She must have noticed the look on my face. "What is it?"

"Do me a favor," I say, handing her the phone. "Check your bank account."

"Why?"

She's a little confused at first. She taps her way onto her bank's site. And then she's completely bewildered. *<that can't be right> <did I enter the right numbers?> <holy crap where's my money?>*

Her account is gone too.

"My account is gone," she says.

"I know."

"You know? What do you mean? What happened?"

I take the phone back, switch over to the email, and then let her read it.

"Holy God," she says.

I have to smile. "Yeah. That's one way to put it."

"What are we going to do?" she asks.

I don't answer. I'm suddenly very aware of the security camera watching us from above the pumps.

"Get in the car," I tell her.

I'm not sure if Preston was bluffing, or if he really can see us through every one of those eyes. I crack open the phone and pull its battery and SIM card. The SIM card goes on the ground and I crush it under my heel. The battery and the phone go into separate pockets.

Maybe I'm being paranoid. But it sure doesn't feel like paranoia now.

It's time to start running.

[10]

As soon as I healed from Leary's assault, I went back for more training. But not with my old unit at Benning. As far as anyone there was concerned, I no longer existed.

I was sent to the compound within the compound at Fort Bragg, where my instructors, like Cantrell, didn't dress in uniforms with rank. They were special ops. They ignored military regs and were encouraged to grow their beards and skip showers. In the places where they traveled, a clean-shaven man was automatically a target. They went deep in the desert and came back with nightmares and scalps. They tracked high-value targets, negotiated with Taliban warlords and Pakistani secret police, and painted targets with high-powered lasers in order to guide smart bombs.

And they taught me how to do all of that too.

They showed me all the ways to inflict pain on the human body, all the pressure points and weak spots where a man will fold or break. I learned how to kill with a gun, a knife, a garrote, my bare hands, and a half pound of strategically placed C-4.

The closest way to describe it was like med school in reverse. Instead of rotations in saving lives, I had short intensive courses in death and destruction.

They weren't my only teachers. The rest of the faculty was stranger. They ranged from neuroscientists to guys who acted like Buddhist monks to men who'd clearly spent some time in prison. They taught me, and the other weird recruits selected by Cantrell, how to refine and use our talents. They called us Cantrell's special-ed class.

We didn't spend much time together outside of training. For starters, we didn't like each other much. You'd think that the weird kids, the perpetual outcasts, would be happy to finally find others like themselves. But the opposite was true. We grated on each other. Being near them for too long felt like chewing tinfoil. I mentioned this to Cantrell once, and he laughed. He said it was the same with every group. Some kind of feedback caused by proximity, like a microphone placed too close to an amp.

"I see one of you smiling and getting along with the others, that's when I know he's not the real thing."

We never quite got over it, but we got used to it. We learned calm and focus from our instructors. Though I never met anyone else with a talent as strong as mine, I finally met people who could tell me how to make it work.

I learned how to dig below the surface of people's thoughts, to burrow down into the places where they kept their secrets. I learned how to separate truth from lies, even when a person might not know the difference himself. I learned to detect hidden weaknesses, to excavate the suppressed memory, the hidden motive, the fear behind the smile.

Most important, I learned how to take pain and give it back.

Cantrell suspected this might be part of my talent after what had happened to Leary. I think that's why he put me with the most sadistic of the unarmed combat instructors. I took many more beatings—all in the name of training—before I lashed out again.

I can remember the moment clearly. An instructor called Fairchild—not his real name, since secrecy permeated everything we did, and we all used aliases, even within our units—was bending my arm back farther than it was ever designed to go. There was no tapping out in our sparring sessions. You either broke the hold or broke a bone.

I felt my frustration well up inside me, along with the pain. I wanted to hurt him. I was helpless. I could feel something about to give.

And so, like I had done with Leary, I took all my pain—the nerves and tendons and bones all screaming—and wadded it into a ball and hurled it at him.

Fairchild let out a shrill yelp and I felt his grip go slack. I spun and reversed the hold, then spent a few minutes getting payback. But when I let him up, it was clear nothing I'd done hurt him as much as the phantom pain I'd thrown at him. His eyes were full of surprise and he kept rubbing his arm in the exact same spot where mine sang with agony. More than that, I could feel the ache, a dull throbbing echo.

That was when I discovered I could inflict pain as long as I was willing to take a percentage myself.

I described this to Cantrell, after Fairchild told him what happened. Every instructor working with Cantrell's class was under orders to report anything unusual with us.

Cantrell was giddy with delight. To him, this meant I was making progress.

So as a reward, I got the crap kicked out of me in a whole new variety of ways. Each instructor would take me right to edge of serious injury, until I reached out with my mind and forced it back on them.

My life got marginally better when I learned I could simply absorb the pain of others rather than endure it myself. At that point, I was sent to witness and experience all the worst traumas the military had to offer. Which turned out to be quite a few.

In a base hospital, I sat at the bedside of a 90 percent third-degree-burn case while his life oozed out of him. In rehab clinics, I held the hands of amputees and talked them through the memories of having their limbs torn away by roadside bombs or stray rounds. In VA centers, I got to experience chemotherapy, appendicitis, bedsores, arthritis, paralysis, and heart attacks—all secondhand.

I found I could absorb the little hurts as well as the big ones. The humiliation of a neglected catheter bag exploding with hot piss. The pretty nurse flinching at the scar tissue that used to be the right side of a man's face. The weakness and helplessness of strong men and women reduced to tears by the simple effort of standing, walking, or feeding themselves.

I filed away every injury, every pain, in a big mental catalog, just as my instructors had taught me. And then, back at the base, I would pull one of these files and share it with someone who rushed me with a knife. If I came away without bleeding, then it was working. If I got cut—well, that was one more pain, one more experience, to go into the files. More practice needed.

After months of this with no end in sight, I went back to the barracks to find my duffel already packed and Cantrell waiting for me. He tossed me a new set of BDUs, with no name or rank, in desert camo that matched his own.

"Practice is over, son," he said. "Time for you to join the majors."

Cantrell used to keep a stack of Iraqi dinars in his desk with Saddam Hussein's face on them. When he was feeling especially theatrical, he'd use one to light his cigar. He picked them up after the second invasion; he was there on the ground not long after the bombing started.

"You hear stories about people carting wheelbarrows full of cash to buy bread after the government collapses?" he told me. "Total bullshit. They dumped this stuff in the street. They wouldn't even use it for toilet paper. When the shooting stops, that's the first thing everyone wants: real money, something with a little faith and credit behind it."

This was his way of explaining why we were transporting a metal case packed with cash through a suburb of Baghdad called Sadr City. I didn't know much about the place at the time. It hadn't yet made the news as a shooting gallery filled with anti-American Shiite fighters. All I knew was what Cantrell told me. We were going to buy off the support of a local militia, and its leader would only accept American dollars.

So I was in the passenger seat of a Humvee, riding shotgun on a million bucks' worth of $100 bills.

It was my first time in a war zone. Or anywhere, really. I'd never even been on an overseas flight before, and now I was riding in a Humvee on the other side of the planet. The invasion was over, but the fighting wasn't. After the first few giddy days, with the statue of Saddam being pulled down and the cheering crowds, things were turning mean again.

There were no lights because there was no electricity. People hid inside their homes. The streets were quiet, but not peaceful.

Cantrell was silent for most of the drive too. Years of working with people like me had given him a lot of practice at shielding his thoughts. There was a standing order among his kids not to read the boss's mind, but we all made a run at it once or twice. Whenever I'd scan him, I mainly saw bits of sitcoms from the eighties, or clips from porno movies on a loop. That night, I got nothing but the streets and the map in his head as he looked for markers in the bombed-out city to find our rendezvous point. I stopped probing. I figured if he had something to tell me, he'd say it out loud.

We arrived at the meeting place, which was an abandoned convenience store. That surprised me. I didn't know how modern Baghdad was before I got there—before the bombing started. I expected mud huts or maybe something from *Aladdin*. Instead, I found scenes from a straight-to-DVD zombie movie: deserted stores and buildings, empty streets and abandoned cars, like it was the end of the world.

Cantrell checked his Rolex and then looked at me. "How many inside?" he asked.

I was about to protest that I couldn't possibly know. Then I realized I did. There were eight of them in the building. I could sense them, their nerves singing out high and clear. The queasy stomach of the youngest one, the lookout on the roof, who'd never been in a fight before. The persistent ache in the leg of their leader, from an old bullet wound that had never healed properly. Their impatience and tension and nervousness, buzzing like flies around all of their heads. I didn't speak much Arabic—my lessons had been confined mainly to a few simple phrases and commands—but I could still read them. I understood the meaning, if not the words.

"Eight men," I said. "One on the roof. He's signaled the others. They know we're here."

"They have radios?"

Again, I wanted to say, *How should I know?* But this time, I knew I could find out. "No," I said after a moment. There was no sign of the spike in mental activity I'd come to recognize when people broke out of their inner thoughts and began talking. They were silent.

Cantrell nodded. "Fair enough," he said. He hoisted the case and got out of the Humvee. I followed.

We were met at the door by one of the men carrying an M16. He escorted us inside. The other men stood behind the empty displays and shelves, using them as cover. They held a variety of weapons: a few M16s, like the man on the door; some old AKs; a couple of ancient Kalashnikovs. Cantrell and I each had our sidearms, and I had an H&K MP5 as well. But even if only half of their weapons worked, we were outgunned.

Still, that was not supposed to be a problem. This was a friendly meeting. We were there to give them money, after all.

It began about like you'd expect from a roomful of armed men. Their leader stood behind the counter, watching us with undisguised hostility. Cantrell was so obviously CIA that he might as well have had it tattooed on his forehead. The leader could remember when the CIA delivered cash and weapons to Saddam, and he had a headful of hard feelings about those days.

But the temperature thawed considerably after Cantrell stepped over to the counter and heaved the case onto it. His Arabic was only slightly better than mine, but there's something about opening a huge suitcase full of cash that transcends language barriers.

The Iraqi leader took out a knife and sliced open the shrink-wrapped packets of bills. They'd been packed in a special facility ten miles west of Manhattan, completely untouched by human hands until that moment. He checked the faces on the stacks, flipping carefully through each one. Then he withdrew a single hundred, took out a highlighter, and marked it. He peered at it in front of a flashlight held by one of his men. I'd seen that back at home at Walmart: he was checking to make sure the hundred wasn't counterfeit.

He nodded, satisfied.

That's when we were all supposed to relax. And I did. I let down my guard, just a fraction of an inch, because I thought the hard part was over. I remember I started thinking about getting back to the Green Zone and wondering where I would sleep that night.

But the Iraqis didn't relax. Instead, I felt a surge of sudden tension, like a current of electricity had passed through them all at once. Their minds were on high alert, open and receptive, ready for one thing to trigger their next move. They were waiting on a phrase, I realized. One phrase. And once the leader said it, we were dead. I could feel them rehearsing the steps in their minds, like dancers waiting for the curtain to rise onstage.

The Iraqi leader smiled and extended his hand to Cantrell. Cantrell was smiling too. I couldn't believe that he didn't see it. It couldn't have been more obvious with flashing lights and sirens and balloons dropping from the ceiling and a big sign reading CONGRATULATIONS! YOU'VE JUST BEEN SCREWED!

Then I felt the leader's mind form the phrase, the signal that would tell his followers to kill us before we could make it out the door. He was already planning his ride back to his grimy little hideout in our Humvee.

I was certain of it. I hadn't questioned my talent in years. Not since I was a kid. And it was fairly screaming at me that this was about to go bad.

But I still hesitated. If I went for the H&K at my side, then they would all start shooting, and Cantrell would definitely get hit in the cross fire. I froze up. I didn't know what to do.

The leader took it out of my hands. He kept smiling. He gave the word: *"Anta lateef." You're very kind.*

I tackled Cantrell and took him to the ground. The bullet aimed for his back caught the Iraqi leader in the chest instead.

There was a moment of shock and horror as the Iraqi leader slowly toppled over, his chest a bloody mess, an exit wound bigger than a dinner plate in his back.

Then they all began shooting.

Cantrell and I scrambled for cover. Bullets tore through the shelving, right by my head. I fired off a few rounds, but it was a small store and we were outnumbered. There was no way to the door.

We were dead. No way around it. I looked to Cantrell, thinking maybe he had a plan, or possibly an airstrike hidden in his pocket. He looked back at me, waiting. He didn't say a word. I scanned him.

All I got was this: <*This is it, John. Showtime.*>

I wanted to scream at him. How the hell did he expect me to get us out of this? I wasn't the one who walked us into an ambush. I wasn't the guy in charge. I'd never even shot at a real, live human being before, and now I was caught between a bunch of trained killers. Only their reluctance to shoot each other kept us alive as we huddled behind the shelves.

That was what gave me the idea. I'd never tried anything like it before. But if the alternative was dying, then what the hell: nothing ventured, nothing gained.

I picked the brain of the nearest Iraqi. I put a picture of myself right into his field of vision, popping up to his left.

He turned and fired, as if by reflex.

And shot one of his own people.

He froze as a dozen different competing thoughts and emotions ran through his mind at once. I could empathize with all of them: he was guilty, he was stunned, he was so sure it had been one of the infidel Americans.

The last thing to go through his head was another bullet. I'd jumped out and pulled the same trick again. Another Iraqi fighter saw Cantrell's face on the back of the first guy's skull and fired.

I did it again, and again. And again. Jumping in, messing with their perceptions, and jumping out again. Each one was convinced they had us dead in their sights. Right before they took a bullet from one of their friends.

It lasted only a minute or so. Then it was just Cantrell and me. Alone in a store full of corpses.

Cantrell stood carefully, gun drawn. When he saw none of them were even twitching, he got up and went to the counter. He closed and locked the case, then nodded to me.

"You coming or what?" he asked.

I was still in shock. I'd just used my talent to kill a whole roomful of men. I felt no guilt—they'd wanted to kill me. I felt elated that I was still alive. But I also felt every one of them die. It was like watching the lights of a house go out, one by one.

I shook it off and stood up. I thought I was fine. I didn't know it yet, but the darkness would wait for me.

I looked at Cantrell, and for a moment, his guard was down. On purpose, I'm pretty sure. I read him like a book.

"You knew they were going to try this."

"Of course I did. Question is, why didn't you?"

"I was following you," I snapped.

"And look where you ended up. You never should have walked in here. You never should have let *me* walk in here. You should have known what they had planned from the second you read them. You should have told me to turn the Humvee around and get the hell back to base." He spoke with the exaggerated patience of an adult telling a child that there's no such thing as Santa Claus.

"But you knew," I said. "And you came in here anyway."

He looked me right in the eyes. "If you didn't survive this, you'd be no good to me anyway, John."

He didn't have to say any more than that. Not out loud. But I knew what he meant, in precise detail. His commanders didn't have any use for psychic soldiers who couldn't really fight.

Cantrell had always aimed for me to be an interrogator, just like the rest of his recruits. Like he said when we first met, he wanted us to pick the brains of our captured POWs, find out their secrets.

His superiors didn't see it that way. They didn't want to put any of Cantrell's special-ed students in a room with high-value detainees. They wanted more from us.

During the Cold War, nobody really minded spending money and time on Cantrell's psychics, even if they only made vague predictions about enemy troop movements and missile silos. Money and patience were nearly unlimited then. But with two actual wars going, there was a sudden demand for results. We had to prove we were worth the line item on our budget by actually using our talents in combat.

That was the reason Cantrell had me with him. To prove that our abilities could be weaponized. And he was willing to risk both our lives in the process.

I tried to keep some of what I was feeling from showing up on my face. I failed.

"What are you looking so pissed about?" he said out loud. "You passed."

I was searching for a response when an angry burst of thoughts suddenly broke into my head.

The lookout from the roof.

He'd heard the gunfire and thought he would come down to see his friends celebrating over our bodies. Instead, he found them all dead.

I felt the shock and rage burn through his mind, obliterating any concern for his own safety. He stepped out into the store from the back room, holding an AK-47 on me.

I could have gotten him. He was even less experienced than I was. A kid, maybe a year younger than me. He was confused and angry, and the AK-47 is notoriously inaccurate. I would have nailed him before he got me. I'm sure of it.

But Cantrell already had him. He dropped the Iraqi with a three-shot burst. I felt the kid's life end before his body hit the floor.

I stood there for a moment, looking stupid for the second time that day.

Cantrell crossed the store, covering the dead kid with his weapon the entire time. He kicked the AK-47 away from the corpse, then rolled the body over with his foot, just to be sure.

He scowled down and pointed at the kid's chest. There were three neatly spaced holes in the kid's shirt.

"Look at that," he said.

I thought he was admiring his grouping, but he was talking about the shirt. Something from Polo or a knockoff. Hard to tell with the blood.

"These fucking morons," he said. "Where do they think their clothes and their movies and their music come from? Guarantee you this idiot was listening to Tupac or some shit on his headphones before he decided to take up arms against the infidels. They should have figured it out by now: they're already living in America. We just haven't changed the names on the maps yet."

He shook his head and straightened up. "Come on," he said. "Let's get the hell out of here."

Sixteen hours later, we were back at Fort Bragg. Cantrell took me out and introduced me to good Scotch for the first time in my life. He told everyone in our unit who'd listen how I'd saved his ass. He told me he was proud of me.

He might have been willing to let me die in that grimy little store in Baghdad. He played off my trust and inexperience. But he wasn't lying. I read him. I know.

Somehow it means more when you get a compliment from a total bastard. It's like you had to pass a tougher exam to get the grade.

ALL OF CANTRELL'S special-ed kids got put on combat missions after that, no matter what our talents. I'll admit, some of us were useless in the field. There was one guy who could sense danger before it happened. In a war zone, that's not a whole lot of help. He'd get ready to go out in a Humvee, and get hit with one of his premonitions of imminent death. At which everyone else in his squad would look at him with the sort of expression that says, *No shit.*

They finally found a place for him in the entourage of high-ranking visitors. If he began to sweat, they knew it was time to head for a secure area. Once I saw him on TV, deep in the crowd while the president visited the troops.

I got a lot of practical experience. I was attached to a unit that did search-and-recovery missions, looking for faces from the deck with pictures of high-value targets on each card. At first the other guys were skeptical. But nothing convinces people like saving their lives a few dozen times.

In close quarters, I could tell you how many men were hiding inside an apartment building or a bombed-out storefront. I knew, instinctively, if a room was clear before we went through the door. It was harder for me to miss a shot than to make one: I could use my talent like radar, and aim my weapon for the center of the target, even through walls. It was impossible to get a sniper scope on me. I always felt it, that sudden prickle of another set of eyes focusing on me. When I hit the deck, everyone in my squad learned to do the same. That's where I learned to trace a sniper's gaze back to his nest, to find him based on his attention to me.

After a while, Cantrell was able to push for more important, more sensitive missions. I was trusted with black ops, attached as a specialist to units that went deep into enemy territory to look for the guys hiding out under protection of the Taliban or foreign governments. We crossed borders that weren't supposed to be crossed. We did questionable things, if any of us had been the kind to ask questions. We came back with captives: fresh meat wrapped and packed for Gitmo and Abu Ghraib and Bagram, as well as a dozen other places no one in the civilian world would ever know about.

I went with them. I began picking their brains, just like Cantrell wanted from the very start.

[11]

The old mall is halfway through the process of being abandoned. The big stores have moved on to newer, shinier homes. The spaces that aren't locked up are occupied by weird, off-brand franchises: a Chinese food/doughnut place; a cash-for-gold pawnshop; and, taking up an entire corner of the mall, a discount mattress store with an enormous, cheap vinyl banner over the old JCPenney sign. It's like seeing insects feed on the body of a big, dying animal.

Inside, the fountain is dry and there are only a few people drifting around. Half the lights are out.

Kelsey and I walk inside the mattress store. A single saleswoman, heavy with sadness, sits behind a desk in the middle of all the beds. She waves but doesn't get up. She thinks we might actually buy something—we still look like healthy consumers—but her knees hurt. Her back hurts. She worries about her next paycheck. There used to be two people on every shift. Now her manager comes in only every other day. *<and how am I supposed to make rent on twenty hours a week> <not even getting commission> <sell your own damn mattresses then>*

I can barely screen out her long list of complaints. There's too much already loaded up against my firewalls. I'm going to crash hard soon.

I just have to hold it together for a little while longer.

An old recording squawks to life, interrupting the bland pop music coming out of the ceiling speakers. The mall is closing in twenty minutes.

I smile at the saleswoman, shrug, and Kelsey and I head for the exit. She barely looks in our direction. It's easy to double back and duck behind a master-bedroom display set. It's even easier to plant the suggestion that the saleswoman head for home without checking the floor one last time. <*not paying me enough*> She sets the burglar alarm and shuffles for the exit. As she does, I read a short menu of the store's security options from her memory. There are no motion detectors—they haven't worked since JCPenney moved out. The owners are too cheap to spring for full-time patrols. Nobody cares about this place. It doesn't have anything worth stealing. It barely has anything worth vandalizing. People can smell neglect. It sends them in the other direction, even if they're not aware of it.

The lights in the mall switch off. The steel shutters on the entrances go down. Locked inside, we're as close to invisible as we can get for the night.

Kelsey is huddled up on one of the mattresses, arms around her knees, staring at nothing. The events of the day are starting to catch up with her too.

But there's a question she's been waiting to ask.

"Can't you get in touch with Sloan?" she says.

There's something plaintive in her mind when she says that, even though her voice remains firm. The betrayal still hurts. She thought Sloan was different. She thought he was her mentor. <*he never even tried to touch me, not even that time in Prague when I got so drunk*> She didn't believe me when I said that Sloan had abandoned us. She wants evidence. Or she wants me to at least try to reach out to him, to give him a chance to prove me wrong.

"You're the one who said he was completely cut off from the outside world," I remind her.

"You're the superspy. I'm sure there's some way you could contact him," she says.

She's right. There are a half dozen ways I could contact someone in Switzerland who could get inside the conference and deliver a message to Sloan. If I were really motivated, I could make the trip myself and show up in his hotel room with his morning croissant and cappuccino.

But honestly, I don't care enough to try. Sloan cannot help me now.

I don't know if Sloan has abandoned us, or if he's really out of touch, like Kelsey thinks. Either way, it doesn't matter. He would make the same coldhearted calculation that Gaines did. His vendetta against Preston is real enough—I could read that much from his mind—but that only means that he doesn't have any leverage to get Preston off our backs. More important, it's not worth the exposure to him to rescue me or Kelsey.

Hiring guys like me isn't exactly illegal, but it's not considered a standard business practice either. If Preston wanted to, he could produce the body of the man I killed, and spin any story he wants. The only reason he hasn't done that is because he wants to keep this quiet. If Sloan was to get involved, bring in his lawyers, or bring pressure on Preston by other means, then Preston could make things very unpleasant for him, in a very public way. Then Sloan might have to face some real questions from real cops. Of course, the odds are against him ever doing jail time—he's rich enough to tie any inquiry into knots. But the media would be all over him, and you can never tell how these things will end up, especially if a politically motivated prosecutor gets the case.

Sloan would look at all the negatives of helping us: the chance of exposure, the legal liability, the sheer tiresome inconvenience. Then he'd weigh those against the potential upside: none. So he'd make the easiest decision, and pull up the drawbridge with us on the other side of the moat. It should be easy for Sloan to write me off—it's an unspoken assumption in every contract I sign. Kelsey would probably be more difficult. Not enough to make a difference, though.

But Kelsey still wants to think her boss is a good guy. And for some reason, I don't feel like shattering that illusion for her.

So I tell her that there's nothing I can do.

I'm not sure she believes me, but she doesn't press too hard. She's smart. She probably knows the truth, same as I do.

In the grand scheme of things, people like us are disposable to people like Sloan.

<cherries jubilee> <Baked Alaska> <screw it, a cheeseburger, haven't had one of those in years, it feels like> <double cheeseburger, giant fries, large vanilla milkshake>

Kelsey is practically singing out a list of comfort foods. It's enough to make me grind my teeth.

<blueberry muffins> <Ben & Jerry's Cherry Garcia> <barbecued chicken> <Szechuan noodles> <Cobb salad> <pancakes> <bacon>

I find the employee break room. Sure enough, two giant vending machines are inside, filled with empty calories.

A minute later, there's broken glass on the floor and a pile of snacks in my hands. I dump them on the bed where Kelsey is sitting.

"It's not cherries jubilee," I tell her, "but it'll have to do."

She looks surprised. "I didn't say anything."

"You don't have to," I say. "I might have mentioned that once or twice already."

"Well, you don't have to listen."

I could almost laugh at that. If only it were that simple. "Yeah, you are really not getting it."

<*oh, blow it out your ass*>

"Heard that too."

"Serves you right," she says. "I was trying to be polite. You know, like normal human beings."

"If I were a normal human being, Kelsey, you'd be dead by now."

That hits her hard. She shuts up. For a moment, the only things going through her head are images of men with guns.

"I'm sorry," I say.

Clearly I need some space. I move to the other side of the room. It's not far enough. It doesn't reduce the volume on the pain and shock working its way through her system. She was working hard to cope. She didn't need me bringing it up again.

For a moment, I fear she's on the verge of losing it. Then she reaches for a bag of potato chips and tears it open. Eating is good. Eating means you still want to live, you're still feeding the organism.

Which reminds me, I really should eat something. But I don't feel all that hungry.

My hands hurt from the fight today. They're barely swollen, so I know that the pain isn't entirely real. This happens from time to time. Most of the ache is psychic. I know it's all in my head. It doesn't help. When you get a bad idea, it might stick with you for a while. When I get one, as a consequence of my very special brain, it grows its own legs and crawls around in my head. It takes on a life of its own and becomes real. Real enough to chew at me and grow bigger and fatter on the meat.

I rub my knuckles, try to shake out the hurt. The pain feels like rot and corruption, spreading in from the point of contact, like some nightmare skin infection, passed on by touch.

This is where the bill comes due, I realize. The feedback from the pain I inflicted on the other OmniVore security people. The thoughts of the salesman who gave us a lift, like touching a used condom.

Kelsey's anxiety and fear, hidden behind her efforts to press it down. And most of all, the dead man.

The pain in my hands is just the way it's all breaking in, getting past my defenses.

I know it's not real, not the worst of it. But it doesn't stop.

"Are you all right?" Kelsey asks.

She managed to get close without my noticing. I'm in worse shape than I thought.

"I'm fine." It comes out almost like a growl. I really need my pills.

"You don't seem fine."

Put it aside. Focus. Lock it down. Get it under control.

"Give me a second," I tell Kelsey.

Over the years, I've come up with lots of little ways to help block out the crazy and the hurt screaming from the people around me every minute of every day. I might take a shower. I have an old-fashioned mug with soap and a straight razor that I use to shave. It's calming. It forces me to pay attention. I spend a good five minutes with nothing but the steam, the scent of the soap, and the sound of steel scraping against my beard and skin. Then I might put on a clean, pressed white shirt, with a decent suit over that. Go to a dark, quiet restaurant, where the waiters don't wear fifteen different kinds of flair and bother you every five minutes with a suggestion to try the Bacon Balls. A place where they know enough to let you enjoy your steak and your drink in peace. And then I can chase my whiskey with enough pills to block out the constant noise of all of you, all of your whining and pissing and moaning and bitching and running in circles as you think about your pathetic little lives. This is how I keep myself human.

Unfortunately, all these rituals depend on stuff that's now gone.

I run through the inventory. Twelve tailored suits in the closet. About thirty good shirts on the hangers. There was an Attolini I had made to measure in Italy. Two backup guns, another Walther and a Glock 9mm, one in the bedside table, one in a drawer in the kitchen.

Not to mention a bar full of whiskey and vodka and a bottle of fifty-year-old Laphroaig I got from a client. Was saving that for a special occasion.

I'm not particularly sentimental, but I'm going to miss that bottle.

Not as much as my pills, if I'm being honest.

My pills. The results of doctor-shopping, duplicate prescriptions, and a half dozen Internet drug dealers. A whole bunch of Vicodin and oxycodone, some antiseizure meds for when the migraines got really bad, and some Ambien, Haldol, and Ativan to help me sleep.

I'd even take an Advil right now, because my hands will not fucking stop hurting.

Out of nowhere, I see it again. Body dropping, blood in the air. That absence in the mental landscape as a man suddenly stops. Stops breathing, stops thinking, stops existing. The freshly made hole in the world where a human being used to live—a little rip that threatens to suck all the warmth and life into the cold and emptiness of the abyss, and take me right along with it.

Every time, I am convinced that this will be the one that drags me down.

I realize I am shaking and sweating. I listen desperately to the sound of my own heartbeat, trying to convince myself I am still alive.

I try to block it out. Not working.

"Are you all right?" Kelsey asks again.

No. No, I am not.

It feels like insects are under the skin now. My bones feel like someone is scrubbing them with steel wool. Everything I own is gone. The idea sits there, in my brain, like a chunk of ice that stubbornly refuses to melt. Everything I own is gone.

I spin and punch the wall, trying to block the fake pain with the real thing.

I look down. There's a hole in the drywall and blood on my knuckles. It didn't work. The insects are still there, under the skin, chewing away. I can still feel the hole, like a sudden increase in gravity, plucking at me, pulling me down.

"Jesus," Kelsey says. Her voice drags me out of my head for a moment. "What's going on? What are you doing?"

"I need my goddamned pills," I snap at her, biting off each word.

Her eyes are wide. She's looking at me like I'm a strange dog blocking her path. She steps closer, carefully.

"Easy," she says. Her voice is very low. "Take it easy."

"Stay back," I warn her. I don't want her picking up on my pain. It can be contagious when I'm like this.

She keeps coming anyway. "I can help," she says. She reaches out, slowly, like a bomb-squad technician, and takes my hands in her own.

She brushes away the dust. I flinch.

"Take it easy. Breathe," she says. "Breathe."

My whole body is a clenched fist now. But I try.

"Come on. Breathe. Listen to my voice. Focus on that."

Somehow it works. I don't know how. She's a calm center in the midst of it all.

She can see me crank down the level of tension, bit by bit. The static and pain begin to clear.

"There you go," she says. "You're getting it back, right?"

I nod.

"Prove it," she says. "What am I thinking?"

I look into her head.

That can't be right.

She's got a look on her face. Half smile, half smirk.

"Maybe we can do something to take your mind off the pain," she says.

"I thought you didn't want to use my body for cheap thrills."

She shrugs. "Yeah, well. Tomorrow we may die, and all that. Besides"—she takes a look around the store—"what else are we going to do in here? Build a fort?"

She leans in, with the same half smirk, and I kiss her.

MOST OF THE time, I try to concentrate on the physical, to screen out the rush of emotions that surges forward with sex. This is where we are still closest to being animals, where we can reliably blot out our thoughts, where we can try to respond only to the basic facts of hard and wet and warmth and comfort.

But with Kelsey, it's different. She's already inside, has already seen the cracks in my defenses. And she does not care.

She doesn't have to ask me anything. I know what she wants the second she wants it. I can feel her get close, and I know just what it will take to push her over the edge. We form a circle together, her excitement feeding mine, over and over, locked into the rhythms of each other's body, shuddering to a finish, and then starting again. Again and again and again.

Honestly, sex with a telepath is pretty great. If you ever meet me, you should try it.

"PROFESSIONAL GAMBLER. YOU'D know what cards everyone was holding."

"God, no. The times I've been inside a casino, it's like rats scratching their way out of my brain."

Kelsey lies with her head on my shoulder, one arm and one leg thrown over me. We're on the mattress, huddled together for warmth under the thin sheets. The store's air-conditioning is brutal. She's trying to come up with a new career for me, new ways for me to use my talent that don't end with me hiding inside a dying mall.

"You could be a police officer. You'd always know exactly who did the crime. Hundred percent solve rate."

"Most of the time, the cops already know who did the crime. It's the guy standing there crying over the corpse with a bloody steak knife. Anyway, I thought the idea was to get away from people shooting at me."

"All right, then. Therapist. You could find out what's really bothering people. Give them exactly the advice they need. You could probably even undo their problems yourself. Go inside their minds and find the clogs and fix them up. Like a plumber."

I laugh at that. "I think plumbers make more money than therapists. And either way, it's not enough."

"Because you need the money for your own island."

"Exactly."

She props herself up a little so she can look at my face. "Is it that bad?"

My voice is a little tight when I answer. "You think I was faking before?"

"No, no," she says quickly. "I'm asking if it's always that bad. If there's no other way to handle it."

I search for the right words. Come up empty. "It's that bad. Yes."

"Is running off to a deserted island really the best idea you've got?"

Good question. One I've asked myself many, many times. "The drugs won't work forever," I tell her. "I've already got a high tolerance for painkillers. The standard antimigraine meds might as well be sugar pills to me now. I've seen the end of this curve with other guys, and it always leads to me with a needle, looking for a vein."

"Have you tried anything else?"

"I'm open to suggestions."

"Meditation?"

"Doesn't work," I tell her. "The quieter my mind becomes, the louder everyone else's thoughts get. It's like that right now."

"Really?"

I nod. "Aside from you, the closest person is a homeless guy camped out at the bus shelter at the edge of the parking lot, about a thousand yards away. Ordinarily, he'd be way out of my reach. He's asleep. If he was awake, I'd probably be screaming about the black helicopters and the Bilderbergers and itching the staph infection he's got on both arms."

"Jesus Christ," she says. "So why haven't you just stolen enough money to buy your own island already?"

She's laughing, but she's not joking. Not entirely. Even someone like Kelsey, with her healthy respect for the rules and love of structure, knows that pain can push you outside the lines of what's good and proper. And she's already seen me break a half dozen laws and commandments, including the big one about killing.

Sloan asked me something similar. It makes sense. It's like the Vegas-act question. If someone can do what I do, why not just take anything I want? I ask myself sometimes.

Sometimes it's good to remind myself of the reasons by saying them out loud.

"It doesn't work like that. You've tried separating rich people from their money before, right?" I ask.

"Oh my God, yes," she says, and I get a quick montage of all the moments when she's had to persuade Sloan's clients and partners to write checks, to make an investment or pay their debts; it's like climbing a mountain every time, even when Sloan was doubling their money.

"So you know. It's like the old joke: a rich man doesn't get that way by reaching for his wallet all the time. It goes against almost everything in their nature. They don't give away their money without a really good reason. And even then it's a struggle. So I could push and prod, and I might fool their brains into accepting some bullshit excuse to write me a check. For a while. But it wouldn't last. Eventually people always go back to who they are. They do what they want to do. They'd recognize that something was wrong. They'd start making noises, asking around with other people who know me. They'd talk to each other, and pretty soon I'd have a price on my head. I already told your boss: I don't want to live that way."

Kelsey takes an exaggerated look around the store. "Yeah, this definitely seems like the safer alternative."

She has a point. "There are degrees of risk," I say. But that's not the whole reason, and she knows it. I'm not sure why, but I decide to tell her the rest.

"Anyway. What would you call someone who does that? Who worms his way into someone's trust and takes a chunk out of their lives?"

It jumps into her head: *<parasite>*.

"Right," I say. "My whole life, everything I ever got, someone was always sure to tell me that it wasn't really mine. There was always some foster parent or social worker or church volunteer who would remind me that my whole life depended on them. My food, my clothes, whatever I had—the money always came from the state or some charity or someone else's pocket. They were so *happy* when they told me, too. I could feel it. Sometimes they wanted me to know how generous they were being. Or they wanted me to seem more grateful than I was. But most of the time, they wanted me to know I was draining the blood right out of their veins. That whatever I got, they could rip it back at any moment. So now I don't take what I don't earn. I do my job, and I get paid for my services. And nobody can ever tell me I don't deserve it."

An awkward silence. She picks up on my discomfort and changes the subject. Which is kind of her.

"Well, at least now I know you didn't ensorcell me into jumping into bed with you," she says.

"'Ensorcell'? Is that even a word?"

"Pretty sure. I read it in a book about witches having a lot of sex with vampires."

"How appropriate."

"Thank you, by the way," she says.

"For what?"

"For not asking. Every guy always wants to know."

"I think it was pretty obvious."

"Don't get overconfident. There's always room for improvement."

"I'm willing to put in the hours if you are."

She laughs again, sits up, and stretches. I see the muscles moving under her flawless skin, feel the animal contentment purring through her body, and share in it for a moment.

Then she turns and sees her clothes—literally the only thing she owns right now—crumpled on the cheap carpeting, and the reality hits her again. How far away she is from home, how far away she is from her actual life. It's like a wave that threatens to swamp her with fear and loneliness.

She shakes it off, almost physically, then turns to me. *<this was fun and all, but . . .>*

"This was fun and all, but now I've got to ask: What's the plan?"

I hate to admit it, but I've run out of ideas. So I've got to do something I never thought I'd do again.

I'm going to call Cantrell.

[12]

I'm not exactly sure when I joined the private sector. One day I checked the bank account where I direct-deposited my paychecks. The money just sat there most of the time. I traveled in government transports and ate in army mess halls. My clothes came from uniform stores, and a packet of spending cash was always included in the kit for any mission. But this time, when I checked my bank's website, I noticed that my account had more money than I expected. A lot more. I looked at the last few transactions, and discovered that my paychecks were no longer coming from the government, but from a private company called Global Travel, LLC. And they were much bigger.

I asked Cantrell about this the next time I saw him. He gave me his usual smile and said, "You complaining?"

We'd turned into a private military contractor somewhere along the line—or, more accurately, mercenaries. I'd done three tours in Afghanistan and Iraq by then. Suddenly I was officially a civilian again.

Other than that, nothing really changed.

We were still backstopped by U.S. soldiers. We still used the CIA's jets wherever we went, or hitched a ride on military transports. And our security clearances still got us into every base, government building, and top-secret black site.

The main difference was that I was now free to go back to the States whenever I wasn't on a mission. I began commuting to the War on Terror.

A lot of the money budgeted for fighting bin Laden and other bad guys went in big crates direct to the Middle East, but there was still plenty left over for salaries and contracts. Cantrell secured us brand-new office space in Crystal City, Virginia, in a corporate park filled with CIA front companies. I found an apartment near Dupont Circle, at the center of a cluster of trendy spots populated by hipsters and young professionals.

I did my best to rejoin the outside world. I studied civilian life like I was reading a mission brief for hostile territory. I learned how to wear a suit instead of a uniform. I began to drink decent whiskey instead of whatever was cheapest on the shelf. And at night, I went out to a lot of places where I faked polite conversation with people while pretending I didn't know exactly what was going on behind their eyes.

One night I was at an embassy party that Cantrell insisted I attend. It was filled with old, very rich men who talked quietly in small groups, dividing up the globe between dirty jokes. Most of the women were escorts, but there was a small group of civilians: interns, think-tankers, and policy wonks who stuck close to the food trays. They were making the Ivy League equivalent of minimum wage, but they all had big plans. This was the ground level for the New World Order, and they intended to gnaw their way to the top.

That's where I met Whitney. She was a low-level staffer in the State Department, but already eyeing her path over to Defense or the White House, where the real power flowed. I assembled a quick picture of her from inside her head: perfectly dull home life back in Michigan, father a big political donor, leveraging her intellect and her sharp good looks into one job after another with a machinelike precision.

She'd had a few drinks, but her first impression of me still came through crisp and clear. Deep tan and buzz-cut hair screamed ex-military. Good suit said private contractor, high-dollar salary. The cheap wrinkle-free shirt underneath said I wasn't quite sure how to spend it yet. The word that kept bouncing around in her brain was *<potential>*.

I've rarely met anyone so focused outside of a firefight. Even reading her mind didn't quite prepare me for how fast she made decisions. Within minutes of walking over to me, she'd already mapped out the dark corner of the party where she would allow me to lift her dress and pull down her underwear. She had plans for me, and not just for the night.

Who could say no to someone like that?

Within a month, we were living together. We were a new-model DC power couple, each with our own security clearances and classified briefing books on our bedside tables. The fact that we didn't actually like each other very much didn't come up that often.

I was still flying back and forth from the Middle East every couple of weeks. She had her own seventy-hour schedule at work as she and her colleagues planned where to send people like me for the next battle.

Whitney put up with what she called my James Bond lifestyle, and I pretended not to notice the cyclonic rages that could sweep through her at a moment's notice. Unhappy with her hair, she would throw her brush so hard it would break the mirror. I learned to budget for things like new dishes and minor household repairs. She screamed over the phone at everyone—subordinates, bosses, friends, her parents—with a scorched-earth intensity that had them babbling apologies. Being on the receiving end of one of her rants could trigger a migraine that would last for days.

I kept my talent from her. I justified it because it was classified. But in truth, I didn't think she'd understand or believe me. And to be totally honest, I just didn't trust her.

Occasionally, I'd catch a glimpse of a fumbled encounter in her mind, usually on the office couch with her boss or a coworker. She thought of it as tension relief when she couldn't get to the gym, and stomped any residual guilt under her heel until it quit whimpering. In return, I slept with her girlfriends, who liked her even less than I did. One of the advantages of reading minds is knowing exactly how much you can get away with.

I figured it was as close to normal as someone like me was going to get.

I GOT THE call at home.

"Son, you know I hate to drag you back into the shit," Cantrell lied, making it sound almost sincere. "But we got a big one. High-value prisoner with beaucoup secrets stashed in his head."

"What, you finally got Osama?" I joked.

This was long before SEAL Team Six killed bin Laden, back when he was still the bogeyman of the Western world, haunting us all with the occasional message from a hidden cavern somewhere. This was when he was still the most wanted man on the planet.

There was a pause, and I could tell Cantrell was deciding how much he could reveal, even on a secure line.

"No," he said. "But they say they got someone who knows where to find him. They think they got Osama's boyfriend."

It was common knowledge in the business that bin Laden was a pedophile with a thing for underage boys. It was the kind of rumor that probably got started as a bad joke, but then took on a life of its own. In Afghanistan, there's an old—and seriously fucked-up—tradition of using dancing boys as entertainment at tribal celebrations, the same way a bunch of drunken frat boys will hire a stripper for a bachelor party. The practice, called *bacha bazi*, gained new life under the Taliban after it came into power, with the boys—as young as ten or eleven—used as sexual party favors by the warlords.

In other words, about what you'd expect from a group that stones women to death for being raped and shoots little girls in the head when they try to learn to read.

Osama was rumored to be a big fan of *bacha bazi*, even taking his favorite boy toy into the caves of Tora Bora with him when the U.S. bombing started.

But it was just a rumor. There was never any hard intel.

Until we got Prisoner #7461. His given name was Fahran.

Cantrell laid out the whole story for me on the plane ride out of Reagan, on our way to Afghanistan.

They picked him up with a bunch of Taliban hard-liners in Nuristan province. Our guys were out on a presence patrol, reminding the locals of the military might of the United States, when the hard-liners attacked. Most of them retreated into the hills right away. But a group of seven were cut off and surrendered.

Fahran was the youngest of the bunch, and one of the U.S. troops—who'd picked up a lot of Pashto in his tours—overheard his friends insulting him. They referred to Fahran as a veteran *bacha*. And then they said something about his boyfriend coming to rescue him from the satanic Americans: the great Osama bin Laden. The soldier knew the rumors as well as anyone in Afghanistan, so he reported it up the chain of command.

The guys in black uniforms with no rank showed up. They were skeptical at first, but they questioned the other hard-liners. Every one of them gave the same answers. How Fahran had spoken of being bin Laden's favorite, how he had accompanied Osama everywhere—even to the Saudi's most recent hiding places.

So they threw a hood over Fahran's head. Before nightfall, he was in a cell.

But the little dancing boy turned out to be harder than everyone else in his crew. From what Cantrell told me, they'd done their best already. They'd worked on him around the clock, using all the standard tricks in the interrogation manual.

Nothing.

The kid knew where to find bin Laden. But he wouldn't talk.

Which was why they had paid Cantrell's insanely high contractor's fee and had me shipped over on the company's jet.

To Bagram.

[13]

The phone rings for a while before someone picks up. "Cactus Bar and Grill."

I rack my brain, trying to remember the proper countersign. "What time is happy hour?"

The guy on the other end sounds bored. "Happy hour is all day, every day."

"24-7," I say. "And is it still ladies' night every night?"

That should be the call-and-response to let the operator know I'm legit, even if it is a couple of years out of date.

"That's right," he says. "Anything else I can do for you?"

"Is Nick there?"

Long pause. "Who wants to know?

"I need to leave a message for Nick."

Another long pause. "Nobody by that name here."

I've been out of the loop for a while, but I can't believe Cantrell would shut down all his old listening posts. He might not be officially CIA anymore, but he's still plugged in deep.

"He was a regular there. I need to get in touch with him. Can you take my number, at least? Just in case he comes in."

"I told you. There's no Nick here. Sorry."

"If Nick comes in, let him know I called."

"Whatever, man."

He hangs up, and I get the impression I annoyed a perfectly normal bartender for no good reason.

I wait for five minutes, then another ten. Then another ten. Kelsey waits, not sure what I'm doing, but not willing to disturb me.

I'm just about to give up and call some other old numbers when the phone rings.

I hesitate a moment. Then I curse myself for waiting. If you've decided to do something, even if it's hard, you do it. Waiting around doesn't make the choice any easier.

I pick up the phone and hear the voice of the man who taught me that.

"You must be desperate," Cantrell says. "Nobody's called the Cactus in a long time."

"Well, you didn't send me a new decoder ring this year."

He laughs. "That's what happens when you quit the official Captain Midnight club, kid. You gotta pay the dues if you want to remain a junior birdman. How's things going?"

I suspect he already knows what's going on, but I give him a brief, edited version anyway. The job, getting burned, and now being tracked with a kill order on my head.

"Sounds like you got a problem," Cantrell says.

"Who's looking out for Preston? As soon as my name came up, they told him to terminate me. What the hell is he into?"

Cantrell laughs again. "You asking me?"

"You always had all the answers."

"So what makes you think I'm going to give them to you? We already covered this. You quit."

"Fine," I say. "Nice talking to you. I'll see you around."

"Whoa, whoa, whoa there. No need to go sulk in your room yet, princess. I might be able to help you out."

"I'll survive on my own. I'm pretty good at that, remember?"

"I'm not so sure anymore," Cantrell says. He drops the down-home glaze, and his voice becomes clinical and cold. "You've got no money, no weapons, no base of operations, and no way to get any of that back without exposure. You're dragging a civilian around. Even with your talents and training, this story only ends with you on an autopsy table. You've fucked the dog pretty good here, John. Honestly, I trained you better than this."

That stings. I'm surprised—and annoyed—by how much I still want Cantrell to think well of me.

"Why do I get the feeling you knew all this before I ever picked up the phone?"

I can hear the smile in Cantrell's voice when he answers. At least I redeemed myself a little bit with that question.

"Well, I thought you might get in touch. Preston asked his friends to check you out. I might not be on the official payroll anymore, but they still come to me when one of my kids is out there causing trouble."

That makes sense. Anyone who wanted information on me would go straight to Cantrell. Which means he's had plenty of time to think about my problems.

"See, your mistake was underestimating your target. You thought your bullshit cover story would hold up. But you weren't expecting someone with real muscle to start looking at it. People with access to classified files. Like your personnel records."

That narrows it down. There are a couple of black-ops agencies with that kind of clearance. But only one that would have the information available that quickly, just sitting on the other end of a search query.

"You're telling me Preston is working for the CIA?"

Cantrell laughs at the tone in my voice. "Not like it's an exclusive club. They hired you, didn't they? Anyway, when those people found out who you were, they immediately gave him the order to drop you because they don't want you peeking inside his head. Too many secrets in there. Lots of stuff they don't want out in the world."

"Like what?"

"Come on, son. That's classified."

"They didn't tell you, did they?"

He laughs. "That's not considered part of my operational area these days. But let me run a little hypothetical past you. You know the CIA has its own venture capital arm, right? Investing in high-tech companies for the good of the nation and all that?"

"Sure." Everyone who reads *Forbes* knows that. It's called In-Q-Tel.

"Right. The guys you're up against, they're like the quiet version of that. The one that doesn't put out press releases. They're the ones backing Preston and OmniVore."

"Yeah, but everybody knows the CIA invests in these kind of companies. It's not a secret. Why would they suddenly start dropping kill orders?"

Cantrell makes a tsking noise, like this should be obvious. "Well, John, why do you think? You've already seen what data mining can do if it's turned against you. Preston's got access to every fact in the public record about you. He had your bank account numbers, your address, your mortgage, your passwords, everything, in just a couple hours. What does that tell you?"

I feel like I'm back in training. But I answer anyway. "That he's inside every one of OmniVore's clients. He built backdoors into all of their data."

"Pretty good guess," Cantrell says. "Now, do you think the CIA might have some interest in the hidden data of every major corporation that's hired OmniVore? You think they might have some use for searching through every financial transaction a bank makes? Every stock sale that goes through a major brokerage? Being able to trace every credit-card purchase of any customer they want, anywhere they go, anytime? Searching through the flight records of every major airline to find a particular passenger? Every email you've ever written, every dick pic you sent your girlfriend, every drug you've ever been prescribed—"

"I get it, I get it," I say. I'm not a complete amateur, the last twenty-four hours notwithstanding. "The CIA can finally compete with the NSA, using America's most trusted brand names to do the spying for them."

"Right," he says, and to my shame, I feel like I just got an A from the teacher. "So you can see how they might be a little leery about having someone like you—a free agent, nobody watching you anymore, totally outside the chain of command—knowing all the same secrets that Preston knows. You can probably imagine the shitstorm that the Agency would have to endure if any of this got out. People are already paranoid enough about their privacy settings on Facebook. Imagine how the Fortune 500 would feel if they discovered that the company they hired to protect their data was actually sluicing everything over to the CIA? The blood would be knee-deep in the streets in Washington. Hell, someone might even have to quit and go get a high-paying job as a lobbyist. Much easier to have him kill you. Which is one reason they've got a squad of heavy hitters following that boy everywhere he goes."

"But they didn't tell him everything about me," I say. "Preston's men had no idea what they were up against."

"Maybe they thought he didn't need to know. You're still considered a pretty big national secret yourself."

"Not as valuable as Preston, apparently."

"I wouldn't say that," Cantrell says, and lets it hang there.

And here it is. Cantrell is not on the line with me out of charity. There's always a motive. Nothing's free.

"Something tells me you're going to offer me a solution here."

"Really? You must be psychic."

God, I am getting tired of that joke. "I've heard you pitch before. I know the rhythms."

"You're right. I can make all your problems go away."

"How?"

"Come back in."

I'm actually stunned into silence. Times like this, I wish my talent worked over the phone.

"You want me to work for you again?"

"And America. Motherhood. Apple pie. The USA and Chevrolet. Truth and Justice. All the good stuff. We invested a lot into you, John. As much as it pains me to say it, you were one of our best. We'd take you back."

"And my problems with Preston?"

"Disappear," Cantrell says.

"You have got to be kidding. You just told me the Agency wants me dead."

"There are wheels within wheels, John, and my father's house has many rooms," Cantrell says. "There are always a shitload of competing agendas. You know that. Someone panicked. Made a bad decision. But we can rectify that now. After all, you'll be on the right side again. Nobody would worry about you running around with their secrets once you're back inside the fence."

He sounds serious. For a moment, it's tempting. There's a lot to be said for having the government on your side. It's like having a big brother to beat up all the bullies in your neighborhood—except he's armed with nuclear weapons and billions of dollars. It's certainly working out pretty well for Preston right now.

There's only one bit of sand in the gears. Kelsey.

"What about the civilian?" I ask.

"What about her?"

"Can you guarantee her safety?"

Kelsey's been listening to my half of the conversation the whole time, but now her attention sharpens on me like a needle.

"She must be a looker."

I wait.

"Negotiable," he finally says.

"Not good enough."

"Whoa, a looker and good in bed too. If she cooks, marry her."

"I'm serious."

"What do you want from me? You're talking about some big secrets here. And she's not part of the family. I'm telling you she's got a better chance of surviving if you're inside the tent than if you're outside pissing in. That's the best you're going to get."

I suspect he's right. Cantrell never lied to me—depending on how you define a lie, of course. This seems like the best deal I'm likely to get.

Not so great for Kelsey, admittedly.

"Son, you're up shit creek and I'm driving the honey wagon," Cantrell says when I don't answer. "You going to jump aboard or not?"

Kelsey is still looking at me. Cantrell waits.

For a long moment, I don't have an answer for either of them.

"Let me get back to you," I say.

"You and your goddamn conscience. This is a limited-time offer. You know that."

"I know. Twenty-four hours. I'll call back at this number."

Cantrell sighs. "If that's what your pride requires. Don't wait too long."

An ugly little suspicion occurs to me. Before I can stop myself, I open my mouth and let it out.

"You know, I have to wonder. All of this seems almost designed to get me out of the private sector and back into government work. My client flakes out on me, Preston steals everything I own and puts a price on my head. It's like someone's cutting off all my alternatives. Then I call you, and you magically have a job offer waiting."

A long pause. "You got a question for me, John?"

"These people you talk about behind Preston—any of them happen to sit in your chair? Did you set me up, Cantrell?"

That brings another laugh. It even sounds genuine. "No," he says. "You give me too much credit. No way I could have planned this. I'm just improvising here, trying to find the silver lining in this clusterfuck for all of us."

Then he pauses.

"But, son, even if I did, do you think I'd ever be stupid enough to admit it?"

He's still chuckling when he hangs up.

Like I said, there are times I wish my talent worked over the phone. Then again, sometimes, it's probably better that it doesn't.

There are some things I don't really want to know.

[14]

We leave the mall via a fire exit—unsurprisingly, the alarm is old and doesn't work—around 6:00 A.M., long before the first shift arrives.

I tell Kelsey about Cantrell's offer when we're in the Escalade. She has a right to know just how deep this all goes.

She takes it better than I thought possible when I tell her that the most powerful covert operations agency in the world is after us.

"Eli's working with the CIA? Really?"

I nod. She looks thoughtful, not scared.

"That's weird," she says. "I thought he stopped doing that a long time ago."

Proving that you can, in fact, surprise a psychic. That stops me short. "He did what?"

"He used to do some contract work for them."

"For the CIA? Seriously?"

She nods, like this is obvious. "With their tech division. Signals intelligence. Decrypting communications, creating viral attacks. That kind of thing. You must know the Agency uses a lot of programmers now, right?"

I did, but I had no idea Preston was one of them. "Sloan said he recruited him out of Harvard."

Kelsey shakes her head. "No. I mean, yes, Eli dropped out. But Everett heard about him through an old contact at the NSA. He hired him from the government. He does that a lot. He says it's good training for the kind of people he needs. It's not something Eli puts on his official résumé, but it was a big point in his career. There's a lot of bleeding-edge programming work being done in the intelligence community these days—"

"And you're just telling me this *now*?"

"It was in the packet I gave you," she snaps back. "The one you said you didn't need." *<you should have done your homework>*

"Hey. Does this seem like an I-told-you-so moment to you?"

She looks away, annoyed.

It occurs to me, not for the first time, that she's handling this differently from most people who've been shot at. Until now, I haven't had the time to examine it. But most people don't respond with anger. Most people go into a mild kind of shock after someone tries to kill them. If they believe the threat is still out there, their top priority is to hide. This is usually followed by at least a month of flinching at loud noises, along with occasional flashes of *<holy crap I can't believe that really happened>*.

Not Kelsey, though. She's just pissed. Which means there's something in her life that let her jump past the usual first stages of trauma and get right to the anger.

"Where did you say Sloan hired you from?"

She stops short. "I didn't," she says, but it jumps into her head. A big building in Maryland. Black-mirror windows, like wraparound sunglasses.

"The NSA?" I say. Christ, is there anyone involved in this who hasn't been a spook?

"I wasn't clandestine operations. I was administrative support."

There's a *<but>* attached to that statement. More than she's telling me. "But it wasn't for lack of trying, was it?"

She shrugs. "I applied for the CIA. I didn't make the cut."

There's a warning there, like razor wire around her thoughts. She doesn't want to discuss it, and she doesn't want me prying either.

So she starts singing to herself again. *<happy birthday to you happy birthday to you happy birthday dear Kelsey>*

I almost laugh. That's pretty damn smart. And a really effective way to keep me out of her head. I hate that song.

I do my best to block it out for a few more miles. Then she speaks up again.

"This is where you say it's time for me to go home, isn't it?" she says.

I must look surprised, because she laughs. "Doesn't take a mind reader," she says. "Let me explain why that's a terrible idea."

I can see her lining up arguments like PowerPoint slides, as if she's about to make a presentation in some midrange hotel conference room.

I try to cut her off before she gets going. "I can still get you back to Sloan," I say. "This can end right here for you."

She makes a face. *<oh horseshit>* "You don't really believe that. I cracked your code when you were talking to that guy on the phone, you know. If I go back to my apartment, to my life, how much time do you think I have before they send someone for me?"

She's right. An impressive mind in there. But it doesn't matter. I choose my words carefully. "I believe it's safer than staying with me."

"Because you're going after Eli now," she says. "You're not going to take the deal."

It's better for her if she doesn't know too many details. It will give her a good legal defense if everything goes wrong on my end, and someone tries to make her pay for what I'm planning to do to Preston. "What makes you say that?"

"I think I know you a little by now. And anyway, I wouldn't, if I were you."

That makes me smile. "Oh really?"

There's a little A-bomb cloud that goes off when she hears the tone in my voice. "Yeah," she says flatly. "Really. I close deals for Sloan all the time. And I'd never take an offer like this. You'd be helpless, totally at their mercy. You hand yourself over, and what guarantee do you have they won't just box you up and put you away? None at all. It's like a cow walking into a slaughterhouse, pretending it's still got a choice."

"I don't have a lot of other options."

"You really think the same people who want us both dead right now will just take you back, and all is forgiven? What makes you think they won't kill you as soon as you show up for your first day on the job?"

"Because I've worked for them," I snap back at her. "At the end of the day, the CIA is just another bureaucracy. Nobody gets promoted for holding a grudge. They could give a crap about me. They care about Preston and his secrets. That's all. Remove Preston from the equation, and they no longer have any reason to care what I do."

She smiles, like I've just fallen into her trap.

"And that's what you're going to do, right?" she says. "You think you've got to go after him, hurt him, or even kill him. That's the only way to end the threat. You think it's all a zero-sum game. Preston pushed you, so you've got to go find him and push him back. Show him you're scarier. That you won't back down. And then he won't back down either. And it just keeps going, back and forth, until one of you gets a bullet in the head. Am I right?"

Sad to say, that was pretty much my plan. I don't confirm or deny it, but she doesn't care. She keeps going.

"That's stupid," she says. "That's what he expects. He knows how you were trained. He won't even have to send anyone looking for you. He knows you'll go rushing after him, dick first and guns blazing. And as soon as you show up, he's going to have a bunch of guys waiting to shoot you dead."

I take a little offense at that. "I've beaten worse odds," I tell her. "You've seen me do it."

"Stupid," she says again. "All it takes is one lucky shot. But sure, let's say you do get past all of them. You get to Eli. Then what—you kill him? What good does that do? What do you win?"

"It will be over. And I'll be alive."

"Alive, but broke, and looking over your shoulder for years, waiting to be arrested for the murder of a Silicon Valley billionaire. Sounds like a real victory party to me," she says. She lets that sink in for a moment. "Or you could get your life back, and even come out ahead on this job."

She's got a point. And an idea she's been working on, in the back of her head. But I know this world better than she does.

"There is no job," I remind her. "Your boss burned me. I've got no client."

She makes a face, like she can't believe I'm this slow. "So go to work for yourself."

And it starts to unfold, behind her eyes. I can see almost all of it. But I want to hear it out loud. "Tell me what you mean."

"Do your job. Don't kick down Eli's door. Be smarter than him. Take the one thing that really matters to him."

I get it now. "The algorithm."

"Right," she says. "Steal it back, just like you were hired to do. And then hold it for ransom."

"I told you, he didn't steal it from Sloan."

"Who cares? No matter where he got it, Eli used that source code as the basis for everything he's built. It's the lifeblood of his company. He needs it to find patterns in all the data out there. The algorithm is what makes Cutter work. And without Cutter, he's not valuable anymore. No more clients. No more backing from the CIA. He'd sell his own mother to get it back. Guaranteed."

I have to admit: I like the idea. It beats the hell out of going directly up against a group of ex–special ops killers.

"You should listen to me," Kelsey says when she sees me wavering. "This is what I do for a living. I analyze problems and come up with the best solutions. And I'm pretty good at it."

"So this is what you'd do, even if I wasn't around?" I ask her.

Another face. "Don't be an idiot. I don't stand a chance. But you do. You have the skills and the talent. And I'm going to do everything I can to make sure you win. That means you're stuck with me."

It could work. But it's still dangerous. She would still be safer hiding out somewhere—maybe in that office Sloan keeps in South Dakota.

Being a gentleman, I give her one more chance to back out.

"You can still go home. Stay safe. You're still breathing."

"How long do you think that's going to last?" she snaps. "You're not the only one at risk here. I'd appreciate it if you stopped thinking like you are. This is my life too. I'm not about to stand around, chewing my cud, waiting for the bolt to the head."

For a brief moment, I worry my talent has been working overtime, gently nudging her into making this decision.

And then I shove the thought aside, because as much as I hate to admit it, I'm not sure I can do this alone. With Kelsey's help, the odds move up from "no way in hell" to "better than impossible."

She's tough and she's smart and her plan's good. I'm not likely to find a better partner.

Even so, the smart money says we both end up dead. But I'll take what I can get. I'm not ready to go quietly into the slaughterhouse either.

"All right," I say. "We'll do it. Any ideas on how we get the algorithm?"

She knew she was going to persuade me. She never had a doubt. Her smile is brilliant. "I can't do all the work. I mean, you're pretty, but you've got to bring something to the table, Smith."

I laugh. Then I ask her, "Jesus, how did the Agency ever let you slip away?"

It was meant as a joke. But it brings up the memories she was trying to guard. She starts singing *really loud* in her mind—*<AND MANY MORE ON CHANNEL FOUR>*—but it's too late.

I see the whole thing, even if it's all in fragments: A man—a senior Agency recruiter—takes Kelsey into a small white room. There's a big-screen monitor on one wall and a desk with two chairs.

I know what happened.

The CIA should have loved her. She's smart. She's attractive and ambitious, and thanks to her father, despite his other failings, she knows how to handle a gun. (They stopped going on those father-daughter hunting trips not long after she found out he'd been cheating on her mom. She told him, "I don't think you and I should be alone in the woods with guns anymore, Dad.")

But the CIA needs one other thing in its field operatives. It requires a certain flexibility. An ability to look the other way, every now and then, for the greater good. The Agency has been doing its job for a while. It knows that not everyone will be able to stomach some of the moral compromises necessary for truth, justice, and the American way. It's had its share of whistle-blowers and public scandals, too many books written by people who turned out to be more concerned with their ethics than with secrecy.

The people behind the Agency aren't complete idiots. They learn from their mistakes eventually.

So now the CIA weeds those people out before they get too far inside, before they're exposed to any really damaging intel.

It's come up with a pretty simple test for this: A senior CIA agent takes a recruit and leads her into a dark room with a chair and a desk. Then he hooks her up to a polygraph and asks her if she'd be willing to torture someone.

And then he asks her again while a big-screen TV shows close-up, graphic images—photos and video—of people actually being tortured.

That's what they did to Kelsey. They showed her the movies nobody will admit exist. They showed her the photos that were never released from Abu Ghraib, from grimy cells in Egypt, and black sites in Eastern Europe.

Polygraphs are funny things. Speaking as someone who always knows when another person is lying, I find them crude and flawed. But they're great at measuring when someone is uncomfortable. They detect the increase in perspiration, heart rate, breathing. They detect anxiety. They know when someone cannot tolerate the actual torture and abuse of other human beings.

Even someone who thinks she'd be just fine with torture, on a purely intellectual level, if it was done for the right reasons. If it meant finding a dirty bomb hidden somewhere in an American city, or learning the name of a traitor who planned to assassinate the president.

What Kelsey learned that day, in that tiny room, was that it's almost never for big stakes like that. It's long, ugly, brutal sessions for the smallest facts, like a prisoner's real name, or an address, or a phone number.

I see it clearly in her memories: Kelsey sat there, watching the images, answering the questions. She knew the polygraph was ticking away. She did her best to be calm. But she couldn't fool it, any more than she could fool herself.

After she flunked, Kelsey was told she couldn't be trusted for fieldwork. She was referred to an admin position in the NSA. From there she went to work for Sloan.

She looks at me as I'm driving. Maybe ten seconds have passed. She knows I know.

"Why?" I ask.

She snorts. "You know why. You saw, didn't you? I failed. I couldn't do it."

"That's not what I meant," I say. "Why did you apply for the CIA?"

That throws her off. She tries to cover with indignation. "Why did you join the army? You think you're the only one who wants to serve his country?"

"I didn't have many other options. I didn't do it out of patriotism, really."

"I did."

"I know," I say.

"Yeah, well, now you know. Good for you."

She turns away, and I recognize the flavor of the anger coming off her. She's ashamed.

It was the first time in her life she ever failed, she thinks. She was a straight-A overachiever, the captain of her debate team, a killer volleyball player, an honor-roll student and summa cum laude graduate. She was supposed to have a straight golden ticket to whatever she wanted to do in life. She really wanted to be one of the good guys. She thought it was the right thing to do. And she thought it was cool. She wanted to be a spy.

"You didn't fail," I tell her.

"Easy for you to say," she says. "You did it. You did the job. You passed the tests." She's really pissed. Looking for a fight.

I make a noise. I suppose it sounds like a laugh.

"That's funny?" she asks.

"No," I say. "They were trying to find out how far you'd go. If you could do the things they were showing you. You couldn't. That's not a failure."

In that little room, Kelsey discovered that her principles—the same ones that led her to apply for the CIA—wouldn't let her cross some lines. No matter how much she might have wanted to.

It's why she got sick and guilty after I shot OmniVore's goon, even though he tried to kill her. There are some people who cannot stop thinking of another human being as human. No matter what. Kelsey is one of them.

"You should be proud of that," I say. "Believe me. That's the test that matters, and you didn't fail it."

She's not entirely sure she believes me. "Oh yeah? How would you know?"

"Because I did."

[15]

I spent a lot of my time during the War on Terror inside one secret prison or another. Gitmo resembles nothing so much as a very well-run animal shelter, the cells like kennels off spotless white corridors, the prisoners looking out the wired-glass windows in their doors with the same mute hope of strays waiting to be adopted, or the snarls of animals daring you to put them down. Abu Ghraib was like a haunted house, with the ghosts from Saddam's atrocities watching hungrily over our own crimes there.

Those places got all the airtime on CNN, but Bagram was the only place that actually gave me nightmares.

The airfield was built by the Soviets during their own attempt to smack Afghanistan into behaving. When we came stomping into the country, we began using the base and rebuilding it to suit our needs.

And we needed cells more than airplane hangars.

At first, we just made cages out of wire and rounded up the prisoners into them. Then the military realized our temporary solution had been going on for seven years. We needed something more permanent, and started building cells in another building nearby. When it was done, it was renamed—more like rebranded—Parwan Detention Center. But everyone still called it Bagram. There were no bars on the steel doors that lined the long hallways; just a single slit window that gave a view inside the cinderblock rooms.

There were around 1,700 prisoners there on my last visit. Most of the men were held in bunk room accommodations.

Then there was the Black Jail: the place where we put the prisoners who no longer existed.

This was where they stashed the high-value detainees, the ones who were believed to hold the really big secrets. The ones who received what we liked to call "enhanced interrogation," since the United States does not torture.

It was not far enough away from the other cells to completely muffle the screams. This was not an accident.

That was where they held Fahran.

BY THE TIME I got to the air base, I was sleepless and edgy and only half drunk, despite my best efforts with a bottle of Wild Turkey. I hated Bagram, and it seemed to hate me right back. The place throbbed like an infected tooth with barely contained pain and rage.

So I admit, I was not at the top of my game when I arrived. Still, it didn't take a psychic to see that the prison staff didn't want me and Cantrell around. As soon as our plane landed, we were treated like prisoners ourselves. They took our bags and marched us, under armed guard, to see the Black Jail's commander.

We were taken into a trailer near the Black Jail, where a man sat with a little window-unit air conditioner laboring mightily behind him. He said to call him Townsend. He was probably Defense Clandestine Service, but it was hard, in those days, to find anyone willing to give his real name. The jail was nominally run by the Pentagon, but Department of Homeland Security, CIA, ICE, Secret Service, FBI,

ONI, MI6, Mossad, ISR, OSI, and a half dozen other agencies wandered through the cells at any given time. Plenty of people willing to give orders, but very few who wanted their names attached if it turned into another Abu Ghraib. It could be terminal for a bright young officer's career. The bureaucracy was like protective layers of Kevlar, deflecting any attempt at accountability.

Townsend was pissed. He covered it well—you didn't get that far in the Pentagon without learning to hide your feelings—but it steamed off him like vapor. *<fucking sideshow carnival con man> <best piece of intel we've had since I've been here> <finally get that son of a bitch> <derail my investigation> <my career> <with this bullshit> <finally get out of this hellhole> <back to Virginia> <have dinner with my wife more than once a year at Christmas> <find bin Laden> <find bin Laden> <find bin Laden>*

"We appreciate you coming to facilitate the interrogation," Townsend said. "But we don't really wish to compromise our efforts at this point with any outside personnel. We are questioning the prisoner and gaining valuable intelligence."

What he was saying, in translation: get the hell out of here. This was his ticket to fortune and glory, and more important, a way out of the country. He didn't want to share.

I didn't blame him. I didn't want to be in Afghanistan either, and I'd spent a lot less time in the country than he had.

Cantrell tried to play mediator. He put an extra layer of shitkicker in his voice, scratched his head, and said, "Well now, if what you were doing was working, we wouldn't be here, would we?"

Townsend's eyes narrowed. "We'll break him. Eventually," he said.

That should have been the end of it. I should have walked away right there.

But I couldn't. Probably it was just stubbornness. I hated it when anyone thought that I was lying or faking. Guys like Townsend were so full of contempt for me that I loved it every time I got to prove them wrong.

Cantrell gave me a look. I didn't have to read him to know he wanted us to have a piece of this. He wanted to keep getting calls like the one that brought us here. He needed a market for our services so he could keep drawing on his no-bid Pentagon contract. If Townsend was an obstacle to that, my orders were to get him out of the way.

I scanned Townsend, looking for something I could use. Nothing classified, but something convincing.

I found it almost instantly.

"Hey," I said, as if out of nowhere. "Refresh my memory. What's the punishment for violating Article 134?"

Townsend wasn't made of stone. His mouth twitched and his eyes went wide for a second. He closed it down fast, but his head was spinning with panic.

<how did he know?> <one time it was one time> <nobody else saw> <no witnesses> <bluffing>

"Come on, man," I said, smiling. "It was more than one time."

Article 134 is the U.S. Military Uniform Code of Justice section forbidding fraternization between enlisted personnel and a higher-ranking officer. It's the rule that says officers can't screw their subordinates. Or, as anyone who's spent longer than five minutes in uniform knows, the most violated rule in the military. Especially when there are officers like Townsend who don't get home for almost a year at a time.

The female soldier's image popped into Townsend's head, hair damp with sweat, uniform wadded in a ball on the floor. Her name and rank went along with it.

"Maybe we should ask Corporal Karen McCowan. She probably knows."

Townsend hissed something foul at me under his breath. "You

think that's clever? You think I'm scared of your act? I've played poker with guys at Binion's who read minds better than you. Everybody's got something to hide," he said. "Like you and those pills you keep in your dopp kit."

It bothered me that he had people rummaging through my bag, but I could hardly complain about an invasion of privacy.

I tried to shrug it off. "Medicine," I told him. "Taken under the care and advice of a physician."

"You're a goddamn junkie," he shot back.

"Now that's a little harsh."

It went on for a while like that, but we finally began talking honestly. Cantrell negotiated another questioning session, this time with me present. Townsend's people would have a chance to prove that Fahran knew bin Laden's location, and I would have a chance to confirm it. We'd all go away with a chunk of the credit.

Townsend agreed. The word <*blackmail*> kept echoing through his brain, but he agreed.

WE SET UP inside what they called the special interrogation room. It was me and Cantrell, a couple of MPs to manage the prisoner, the camp doctor to monitor his health, and Townsend's lead interrogator, a corn-fed engine block of a guy named Hatcher.

Nobody was happy to be in there. The MPs were nervous, for obvious reasons. The officers didn't serve any time after Abu Ghraib, but the MPs did.

The camp doctor was young, barely out of med school, where he was not exactly at the top of his class. It's hard to find quality physicians when the job description includes keeping people alive while they're being tortured. He was supposed to check the vitals of everyone who went into the Black Jail's interrogation rooms. A brief dip in his head told me he thought signing up for government service was a good way to get out of his student loans. He regretted that decision roughly every four seconds.

Hatcher—not his real name, of course—was angry. He didn't want me looking over his shoulder. Partially because he didn't want to share any credit and partially because he thought I was a fraud. He wasn't a sadist, or a particularly vicious guy, underneath his training. He didn't like his job, or dislike it. He was simply convinced that it was necessary. As far as he was concerned, he was doing the right thing. He wanted to get bin Laden, by any means necessary.

And on a professional level, he was a little embarrassed that he had not been able to make the subject talk yet.

But he had the solution to that. An inclined bench had been brought into the room, along with a five-gallon bucket and a basin. There was a box of plastic bags sitting on the floor, the same kind you'd use to line an office trash can.

Time for the waterboarding.

Something I ought to admit right now: I'd been in interrogation sessions before and watched them devolve into outright torture. It happened more than anyone would admit. I was usually tied in close to the subject's brain stem while they were having the shit kicked out of them. It hurt. I always got a piece of their punishment.

One of the few people I could stand to hang out with when I did government work was a shrink. He oversaw interrogations, and it was in this capacity that we met, when he was one of my trainers. We weren't friends, exactly, but we ended up spending time together off duty. He was not, by any stretch of the imagination, a good person. He once personally blinded a detainee in one eye when he felt the man was holding back. But his thoughts had a calm order to them that made him tolerable to be around, and he had a wide range of knowledge, both from theory and practice, about how the human mind worked. I learned a lot from him.

He told me it was possible to do terrible things to other people, despite listening to them beg for mercy, because of the fail-safes that evolution and civilization have built into the human mind over the past ten thousand years or so. We take a series of steps to wall ourselves off from the consequences of our actions.

The first, and most important, is dehumanization. We decide, consciously and unconsciously, that our enemy is not actually human, that they've chosen a path that reduces them to the level of animals or vermin or robots. *It's their own fault. They don't feel pain the way we do. They're not like us.* And so on. Once we do that, it's pretty easy to justify any other actions in the name of the greater good.

This is how we can continue to think of ourselves as good people even after we put a scalpel into the right eye of a young man from Lahore suspected of being part of an al-Qaeda sleeper cell.

I could never manage that trick. My talent wouldn't allow it. Some of the people we dealt with were unquestionably evil, but I always had a hard time seeing them as inhuman.

Even the man who'd gleefully beheaded a captured U.S. contractor. He smiled as he brought the machete down, felt light-headed with joy when the shock of impact ran up his arm. I knew. I could feel it all, in his memory. I knew he was one of the bad guys, no question. But he still pictured his infant son in his arms as he looked for the strength to resist our questions.

He broke, in the end. Everybody breaks.

No matter what I knew about the prisoners, I couldn't shut down my empathy, as much as I wanted to. So I blamed the prisoners for that, on top of everything else. Just one more thing I had to deal with, along with the bad food and lousy accommodations and stifling heat and freezing cold. I had to carry their pain too.

I complained about it to Cantrell once.

He listened to me carefully, then smiled. "Well, sheeeeit," he said, turning it into a five-syllable word. "Nothing in this world's free, son."

I learned to live with it.

THEY BROUGHT THE prisoner—Fahran—with a black blindfold covering the top half of his head. The MPs carried him, feet off the floor, without difficulty. He looked like he weighed maybe a hundred pounds. They stripped off the blindfold so he could see what was next. He started moaning in fear. He was bruised and shaking and utterly broken. He was in pain and terrified and convinced his god had abandoned him, left him to the demons. He stank of piss and sweat and fear and there was snot crusted into the wisps of mustache he'd tried to grow to prove he was a man.

He was seventeen, according to his paperwork, but looked about twelve. It was easy to see why he'd been called a *bacha*.

I looked at Cantrell. He was thinking the same thing: This was the hard-ass who had resisted all the questioning so far?

They strapped him down and inclined the bench over the basin. Then Hatcher got to work.

The thing is, waterboarding doesn't look like much. It doesn't seem that terrible from outside. Hatcher was almost gentle as he put the plastic bag over the lower half of Fahran's face. He poured water from a bottle over the plastic for less than ten seconds. It's like a magic trick. One moment you're pouring water in a guy's face, the next he's promising to kill his own mother if you'll only stop. I imagine it makes normal humans feel like they can do what I do.

Despite that, and what some overpaid talk-show hacks would have you believe, waterboarding is torture.

Inside Fahran's head, bombs were going off. He could feel the water on his face, in his nose. He couldn't breathe. He sucked desperately for air and got only the taste of cellophane. He tried to break free, but he was strapped down securely. Every reflex in his body told him he was drowning. He devolved into an animal in mere instants, thrashing and desperate. He was sure he was dying.

Hatcher stripped away the bag and let him have a few mouthfuls of precious oxygen. He spoke enough Pashto for Fahran to understand him. But he wasn't asking any questions. He wanted to soften Fahran up first. Let him know who was in charge.

He slammed Fahran back down and poured the water again. He did this maybe ten, twelve times, before he asked anything.

Fahran prayed. He whined. He begged. But he didn't give anything close to a useful answer.

Inside his head, I wasn't doing any better. It was nothing but fear and pain and prayer.

Hatcher's rage kept growing. He started using his fists instead of the water. He leaned over and punched Fahran in the head several times.

As if on cue, the camp doctor tried to step in right then.

"He's not doing well," the doctor said. "You should consider stopping."

Hatcher said, "No."

The doctor crumpled inside. He was used to being overruled, and it took a little more out of him each time. He left the room.

Hatcher went back to screaming at Fahran. He got nothing but more babble. I began to have a bad feeling about all of this.

Cantrell gave me a look again. <*Time to pull a rabbit out of your hat, kiddo*> came through as clear as if he'd spoken it.

"Let me try," I said.

Hatcher wheeled on me. For an instant, I saw the impulse to punch me instead of the prisoner. But he pulled back at the last second.

"Be my guest," he snapped.

I focused and went into Fahran's head.

With the break in the physical assault, I could read him in a second. He was an open book with big Day-Glo letters on the pages.

Oh, sure, he hated us. In his head, he was some kind of holy warrior, fighting against the latest oppressors who'd come to Afghanistan to defy the word of God.

And so on. If you think religious fanatics are boring when they talk, you should try hearing it inside their own personal echo chambers. It's even more tiresome.

If he'd had access to movies or comics or anything normal, he might have seen himself as Luke Skywalker, fighting the evil empire with an old AK-47 instead of a lightsaber. He was a true believer, ready to strap on a suicide vest if anyone gave the order.

But he didn't know a damned thing about bin Laden, outside of what he'd been told. In his mind, Osama was a near-mythical figure. He knew nothing about the man in real life.

Fahran wasn't going to lead anyone to bin Laden. He was a follower. He barely knew where to take a piss when he was out on patrol with the other hard-liners.

They hated him. He was weak and he was slow and he was not very bright, so they called him *bacha*. When they were captured by our troops, they blamed him, and then one of them had made the joke about Osama coming to rescue his little boyfriend.

That started the whole thing. The others in his group saw a chance to save their own skins, so they lied about the kid.

He wasn't resisting interrogation. He was telling the truth. He didn't know anything. If he'd been smarter, he would have lied.

The kid was not innocent, as I said. Fahran would have happily unloaded a full clip from his rifle into me if he got the chance.

He wasn't innocent. He was ignorant.

I jumped out then, took a glance in Hatcher's head. He was still convinced. As far as he was concerned, they'd found Osama's boyfriend. Getting him to let go of that idea would have been like getting a pit bull to unlock its jaws from a rib eye.

They would keep at him. They'd torture him to doomsday. He'd lie to buy time or a break in the pain, and then they'd figure out he was lying, and they'd start it again. He was going to spend the rest of his short, unhappy life locked in a cycle of pain and abuse and humiliation.

But the kid simply didn't know what we wanted to know. Like it or not, I was the only friend the little bastard had.

So before I could talk myself out of it, I told the truth. "He's got nothing."

"What?" I think Cantrell and Hatcher said it at the same time.

"He doesn't know anything," I told them. "He's never even seen bin Laden, outside of a photograph."

It didn't go over well.

"Bullshit," Hatcher said. He got in my face. He had to lean over. He was a good eight inches taller and fifty pounds heavier than me. I knew I'd see his punch coming. I wasn't sure that would be enough.

Instead of hitting me, he went back to the prisoner and grabbed him and shook him. "Tell me what you know!" he shouted, first in Pashto, then in English. "Tell me about bin Laden!"

"Bin Laden will make all of you pay!" Fahran wailed in Pashto.

Hatcher shoved him down on the board. The board tipped toward the basin, which was still full of water from the earlier sessions.

Hatcher kept screaming for Fahran to talk. He was dangerously close to the edge of something. I saw it in his head. There was no future there, just a big black wall like an approaching thunderstorm.

In desperation, I sent a message to the kid, direct into his brain. *<Give him something.>* *<Give him anything.>* *<Christ, don't you know anything?>*

Fahran looked at me, his eyes full of terror. He didn't know how he could hear me inside his brain. He was one generation removed from shepherds. He'd been conscripted by the Taliban and given an automatic weapon. He'd never even made a phone call in his life. This was all black magic to him. He couldn't lie properly when his life depended on it. He could only fall back on one word, practically the only word in English that he knew.

"No," he said.

Absolutely the wrong word, as it turned out.

Hatcher heard defiance. And he snapped. He began pounding on the kid again. Big, swinging, meat-hook punches to the head. He grunted with the effort each time he pulled his arm back.

I was still off-balance, and now I was getting a fraction of each blow, sending my head spinning. I was still too deep in the kid's brain. I put my hand on Hatcher's shoulder, told him to stop.

He shoved me hard into the wall. My skull bounced off the cinderblock. Black dots swarmed around the edges of my vision. The room became a tunnel. Cantrell shouted something. Hatcher ignored him as he lifted the kid bodily from the board and plunged his head into the basin.

I felt the water around the kid's chin, the sudden rush of it up his nose and down his throat, no plastic in the way this time, the jangling alarms going off in his nervous system as he desperately struggled to get back up. Hatcher held him down.

I heard Hatcher scream both in my ears and through the kid's, a garbled stereo: "Give us a location! Where is he! Where is he!"

Cantrell was still shouting at Hatcher. The others were trying to pull him off the kid.

Like I said before, I'd always felt the pain of the interrogation sessions. But in that instant, with the kid underwater, dying for a breath, the reality behind them finally broke through. Up until that moment, I felt it only as another burden inflicted on me, another injury heaped on top of my own. At that moment, I finally understood that there was an independent human being out there, going through everything I felt, and that I was getting only an echo of their trauma. He was experiencing far worse.

I got it. True empathy. Being in the place of another person. Just as Hatcher put the kid under for the third time.

I've never had good timing.

The kid choked and gasped. I felt the water enter his lungs.

He was drowning. I was drowning with him.

I pulled back as hard as I could, told myself there was no water, my lungs were clear, I was out in the air. It was no good. I couldn't get a breath.

Something kicked me in the head. And mercifully, everything went black.

I WOKE A few minutes later, in the corridor outside the cell. Cantrell was there, looming over me. I realized I was on the floor.

For a moment, I thrashed around like I was trying to swim.

"Easy," Cantrell said.

My mind cast out immediately, instinctively. As always, as I'd been trained, to find the nearest people and assess the situation, to present an intuitive and immediate picture of my surroundings.

Silence. Fear. And a hole where the kid's mind used to be.

Cantrell had put me into the recovery position. I sat up and regretted it instantly. There was a lump, getting bigger, at one temple.

"Knocked you out," Cantrell said. "Your face was turning blue. You weren't breathing. Seemed like you were having trouble disconnecting the wires."

"Thanks," I managed.

Hatcher was gone. Well out of my range. Probably on his way to a plane off the base, if not already in the air.

The camp doctor was there too. Cantrell stepped back, and he went to work. Checked me with everything in his kit.

"You had an event," he said.

"What do you mean by 'event'?"

Seemed like a reasonable question at the time. He looked away from my one eye that could focus. The other one I kept shut because it felt like the light was too bright on that side. When I finally got in front of a mirror, I discovered my pupils were different sizes. One looked as big as a Frisbee.

The doctor hemmed for a moment. "I think you've had some bleeding in your brain. I don't have access to an MRI, so I can't really say for sure. You're presenting like someone who was badly concussed."

"But you don't know for sure."

He shrugged, misery coming off him in waves. "You need to get to a hospital. A properly equipped hospital. You need proper care. You could have an aneurysm waiting to burst. Or there could be ongoing damage. You might stroke out any minute, for all I know."

"And he might be fine. I've seen him look worse with a hangover," Cantrell said. "No offense, doc, but you know you're kind of a Chicken Little around here. You're always saying we're going to kill someone sooner or later."

The way Cantrell said it, it almost seemed polite. The doctor bit back something that sounded like a scream. <*You DID kill someone!*>

He didn't say it out loud, of course. Instead, he went into the cell. A moment later, I saw the doctor escort a body bag, along with the two MPs hauling it. None of them glanced in our direction.

I looked at Cantrell. He shrugged. "Yeah," he said. "We lost him. Bad day."

Sometimes being a telepath means knowing exactly what someone else means. It's the complete erasure of ambiguity. There were a lot of different concerns competing for attention in Cantrell right then. He was worried about how Townsend would handle the incident. He wanted to make sure this didn't become another scandal somewhere down the line. He had a brief vision of himself hauled before a congressional committee live on CNN. But mostly he felt a burned-out regret.

Not for the loss of the kid's life. For the missed opportunity. This could have been thousands of man-hours, all billable under the contract.

<*Nothing like chasing a rabbit to fill the hours*> slipped out of Cantrell's head.

"What was that?"

He looked at me. He knew he hadn't said anything.

"You know you're not cleared for everything that goes on between my ears," he said.

It was too late. I knew what Cantrell knew. What he'd known before we ever set foot on the base.

"You never thought he knew where bin Laden was."

Cantrell shrugged. "I had my doubts."

I took a good long look inside Cantrell's head. I could see it clearly. The word from above was that bin Laden was safe in Pakistan, protected by the ISI. The question wasn't finding him. It was finding the nerve to kill him, and possibly start a war with an unstable country that was supposedly our ally.

I didn't quite know what to do with the information. From where I sat, I could see into the interrogation cell. There was discarded sterile wrapping all over the floor. A defibrillator sat on its crash cart, paddles hanging off the sides. The basin with the water was still half full.

Or half empty, I suppose. Depending on how you looked at it.

"He didn't know a thing," I said, mainly just so someone would say it out loud.

Cantrell made a face like his lunch was repeating on him. I felt the stone wall go up, along with weariness and contempt. He began thinking of a scene from *Debbie Does Dallas* to block me out. "Well," he said, "we'll never know now, I guess."

"I'll know," I said.

He considered several replies and discarded them all. "You need some leave," he said. "Get your head on straight. See a real doctor. Spend a little time in bed with that pretty girl of yours."

He signaled to another one of the soldiers nearby, who helped me to my feet. I couldn't walk on my own.

Eight hours later, I was checked out by a confused doctor at the army medical center in Darmstadt, Germany. He said the MRI showed head trauma: tiny blossoms of blood flowering in my skull. They were healing rapidly, on their own, without clotting, so he thought surgery presented more risks than benefits. "Nothing too bad, really," he said. He mostly got patients who were missing actual sections of their skulls, so I could see his point. He gave me a full bottle of OxyContin for the headache, and then signed me out.

Sixteen hours after that, I was back in Washington, D.C., and back in the world. As if nothing had changed at all.

[16]

First things first. We need money, and we need clothing, and we need transport.

Getting the money is the easy part. Preston thought he'd cut me off from the civilized world by taking away my cash and credit cards, and in a way he did. What he didn't understand—what his handlers apparently didn't know about me either—was how little that actually matters to someone with my talents and training.

I try to follow the rules and color inside the lines most of the time. But I was taught how to steal and cheat and lie by the very best criminals our government has to offer. All Preston has done is liberate me to use those skills again.

I don't feel the need to inflict myself on any innocent bystanders today, so Kelsey and I drive deep into what they call Pennsyltucky, the rural areas that make up most of the state outside of Philadelphia and Pittsburgh. At first glance, it's idyllic. Old barns, small towns, green pastures. It's also home to a booming meth trade, liquored-up violence, and cash-only gun sales.

We drive around until we find just the right kind of bar: one with too many cars out front in the morning, paint peeling from rotten wood, and windows dark with grime, like cataracts in the eyes of an old man. We park next to the run-down beaters in the lot, and I can practically smell the bad vibes coming from the building. Exactly what we need.

When we walk inside, I can tell the place was gorgeous once. Hundreds of square feet of deeply polished pine flooring, a wide bar cut from a single log, antique copper-plate ceiling. All of it now pitted and stained and yellowed with neglect. I am not one for feng shui or any of that mystic crap, but a place takes on the characteristics of the people who inhabit it, and the defeat in here is so thick I can almost see it hanging in the air with the cigarette smoke.

Despite our dirty clothes and lack of a shower, we're still the best-dressed and cleanest people here. We get hard looks from the crew holding down the seats before noon. There's an immediate wave of hostility. They've seen people like us before. Tourists. We might as well be from another country. They think we're here to score drugs and gawk at the locals. A little tale of adventure to bring back to our equally rich and useless friends in Philly.

The bartender looks like your grandmother, if your grandma ran with biker gangs and kept little envelopes of crystal in her purse instead of hard candies. She ignores us for as long as she can, but eventually brings her attitude over to our end of the bar. I smell food cooking, and I'm hungry enough to order the chicken-fried steak without thinking too much about the kitchen. Kelsey orders a Pabst Blue Ribbon. The bartender practically spits with contempt. That would have been on tap here twenty years ago. Now it's a hipster brand that sells for four bucks a glass. Kelsey changes her order to a Bud.

There are some ugly words muttered from the tables in the back. I take a look around and scan the watchers in the booths and chairs. No real danger. Life beat the crap out of these people long before they came in here. They're not likely to stand up or make trouble. Most of them are already buzzed, their minds soft and bloated as their bodies, sloshing around in puddles of warm draft beer.

But one gleams, shiny and cheap, like a brand-new penny. It's almost like he's a tick, sucking life from the skins of everyone else in here. He locks on to us, eyes hard, a tight grin pulling his face in half. The local dealer. This is his office, and he thinks he sees new customers.

No. He thinks he sees new victims.

I pluck out his name: <*Tyler*>. His thoughts are about as friendly and inviting as razor wire.

I'm about halfway through the greasy steak when he slides up to us, that grin even tighter.

"Hey there, folks. How's it going?"

He stands provocatively close to Kelsey. Challenging me already.

We chitchat for about a minute before we get to business. "So," he says quietly. "You looking?"

Kelsey giggles. God bless her, she's a natural at this. "Looking for what?"

"You're too pretty to play hard to get," he says, moving even closer. "You know what you want." Tyler is not exactly subtle. He figures we'll let him do whatever he wants as long as we get the meth.

The bartender stands at the other end of the bar, her back turned as if she's trying to ignore us. But she's in on it. She gets a cut of every sale Tyler makes in the bar. And she plans to back whatever play Tyler makes with the sawed-off shotgun she keeps under the register.

We negotiate for an eight-ball, with him steadily raising the price. Thoughts of money give me a way into his finances. He's got about $500 in his wallet, and about three grand in a brick of small bills in his car. That should do.

We walk out through the back door. Nobody looks at us. Even if I couldn't see the plans in Tyler's head like they were on a movie screen, I would know what's coming next.

Tyler uses the bar's rear exit, which opens onto another gravel-and-dirt parking lot. Kelsey almost goes through the door after him, but I hold her back a little. I go out instead.

I'll give Tyler this: he doesn't waste any time. As soon as I step over the threshold, he rears back and throws a roundhouse punch at my head.

It's always worked before when he's ripped someone off. And it's not a bad tactic, as long as the intended victim doesn't see it coming.

But I do. And I am suddenly so grateful to Tyler for being stupid and vicious enough to do this.

I slip the punch, step inside the swing, and knock my shoulder hard into Tyler's chest, driving him back. He nearly loses his footing, but manages to throw a left instead. He's off-balance, wrong-footed. He doesn't know how much trouble he's in.

I block the left and put the heel of my hand right in his face. His head snaps back, his feet start pedaling like he's on a bicycle, and I help him the rest of the way to the ground with a leg sweep.

He goes down into the gravel. Instead of finishing him, I wait.

I realize now I could have raised the cash a half dozen easier ways. Swiped an ATM card from someone's pocket and the pin number from his head, for instance. Found a poker game and bankrupted the other players. Sold the Escalade to a chop shop. Pawned my watch.

But I'm in a foul mood, and it feels pretty good to fight back instead of running.

I can hear Kelsey's small voice of alarm when I allow Tyler to get up. <*what are you doing?*> Then she understands that all I really want is to hurt someone, and Tyler's been elected. It feels like a knot slipping loose as she figures it out.

He struggles to his feet, blood pouring from his nose and a gash on his forehead. He lifts his arms and snarls and gets ready for his last stand.

Unfortunately, at this range, I also get a solid connection with him, and his memories begin crashing into my head.

I see the death of his father when he was eleven, creating an absence that still hurts every time he thinks of it, like probing a broken tooth with his tongue. This was followed shortly by the disintegration of his mother, who retreated into herself and left nothing behind for her kids. He still brings her a carton of Marlboros every time he visits, about the only thing in her life that seems to give her any joy. He was a welfare case, a skinny little runt in church-bin clothes, a frequent victim of bullies. And then, by the miracle of puberty, he shot up six inches and gained fifty pounds and turned into a bully himself. He was just smart enough to realize the best business in town was helping other people deaden their pain. He started out buying beer for the other kids in his high school, then branched out to bad weed, then pills, then meth. He's also smart enough to realize he's never met a successful small-town dealer over thirty, and he knows he'll be looking at the end of a gun or prison pretty soon.

None of it excuses his sins—and there are many. But nobody's the bad guy inside his own mind.

I focus on one of the bad memories. Tyler once stomped on a guy's knee until it folded the wrong way. The guy was on the floor of the bar, about ten feet and twenty months from where we are standing now. He'd given Tyler some smart-ass comment. Tyler doesn't even remember what, but the guy walks with a limp to this day, and everyone remembers the incident. There's a glow of accomplishment surrounding the memory, and he hears Kid Rock's "American Bad Ass" on his personal soundtrack every time he thinks of it.

That helps. That helps a lot as I duck under his final weak attempt at a punch and elbow him hard in the back of the skull.

He hits the ground face-first, not even putting up his arms to soften the blow. He's done.

Without pausing, I reach under my shirt and take out my gun. I point it at the bartender before she can aim the shotgun at me.

Kelsey gasps. She didn't see the bartender coming. She was too busy watching the fight. But I've said it before: it is nearly impossible to sneak up on me.

The bartender figured she'd bail Tyler out as she's done in the past—they're business partners, after all. Now, looking down the barrel of the Walther, she's questioning the wisdom of that idea.

"Go back inside," I tell her. "Leave the shotgun."

She thinks about it for a second. *<I got the shotgun> <bet that shitty little piece will jam up on him> <I could still get him> <damn, is Tyler dead?> <I could still get him>*

"Jesus, is there something in the water in this town? I said *leave the shotgun*, Mona. You don't want to die today."

Using her name finally wakes her up. *<cop? is that a cop?> <fuck this>* She puts the gun on the ground and backs carefully into the bar.

When I feel that she's gone, I step over to where Tyler is snuffling and bleeding into the gravel. He's beginning to come around, but he won't be able to get back on his feet for some time.

I shift him onto his side—he's going to puke at least once—and fish his wallet and car keys out of his jeans.

I pop the trunk of Tyler's car, a nearly new Ford Mustang that he's already filled with empty beer cans, dirty clothes, and the wrappers from a few hundred Extra Value Meals.

I find the ziplock bag of cash under the spare. There's a ten- to twenty-year sentence worth of meth in the trunk as well, plus a few guns wrapped in old towels.

I also find a bag of his second-most-popular product: Oxy. A lot of his customers use it to take the edge off a meth high.

I grab that, along with the ziplock full of cash, and slam the trunk closed.

"Mission accomplished," I tell Kelsey. "Let's go."

Kelsey looks at the bag of pills, then at me.

"What's that?" she asks.

"Let's talk about it in the car, all right?"

"Jesus Christ, all of this—did you do all this just to score drugs?"

"I need it," I tell her.

She doesn't say anything. Just looks down at Tyler, still barely moving on the ground.

This isn't the place for this conversation. I feel like shouting, the adrenaline still surging through me from the fight. But she's not the enemy. I keep my voice under tight control. "It's not the same," I tell her. "Believe me, you do not want me to lose it, and these"—I hold up the bag of pills—"will keep that from happening."

She looks uncomfortable and turns away quickly. "Let's just get out of here," she says.

She walks around the side of the bar, headed for the SUV. I don't read her thoughts. I don't have to.

I start to follow. But for some reason I'd rather not explore, I reach into the ziplock and pull out a couple of twenties. I drop them next to Tyler.

At least he'll be able to buy his mom her smokes.

[17]

I walked away after Bagram. I'm sure there are some people who would have quit the moment they saw that body bag being hauled out of the room. Or at any time before that, when they knew for a fact that they were being used, when their conscience couldn't take it anymore.

I'm not quite that stupid. You don't tell the commander of a black-ops unit to take his job and shove it inside a secret prison seven thousand miles away from the right to due process.

I didn't wait long, though. I made the call to Cantrell from the airport as soon as I got back to D.C.

"I'm done," I told him.

He was less than thrilled. "You seriously think you can quit?"

"Pretty sure I just did."

He sighed, and I could tell he was thinking of the right way to phrase what he wanted to say, given that we were on an unsecured line.

"I told you to get your head on straight. Get back to me when you've had a little more sleep."

"I'm wide awake now. I don't need any more time. You need to believe me on this: I have had enough."

He made a noise. Almost like gagging. "Oh stop it. You going to tell me you're getting misty over that little stain we left on the floor? Bullshit."

"Too many stains. Too much blood on my—"

Cantrell cut me off before I could finish the sentence.

"No. You don't get to make that speech. You want out? Then go with God. You've done your time, and I've had damn few complaints about you, which is more than I can say for most of your fucked-up brethren. But don't use this as an excuse. You've seen worse. Hell, you've done worse."

"Not when the other guy was in handcuffs."

"You want a fair fight now? Be honest. You haven't been in a fair fight in your life."

He had a point. But he wasn't about to change my mind.

"Tell me something," I asked him. "You think what we did in that room was right?"

"Fuck yes, I do. No, he wasn't Osama bin Laden or a Taliban warlord. Yes, he was weak and young and pathetic and stupid. But he was still the enemy. He had chosen to take up arms against the force and power of the United States military and he was absolutely going to die for it. He was born to be a corpse. Now, personally, I'd rather watch him die strapped to a table than have him out in the desert waiting to put a bullet in my skull. Maybe you'd feel better if a Predator dropped a Hellfire missile on his ass from twenty thousand feet. But the result is the same. There's no such thing as a fair fight, John. There's just us and them. Today there's one less shithead for the enemy to throw at us. Bottom line, I can live with whatever road we took to get there."

I knew that if we were face-to-face, I would get absolute certainty from him. I couldn't read him over the phone, but I knew. There was no question in his mind.

And there were too many questions in mine. Maybe it was selfish. But I was done being Cantrell's weapon.

"I can't," I said.

There was a long pause on the line. For a moment, I wondered if he'd hung up. And then Cantrell's voice came back. His southern accent had thinned, which was how I knew he was deeply angry.

"You've been the beneficiary of a lot of investment. We've put a great deal of time and training into you. And we've trusted you with a lot of—well, let's call them trade secrets. Now, you can understand why we'd be reluctant to allow you to leave, given all that you've got in your head."

"You don't want to send people after me."

I heard a fat, happy chuckle over the phone. "Do I hear an 'or else' at the end of that sentence? You think it's gonna be like *Rambo*? Lot of body bags, is that it?"

"I was thinking more like *Night of the Living Dead*. Only a lot less living, a lot more dead."

He laughed at that. His way of buying time. Then he made his decision.

"You've seen too many movies, John. We try to do right by our people. You did your bit. Uncle Sam's got no more legal claim to you. You want to walk away now, I promise, there's no need to look over your shoulder."

"I never need to look over my shoulder. Remember?"

"Don't lecture me, son. I know everything you're capable of, better than you do."

"Then we're done?"

"What do you want, a going-away party and a cake? We're done."

I believed him, even if I couldn't read him over the phone line. I suddenly wasn't sure what to say. He filled in the gap for me.

"Just remember this: you've had us clearing the way for a long time. You might not like it out there on your own."

That sounded like a threat again. I didn't like it.

"Hey, Terry," I said, using his real first name, the one he didn't ever tell anyone. "I've always wondered, why the hell do you use that accent? You're from New Jersey."

That made him laugh out loud. "Shit, John," he said, accent thick as molasses again. "Shut up before you make me miss you."

He hung up.

By the time I got back to our apartment, Whitney was gone. Her closets were empty, and her side of the bathroom was so clean it looked sterile. At some point while I was out of town, she'd made the decision to move on with her usual ruthless efficiency. For her, there was never any sense in hanging around after she'd planned her exit strategy. There wasn't even a note.

I never saw it coming.

She didn't vanish from the face of the earth. I admit, I've run her name on Google late at night. She's the director of a think tank and the wife of an up-and-coming congressman who swept into office as part of the backlash against Obama.

But I've always wondered about the timing. Did she leave because she knew me so well? Did she realize before I did that I'd reached my expiration date?

Or did she leave because someone told her what happened at Bagram, and it was time for her to get out? Was she always a minder from the Agency, or someone else? Did they decide I wasn't worth her time if I wasn't with Cantrell's group anymore?

I don't know. That's the kind of useless paranoia that crawls around in your head when you've been in the community for any length of time. You tend to ask yourself a lot of questions that will never have a good answer.

Either way, it didn't really matter. She was gone.

And just like that, I was alone, out in the world, for the first time in my life.

I CONSIDERED MY options. I could have gone back to being a soldier, only for a private corporation like Blackwater. I could have used my talent for blackmail or gambling, like so many people have suggested. I could have found a normal job, stuck behind a desk or a counter somewhere, dealing with all the mouth-breathing, slow-witted people like you, every day of my life, until I finally put a gun in my mouth.

But I knew what I really wanted. I wanted to be alone. And I wanted to have enough money to do it in style.

There are a lot of other guys with my military training. I'd met some of them. They rented their skills and their lives to the very rich, solving problems that the One Percent didn't want to trust with the proper authorities. That is the point of having money, after all: you get to hire someone to deal with the inconvenient things. Rich people don't have to scrub their own toilets.

I had the same skills as those other guys, plus one definite market advantage. So I went to work for myself.

I moved to Los Angeles because I was sick of bad weather. In a short time, I got clients. Word gets around among the very rich. I bought some good suits and a decent place to live. I even put a little cash away for the day when I'd finally retreat completely from the world.

It all seemed to be working out pretty well.

Until now, anyway.

But I'm not dead yet. And as smart as Preston is, even with the CIA and the government and a billion dollars on his side, he's still only human.

I'm not.

It's time for me to remind him just what that means.

[18]

Kelsey's hand is clenched around my forearm tight enough to hurt.

"This is never going to work," she whispers at me.

We are both in the best suits we could buy at Ross Dress for Less. We showered and changed at a Motel 6, and we've got two cheap wheeled suitcases behind us as we walk from long-term parking to the entrance of Philadelphia International Airport. We look like a couple of ordinary professionals on their way to a conference or a sales meeting.

We get all the way to the doors of the terminal before Kelsey freezes up.

"Just relax," I tell her. "Just breathe."

She sucks in a deep lungful of jet-fuel-scented air, but she still gives me a look. <*this is never going to work*> "Maybe we need to reconsider this."

"This is where you start to question me? After everything you've seen me do?"

"This isn't some backwoods meth head, or a bunch of guys with guns. I know you can handle that," she says. "This is an airport, for Christ's sake. They don't even let you bring a water bottle on the plane."

"You're right," I tell her. And she is. This should be absolutely impossible.

Everyone is supposed to be on full alert these days, if not for terrorists, then for the random lunatics who decide that the airport is the place to work out their issues against the government and the IRS.

But in reality, 9/11 was a long time ago, and human beings are wired to think short term. Passengers care more about getting to their flight than they do about terrorism. The security guards, in turn, just want to get everyone through the line with a minimum of pissing and moaning and threats of litigation. So everyone in the airport is already distracted, preoccupied. They want routine. They want order. They want everything to go as expected. And their brains will work overtime to make sure that illusion becomes a reality.

They're going to do most of the work for me. I'll only have to give them the smallest push.

Preston's machines—and through him, the CIA—are the real problem. He's got his software looking for me and Kelsey in every digital form possible. His programs know our purchasing patterns, our travel history, our seat preferences. Even if we use new credit cards, his algorithms will identify us by matching us to habits we don't even realize we have. If we try to avoid credit cards and use cash, we'll automatically be flagged as drug dealers, and that will raise our profile as well. If we use fake photo IDs, our pictures will still be on them, and the facial-recognition software will pick us out of the crowd better than most humans.

So I decided to bypass all that. We're not going to show any ID. We're not even going to buy tickets.

We're going to just walk past the TSA and get on the plane. I'm even going to bring my gun with me. And nobody will say a word or stop me.

At least, that's the plan.

. . . .

We're blocking the doors. Other travelers move around us with barely restrained sighs and curses. We're being noticed. That's not what I want. I gently lever my arm out of Kelsey's grip: we're not playing husband and wife here. "Let's go," I say.

I pick up my carry-on and start walking confidently toward the security checkpoint.

At least I'm confident. This is where Kelsey is closest to freaking out. She's almost humming with anxiety, like a high-tension wire. She hesitates and then crosses the threshold into the airport, like she's just stepped onto a minefield.

I think she was less worried when people were actually shooting at us. But she was raised in a polite family. Her respect for the rules goes deep. To her, this is like stealing, cutting in line, and cheating on a test, all rolled into one.

It's understandable. Completely annoying, but understandable.

<Will you fucking relax?> I send to her as we walk.

She has to relax. If she doesn't, she'll draw additional attention to us, and that could be a problem.

"I'm fine." *<this will never work> <this will never work>*

"Yes, it will," I whisper.

We stop for a moment so I can scan everyone in uniform. Quickly, I sift through all their thoughts. I don't want the good agents. I don't want the alert and conscientious employees, the ones who take their jobs seriously. I want the guy at the end of his shift, the one who drank too much coffee on his last break and now really has to go to the bathroom.

And there he is. I steer Kelsey over to the line that's the longest. When we reach the TSA agent checking boarding passes, he looks up at us.

He's irritable and tired. He fought with his son this morning, and his mind is still back there. *<so don't take the scholarship, don't even go to college, but just make a decision> <I said I'll pay for school and I will, I'll find the money somewhere> <but why pay if he doesn't want to go?>*

Then he sees Kelsey.

I didn't need to worry about her. When the moment hits, she's perfect. Her anxiety vanishes. She's calm and confident. She gives him a heart-stopping smile.

The agent straightens up a little, wonders if she notices his receding hairline. *<nice tits> <nice smile>*

I hand over two perfectly blank pieces of paper to the agent. At the same time, I push a message into his head, as hard as I can. I actually picture myself taking it in one hand and hurling it at his brain like a fastball at the strike zone.

<air marshals> <don't make a scene> <special assignment> <let us pass>

He looks hard at the paper, then looks at me, his face suddenly grave.

For a long instant, I worry I'm losing my touch.

Then he nods, scribbles something on the blank paper, and immediately stands up and gestures for us to follow him. "Right this way," he says.

He whispers something to the other agents on duty. They're so busy checking for water bottles and shoes that they don't see us. Not really.

He escorts us past the X-ray machine with a respectful nod. And then he goes back to his post, counting down the last fifteen minutes until he's off the clock, back to worrying about his kid and his bank account and everything else. He won't even remember us.

From the playbook of Wolf Messing, ladies and gentlemen. This is how you deal with the mind of someone in authority: you give them a higher authority to obey.

We go to the gate. I selected the flight by checking passenger loads on the Net. It's underbooked, one of a dozen planes that travel daily to Los Angeles. Plenty of open seats, which is bad for business, but like a vacation to the gate crew. They're relaxed, easygoing, and easily distracted. They open the flight to all seats, all rows for boarding, and then go back to gossiping and laughing behind the counter.

We walk up to the employee taking boarding passes. I hand over my blank sheets of paper and send a new message.

<airline execs> <quality-control check> <don't make a scene>

We get seated in an exit row and free drinks from the flight attendants.

I think Kelsey might be more impressed by that than anything else I've done.

WE ARRIVE AT LAX, even though Preston has wiped out my savings and stolen my home.

I'm not so arrogant as to think I can hide from Preston's machines. Believe me, I'm convinced by his demonstrations so far. Anything we do can be traced as long as it goes through the Internet somewhere.

I'm certain that any time I show up in the electronic ether, a siren and flashing lights will go off at OmniVore headquarters, followed shortly by a hit squad heading out the door.

So, whenever possible, I've stayed out of the digital age. That means Kelsey and I have had to dig up phone books and use maps instead of letting our phones give us information and directions. I've been surprised how hard it is to work without the net. It turns out my map-reading skills were mainly good for figuring out how many klicks between checkpoints. We got lost a lot driving to the Philadelphia airport. I have no idea how the Amish survive.

Now we need a car again, and I can't use my license or a credit card. The Internet ride services, like Uber or Lyft, would be even worse; I might as well call Preston and tell him where to find us. No taxicab will drive us all over town for cash, no matter how much we offer. And while other airports have off-the-books drivers hanging out around the terminals, LAX was never a good market for those guys. Everyone here owns a car.

Except me, thanks to Preston. The moment I try to buy anything, I'm screwed. Preston's smart little programs have cracked the code of my life. They can predict where I'll go by looking at what I've done in the time I've lived here. It's like Preston has a watcher at my favorite hotels in the city, my usual restaurants, the places where I shop.

If I was trying to hide, this should be the last place I would show up. There are a hundred other places where I could go and vanish, simply disappear into the mass of humanity. I hear Omaha is nice.

But I'm not hiding. This is my city. It's as close to home as any place I've ever known, and I have resources here that don't show up on any Internet search.

For starters, I have a line of credit in the favor bank with a lot of people. Low tech, but untraceable.

Time to make a few withdrawals.

I NEED TO make a call, but not on my gas-station smartphone. I want a landline, something that still uses cords and copper wires.

It takes me ten minutes to find a working pay phone in the terminal at LAX. It takes Armin Sadeghi only twenty to arrive with a freshly washed, almost-new Audi.

I asked him for an inconspicuous ride. For Sadeghi, I guess this qualifies.

One of his many businesses is a small chain of car lots. And my rescue of his daughter is still fresh enough that he doesn't ask questions when I tell him I need untraceable transportation.

He shows up himself, along with a couple of his security people riding along in his car, an honest-to-God Rolls-Royce. He's spent most of his life here, but he's still very Persian in this: he takes the payment of debts seriously. It's meant to be done face-to-face.

He greets both me and Kelsey with a brief embrace. Then he puts the keys into my hand and closes my fingers around them.

"Thank you," I tell him. "I'll try to get it back to you in one piece."

He waves this away. "As long as you need it. Anything else, you only have to ask."

"How is Kira?"

I see it in his head: a fairly epic tantrum, right before she was sent to Passages in Malibu to get clean.

"She will be fine. Thanks to you."

He excuses himself quickly. He's a busy man. He plans to say the Audi was totaled on a test drive, then write it off as a business loss at the end of the year. He honestly never expects to see me again.

I hope he's wrong.

AILON TIDHAR SMILES when he sees us, even though I show up unannounced.

He lives in a small, Spanish-style two-bedroom in Beverly Hills. It was built in the 1920s. I've been here before. He's very proud of the stucco archways. "They don't even know how to make these anymore," he told me the first time I visited. In any other city, they would have torn this house down years ago. In L.A., it's worth nearly $2 million.

Tidhar himself is a big guy with only a little gray in his hair, even though he's got to be in his sixties by now. Depending on how he wants you to think of him, he either speaks English flawlessly, with an almost British reserve, or with a thick layer of Hebrew over every word. He could be like any Israeli immigrant in his neighborhood; a businessman, an investor, a restaurateur. And sure, he dabbles in all of that.

He just happens to be a spy as well.

We met after some unpleasant business involving his son. Ailon is deep-cover in the U.S. these days. He might even be retired, for all I know. I'm reluctant to get him involved in this. But he's far enough back in my history that I don't think Preston's algorithms are going to be able to track him.

And he is a spy, after all. He's going to have what I need.

He feeds us and gets us drinks, moving his bulk around the tiny yellow kitchen. His wife isn't here—she's out with the grandkids, helping out their daughter-in-law. I'm grateful. I still don't think she will ever forgive me for the last time I showed up.

He's telling Kelsey about the original tile on the countertops. "Covered in dirt an inch thick when we bought the place," he says. "Now look at that. Looks brand-new. Have you ever seen that shade of green before?"

Eventually, when he's done playing host, I tell him why we're here. I give him as much information as I think he needs. Hopefully not enough to compromise him too much if Preston—or worse, the Agency—does track us here.

He's silent for a moment when I finish. I worry that I've asked for too much. I begin apologizing.

"I'm sorry to come here, to you, but we need help. If you can't—"

He turns, and I see that he's been considering how to respond. He's a little annoyed. I shouldn't have rushed him.

"John," he says. "Please. Who do you think you're talking to here?"

HE DRIVES HIS own car and we follow. He takes us to a small collection of storage units not far off the 10. It's not one of the big national chains, and it's half-hidden by an off-ramp and an overpass.

He has a key and an electronic token that gets him past the gates and the doors.

"You own this place?" Kelsey asks.

Tidhar and I both give her a look.

"Sorry," she says. "Just making conversation."

Tidhar takes us down a series of corridors. The air is hot and stale. Then he finds the unit he's looking for. He inserts the key into a hole on the wall, and the door rolls up with a mechanical noise, but smoothly, easily.

He steps inside, and we follow him. The walls are stacked with crates and boxes, all unmarked.

It makes no difference to Tidhar. He knows exactly what he wants. He hauls one of the crates away from the wall, seemingly at random, and a blast of cool air hits us.

Inside, carved out of several other storage spaces by knocking down the walls, is a small apartment. It has a bed, a kitchenette, and a toilet and shower shoved together in one corner.

There are a few more crates. He heads straight for the box he wants and lifts the lid. He beckons me over.

Inside is an Uzi submachine gun, packed in foam. "I know you prefer those German toys," he says. "But you'll have to get over that fetish sooner or later."

This is more than I expected. Much more. I was hoping to get a little intel, maybe a loan or a place to stay for a couple of nights. I had no idea he was still this deep.

Looking at the gun, I wonder how many felonies can fit in a space this small. Enough to get Tidhar deported, at least. Maybe enough to get him killed, if my presence here screws up whatever he's got going.

"Look," I tell him. "You know you don't have to do this. You don't owe me this much."

Tidhar stops digging in the crate and turns to look at me. His face is stony.

He's suddenly, volcanically, angry. I can feel it rolling from him, washing over me. He tamps it down fast, so I'm not quite sure why. But it's sprung up from a place as deep as if I just insulted his mother.

Then, just as abruptly, he turns to Kelsey. "He tell you how we know each other?"

She shakes her head. She can tell he's pissed too. You don't have to read minds to notice the shift in the room. I'm on guard, because Tidhar is no one you want to mess with, even by accident.

His tight self-control falters a little as he searches for the right words, how much he can safely tell a civilian.

"My son Adi was an interpreter. Not a spy, not a soldier, even though he was military. He was going to do his service and get out. And I was glad. He didn't want the same life I had, and I didn't want it for him. He was loaned to a group of U.S. Special Forces soldiers, because he spoke a dialect they needed in Afghanistan. There were never enough translators. He was smart. Had a gift for languages. He would have been an excellent teacher."

He pauses for a moment, and then nods his head in my direction.

"Your friend here, he was in the unit that my son was loaned to. They were sent out to the Afghan border, near Pakistan. I wasn't told many of the details, and even with my contacts, it was difficult to get many answers. But I understood it was supposed to be a routine prisoner transfer. A tribal warlord had captured one of the Afghani militants, then traded him to the Pakistani ISI, who were then supposed to hand him over to the CIA for questioning. Routine. Happened all the time. But something went wrong. Again, I wasn't given many details. But I was later told that the warlord switched sides again. Or perhaps it was the ISI who switched. Nobody could really say. Your friend here, he was no help when he told me about it. He wasn't there, at the border."

He's right. I wasn't. At that point, Cantrell had curtailed my duties in the field considerably. I was too important by that point, and I'd already had one too many close calls. He didn't want anyone to put a bullet in my valuable brain. I still might have gone on the mission anyway. It was supposed to be routine, just like Tidhar says, and I could use my talent to piece together enough of what the militants were saying even without knowing their exact dialects. I'd done it plenty of times.

But I didn't have to, because they found Adi Tidhar, and sent him with my unit instead.

Now his father tells Kelsey what happened next.

"The people who were supposed to hand over the prisoners to the Americans turned against them instead," Tidhar says. "They probably got a better offer from the Taliban. Whatever the reason. The Americans, and my son, found themselves outnumbered and ambushed. Six men were shot before they could escape."

He goes quiet again.

"Adi was the only one who died."

The agony is still fresh. I don't get any words. Just a pulse of raw loss coming from him, centered on the image of a coffin under an Israeli flag.

Then, abruptly, Tidhar shuts it down and resumes his story. "I'm not a spy anymore, but for a while I hit up every connection I ever had. I wanted them to get me out there, to Afghanistan. That should tell you I wasn't in my right mind. Fat, retired guy like me, taking his guns out of the safe, booking a flight to the Middle East. My old friends, my wife, they finally talked me out of it. They said it wouldn't do Adi's memory any good for his father to go and get himself killed either. Besides, no one could find the Afghans and the Pakistanis. They'd vanished. The Afghans went back into the mountains, the Pakistanis disappeared into the ISI."

Tidhar is giving Kelsey the censored version here. For one thing, if he was really retired, he would have been back overseas as soon as he heard about his son, and I don't doubt he was capable of finding a good number of the Afghans and Pakistanis on his own. But the Mossad told him what was really going on. It was an embarrassment to all involved, and the U.S. wanted it forgotten. Relations were tense between the ISI and the CIA at the time. The Pakistani government's spies covered for all manner of crimes by the Taliban and its assorted groupies. They hid Osama from us for years, among many other things. So everyone was encouraged to let it drop, for fear of cutting off the steady stream of intel we were getting from Pakistan. Adi Tidhar was just one of the unfortunate victims caught in the cross fire.

"Then, one day, I'm told that four men in the ISI are dead. But before they died, one of them gave up the location of the warlord. And within a week, a drone strike wiped him from the face of the earth.

I'm ashamed to tell you how happy that made me. I am ashamed to tell you I smiled."

Kelsey is staring at Tidhar with wide eyes now. She's not exactly enjoying this story, but then, it's not for her benefit. Or even mine. I know how it all went, after all. Tidhar simply wants to say some things out loud.

"I asked my friends, how did this happen? And they told me that one man made it possible. One man was able to squeeze the truth from the ISI agents. He would not let it go. Even though it caused considerable discomfort to his bosses. He avenged my son. I don't know how, but he made it possible. I never thought I'd be able to thank him. Then your friend shows up and introduces himself to me, and says he knew my son. And do you know what he did? He apologized to me. He apologized because he wasn't there. He didn't tell me the rest, of course. He left that to me to find out on my own. I had to run his name to learn who it was that questioned the ISI agents."

Tidhar's thoughts are complex and muddled and not easy to read. He says he is grateful, sure. But I remember the look on his face. How can you ever really forgive the man who tells you how your son died? Even if he wasn't there? *Especially* when he wasn't there?

He and Kelsey both seem to be waiting for me to pick up the story. I don't know what to tell them.

"He deserved better," I say. "I felt like he deserved better. That's all."

"Yes," Tidhar says. "He did."

His rage, which had subsided, is back. He looks at me again. "So fuck you very much."

"What?"

"Fuck you and your apology," Tidhar says. "Fuck you, I don't owe you. I will decide who and what I owe. That is not your decision. It is mine. And I will decide when I am done owing you. But you haven't reached the end of your credit with me yet."

He turns and takes a moment to get himself under control. Then, when he turns back, his mind is as clear as the sky after a storm.

"Right," he says. "You'll need ammunition."

He starts rummaging again. I look around the room, taking inventory. You could outfit a good-size platoon with what's in here. Then I see a box marked with a familiar brand name.

It's perfect. "Actually," I say, "we don't need guns."

He scowls. "Right, I keep forgetting, you are a living weapon, you have the power to cloud men's minds. You make your bullets out of bad attitude now too?"

I shake my head. "No. I'm already outgunned. I was thinking about something else," I say, and point at the box. "That ought to level the playing field."

Tidhar looks over his shoulder, sees the box, and smiles. "Oh, it can level a lot more than that."

Kelsey looks at the box. She doesn't know what it is. She's getting impatient.

"So you've got a plan?" she says.

It's more of a half-assed idea than a plan at this point. But it's coming together. Now I'm starting to see a way I can make it work.

"Yeah," I tell her. "I've got a plan."

[19]

OmniVore Tech's main offices are not where you'd expect to find them. Offices are where your father worked. Tech companies are supposed to be on campuses like Facebook and Google, little pockets of the future plunked down in the present.

But those companies don't have the CIA as their primary backer, which does not want its secrets splashing out all over the place, burdening the public with too much knowledge. A single location is easier to secure than a group of buildings spread out over several acres.

So OmniVore is stuck in an office tower in downtown San Jose.

I watch the exterior of the building from a safe distance for several days. Never too close, and always wearing a ball cap and sunglasses against the surveillance cameras mounted above the doors, or in case anyone remembers me from the corporate retreat.

I don't have to get closer than a hundred yards to see that there is serious security protecting the place. We're talking state-of-the-art everything: alarms, cameras, keypad locks, doors with palm-print ID and retinal recognition, pressure-sensitive floor panels, motion detectors, thermal scanners, and, of course, big guys with guns.

Ordinarily, this is what you'd need to get past all that:

You would have to hire at least four subcontractors, experienced people who'd done hard and soft entry before. They would approach the offices in a variety of disguises: FedEx courier, temp secretary, bicycle messenger, homeless man. They'd spend a couple of weeks taking discreet pictures on their phones, exploring fire stairs and exits, measuring security's response time. Then you'd get the building's blueprints from the city or county and check the design against any remodeling that had been done since the building went up. Once you'd made and memorized a detailed map of the premises, you'd have your whole team take positions on the day of the actual breach. You'd have your homeless guy start a fire or something outside the lobby, create a nice distracting layer of chaos, the kind that brings firefighters and EMTs running in response. You'd have your FedEx guy and your bike messenger and your secretary waiting inside with their gear. They'd hit the fire alarms, and everyone in OmniVore's offices would run like hell to avoid being gassed to death by the Halon fire-suppressant system that automatically triggers to protect the computers. Then they would switch into helmets and fire coats and oxygen masks, and race up the fire stairs and smash-and-grab as many computers they could find before the real firefighters and the cops showed up.

Even if you did all this perfectly, with the best operators you could find, it would take two months, minimum, and maybe a hundred grand in up-front costs. And you'd still have only a fifty-fifty chance of actually pulling it off.

Fortunately, I'm not a mere mortal like you. For me, it starts with finding just one guy.

A FEW DECADES ago, Max Renfrow would have led a very lonely life. He would have been a math geek and the president of the chess club, and nobody would have understood his references to Monty Python and Doctor Who.

But that's all changed, thanks to the Internet. It's created a world where his talents are valued and people can Google his jokes if necessary. Tonight, Max is filled with the confidence of a high school quarterback as he enters the trendy little craft-cocktail bar in downtown San Jose. He knows the secret language of machines and he's got a six-figure salary with stock options. He views every woman in the bar as his property; they just haven't realized it yet.

So when he sees the insanely hot woman sitting alone, he immediately heads over to her.

He smiles and takes the seat next to her. He orders a drink for himself—"and another one of whatever she's having," he tells the bartender. <*Women like that*> <*shows them you're in charge*> he tells himself.

Kelsey smiles at him and says thanks. I'm a few seats away, but to Max, I might as well be invisible.

He doesn't know it, but he's exactly the guy we've been waiting for.

I PLUCKED MAX from the mess of OmniVore programmers, purple IDs on lanyards around their necks, dribbling out of the building in irregular spurts for lunch and dinner. Most of them went right back to the office with a Subway bag in hand, ready for another twelve hours of work. It's still considered bad form to put in anything less than a sixteen-hour day in Silicon Valley. Even stepping out for a sandwich is a tiny form of rebellion, a way of saying they value fresh air and sunlight more than the free snacks in the break room.

A brief, surface read of their thoughts showed that most of them didn't have room in their lives for anything but data analysis or network access. And those who did were usually new hires, lacking the kind of seniority I needed.

But there were a few who were secure enough to risk going out after work. They put on fresh T-shirts and jeans and headed out to the bars, ready to prove their alpha-male status and bring home a mate.

Out of those few, I chose Max.

Max is a senior programmer, positioned just right in the org chart to have access to what I need to know, but not so high that he belongs to Preston's inner circles. Looking into his head, I saw his identity, his self-image, wrapped protectively around his job, that purple ID card like a badge of honor on his chest.

I scooped his weekly routine from his brain and stationed Kelsey at his favorite after-work spot.

"Get him to talk about his work," I told her.

She rolled her eyes. "Ask me for something hard."

"I'm serious. I mean specifics. Get him to drill down into his job as much as possible."

"I got it."

"Are you sure?"

Lens flare of irritation, which I'm starting to see whenever she thinks I underestimate her. "I talk to people like this for a living," she reminded me. "All they do is talk about their work. Believe me. I got it."

For a moment, I'm worried.

Max has read a lot of advice about women on the Internet, none of it good. He's filled with strategies and methods, all of which are supposed to guarantee that women will melt into puddles of submissive goo at his feet.

Case in point: his opening line. "Your boyfriend teach you to drink that stuff?" he asks, pointing to Kelsey's whiskey. This is supposed to put her on the defensive, make her crave his approval, and get the conversation started.

She stares at him for a long moment. He waits for her reply. And waits. And waits.

He loses his nerve after about ten seconds of silence. "Uh, I mean, you know, women usually, like. Drink white wine. Or something fruity."

"Maybe you need to meet more women," Kelsey says.

There's a feeling that ripples through him. It's hard to put into words. It sort of sounds like a sad trombone.

I'm afraid this means we're going to get nothing but bad pickup lines from him. Kelsey, however, reads him as well as I do, and she doesn't even have any superpowers. She finds just the right key to wind him up.

"So what do you do?" she asks, and he lights up. (Literally. His brain suddenly switches into high gear, all kinds of neural activity waking up, and I can see all of it.)

"I'm in development at OmniVore Tech," he says, with the right combination of humility and pride.

Most people around here have heard of the company. Even if a woman is interested in him only because he might be rich, she'll know the name. Most people also automatically assume he's doing something incredibly cool and cutting edge from the seat of his Aeron chair. This is where he usually shines, where he gets to tell people how he's making the future right in front of them.

Kelsey restrains a yawn. "Oh yeah. I know those guys."

He's stunned. It's like a small car wreck happened in his brain. He can see she's not some ditz who doesn't realize there are companies behind Twitter and Google. But she's not impressed. He doesn't know what to say next. He charges ahead with his usual next line, even though she didn't ask.

"Uh, yeah, I'm in charge of interfacing over different network architectures," he says. (This is a small lie. He's not in charge—there are five people in his section alone who tell him what to do—but he's high enough, which is why I picked him.) "See, what we do is—"

Kelsey scans the crowd over his shoulder. "Oh, I know what you do. I'm in finance. I sat through your CEO's presentation when he was looking for his last round of funding."

He smiles. "How much did you end up giving him?"

Kelsey smiles back, her teeth much sharper than his. "Nothing. We passed."

"Oh," he says. That stops him short. His company is supposed to be the Next Big Thing. It was on Re/code and everything. He's got stock options. Everything he knows about the company says that it will make him rich when OmniVore's IPO finally hits. But Kelsey doesn't seem impressed. This worries him. "Did you say you passed?"

Kelsey nods. "No offense, but we decided OmniVore isn't really equipped to be the market leader."

Now I'm sure she's gone too far. *<whaaaaaaaat?> <you have to be shitting me>*

"Oh come on," he says, his pride rearing up and thumping its chest. "Who else out there even comes close to us?"

Kelsey starts reciting a list: "Axciom, UpDog, Palantir—"

"We are so far ahead of those guys—"

"And of course, eventually Google is just going to start grabbing everything that comes through its search portal, analyze it in real time, and stomp the market flat for the rest of you."

"Google? Let me tell you why we laugh at Google. Are you ready for this?"

And he's off. Max's eyes are bright, he's slurping his drink instead of sipping it, and the facts of his job are rolling through his head like bowling balls down the lane. When Kelsey casually mentions the words "passwords" and "security" and "access," those sections of his mind open up and I'm free to root around in his best-kept secrets.

An hour later, Kelsey glances over Max's shoulder again, and I nod. I've got everything I need.

She thanks Max for the drinks and stands up. She's even kind to him when she turns him down. He's a much more interesting guy when he's geeking out than when he's playing Buddy Love. He's given me everything we need, and more.

I'm sorry I ever doubted her.

[20]

I make my entrance into OmniVore headquarters the next evening at 11:00 P.M. I walk in through the front door.

Just for tonight, I'm part of the cleaning crew, which is mostly staffed by illegal immigrants. Their bosses squeeze the maximum square footage of clean office space out of each worker, so they usually end up alone and unsupervised, trying desperately to clean a whole floor before moving on to the next building on the night's schedule.

And each one of them has an all-access pass to every office in the building.

Most corporations already know about this glaringly obvious hole in their security. The guys who spend millions to protect their corporate secrets still can't resist cheaping out on their cleaning contracts, however. The worst they can imagine is one of the janitors going through a desk for valuables. Other than that, they don't think about it. The people in coveralls and uniforms barely register to the men who hire them; they hardly even exist.

I found my janitor the same way I found Max: hanging around outside the building and watching the crews as they emerged after work. I got a good look into their minds as they headed back to their van. Even at 1:00 A.M., most of them were on their way to a second job, which meant they'd work more hours in a day than any programmer, and not while sitting down either. Most of them had families. That's why they were sweating all night: to put some cash away to give their sons and daughters a better life than they'd ever see. I could feel the hope and the exhaustion coming off them like steam.

They were useless. They had too much to lose.

Fortunately, there's always at least one guy who's looking for an excuse to get fired. That was Anthony.

Anthony left work every night in time to catch the last shift at the strip club. He was already planning ahead for the weekend, when he'd drive his rebuilt Camaro across the state line into Nevada and blow whatever was left of his paycheck at the craps tables.

I approached him with cash in hand, and rented his uniform and his place on the night shift for five hundred bucks.

The supervisor and all of Anthony's coworkers look right at me, but they don't see me. They see the picture I'm putting in their heads: Anthony, slouched behind his cleaning cart, filling out his uniform as usual.

This is my version of an invisibility cloak. The technical term is "inattentional blindness," a kind of cognitive dead zone in your visual field. Your brain is constantly bombarded with more stimuli than it can possibly handle: about fourteen million bits of information a second, according to the guys who keep count of that sort of thing. It has to narrow all those millions of bits down to a manageable amount just so you aren't paralyzed by all the incoming data. So it takes shortcuts. It cheats.

Your vision, for instance. Over a third of your brain is dedicated to processing the details streaming in from your eyes, and it's still not enough. So your brain ignores most of what you see. The couch in the living room, the tree outside your office window, the people standing with you in line for the ATM—your brain skims right over them to save time and energy. It fills in the gaps with the same images over and over, like the scenery behind the characters in one of those old Hanna-Barbera cartoons. That's the reason that you don't see your missing car keys on the front table, even when you've looked there a dozen times. They faded into the background.

In other words, you really only see what you expect to see. And I can manage those expectations. Everyone here expects to see Anthony, and their minds supply all the details I need to hide in plain sight. To them, I'm as invisible as chewing gum on the sidewalk.

Unless they step in it, of course.

We push the carts into the elevators, past the security guards at the front desk. I'm subtly reinforcing their apathy by broadcasting *<nothing to see here>* in every direction. Sure enough, they don't give me a second look.

I can't fool the cameras, though. They're everywhere now. I'm pretty sure my ball cap and three-day stubble are enough to beat any facial-recognition software that OmniVore might have, but it won't stand up when a real person checks the video tomorrow.

It won't matter. Tomorrow will be way too late.

I BREAK AWAY from the rest of the cleaning crew, taking my little cart up twenty-six stories to OmniVore's offices.

Anthony's key card opens the doors, and I walk inside. I remove a steering-wheel lock hidden in the cart and stick it through the door handles. The doors themselves are wood paneling over a fireproof steel core; the building code requires it. It would take a forklift to break them down, so I should have time to work.

OmniVore's space is set up along an open floor plan. It doesn't have cubicles, let alone offices. The desks are arranged in some kind of fractal pattern, probably designed by an industrial consultant at $350 an hour to maximize efficiency and proper communication. The whole place hums with raw computing power: there's a rack of machines in one corner, hooked to the workstations, quietly processing terabytes of raw data. There's a kitchen area devoted to snacks, with espresso machines, Sub-Zero refrigerators, and smoothie makers. There's a gym area, including a climbing wall built into the concrete that goes all the way up to the ceiling. There are sofas with pillows for power naps. In another corner, there are foosball tables and classic arcade games—which should be a little too dot-com for a company like OmniVore, actually. The whole place is an adult version of a preschool, filled with soft corners and fun toys.

There's only one office with actual doors and walls: it's a huge, two-story atrium, like a glass rocket aimed at the ceiling. It surrounds a couch, table and chairs, and a desk cut from a massive slab of redwood. There's only one screen in the room, a giant HD display on the desk, with a tasteful little brushed-aluminum keyboard in front of it.

Preston's inner sanctum. Big glass windows so he can see out, but I have no doubt that the glass goes opaque at the push of a button whenever he decides he wants privacy.

There's a clear line from Preston's office to the fire exit. That's good. I use a metal wedge to jam that door shut so no one can sneak in behind me. Then I make a quick circuit of the rest of the area.

There's food on the floor, trash everywhere, and gum stuck to the desks. These guys are slobs. If I was actually here to do Anthony's job, I'd be in trouble.

Instead, I remove my packages from the cleaner's cart and place them close to any computer I find. The open floor plan helps. Walls might have seriously screwed up the range and impact.

I head back to Preston's office.

Unsurprisingly, Anthony's key card does not work on the reader on Preston's door. It blares loudly at me, a warning not to try it again. I'm sure the unauthorized entry was logged somewhere, but nobody's going to come running for an honest mistake by the janitor.

There's a keypad. Just for fun, I try the passcode I fished out of Max's head.

The door alarm blares again, louder this time. Two strikes. Now I'm sure that another attempt will bring security.

I didn't really expect the passcodes and key card to work. Just like he's the only one in the office with a door that locks, Preston's the sort of guy who has to have control of his own secrets.

I wasn't able to snag any of his passwords or security codes when I went on my raid inside his head. Even if I had, it would be stupid to expect that they remain the same from day to day. A guy like Preston understands security. He knows you need a constantly shifting passcode, keyed to an authentication token, like a chip on a smartcard. Or, even better, something like retinal scanning.

I don't have that. I have a short-handled sledgehammer. It breaks the lock on the door with one swing.

Alarms immediately begin shrieking. It's annoying, but I've worked with gunfire going past my head, so it's not enough to distract me. I drop the sledge and wheel the cart through the door, then get behind Preston's desk.

I pick up the desk phone and dial a number I've been saving in the back of my memory.

A voice on the other end. "Hello?"

He sounds groggy. Well, even boy billionaires need their sleep.

"Hello, Preston," I say.

I didn't get passwords, but I did manage to retain Preston's personal cell number. I know he keeps it with him constantly—he's got the same complicated, needy relationship with his toys as any other geek—and he'll always pick up for a call coming from work, even at three in the morning.

"I thought you'd want to know that in less than five minutes, you're going to get a call from security, letting you know that someone has broken into your office," I tell him.

Preston knows this isn't the protocol. This isn't how he should be alerted to a security breach. And that wakes him up fast.

"What? Who is this?" he demands. His voice is instantly alert.

"I'm the guy who broke into your office, genius," I say. "It's John Smith. It's time we had another talk."

"YOU'RE A FUCKING dead man," Preston says.

I'll be honest. I didn't have to make this call. But it's worth it just to hear the rage.

"Yeah, I've heard that before," I say. I follow the cords from the monitor into a hole in the big slab of the desk.

"I mean it," he snarls. "You're so fucking dead. I didn't think you were smart, but this is just stupid. What are you going to do? You're stuck in my office."

"I might surprise you," I say.

"You can't surprise me," he snaps. "I know all about you now."

"Really? What's my favorite ice cream flavor?"

"Fuck you."

"So close. It's strawberry."

There it is. The computer's hard drive is located underneath the big slab of wood behind a hidden door. It's big—industrial-server size—and custom built.

"I know about you," he repeats. "You're supposed to be some kind of psychic."

That is interesting. His CIA contacts have decided to bring him into the loop about my talents. Which tells me that they've decided he's more valuable than whatever secrets I used to hold.

"I don't like that term," I say as I drag the hard drive out from under the desk. "See, what we call the mind is actually a metaphor for all the different processes—memories, physical sensations, emotions, thoughts, and reflexes—running inside your head, and what I do is—"

"Spare me," he says. "I've read your file. Whatever it is you do, I know you're not bulletproof. That's all that matters."

"Come on, Preston," I say. "Do you really think I'd call you up without a good reason?"

He takes a deep breath. I can almost hear him trying to regain control.

"All right," he says. "Tell me. What do you want?"

"I'm giving you one last chance to end this peacefully," I tell him. "You give me what I want, and I go away."

"I assume you've got a list of demands."

Now he's stalling. He wants to give his security team plenty of time to reach me. If I had to guess, I'd say he was talking to me on his personal phone, and frantically texting on another device, telling his goons to get here as fast as possible.

Doesn't matter. They'll be too late.

"Nothing too difficult for a guy like you," I say. "Call off the hit on me and Kelsey. Restore my house and my bank accounts. And then add one million dollars for the inconvenience."

"And if I don't?"

I use my Batman voice. "Then I'll destroy everything you've built. Starting right here, right now."

He laughs at me. Remember what I said about the essence of a good threat? The target has to believe you can carry it out. And Preston clearly does not believe me. "Well, that sounds reasonable. Thing is, I don't have that kind of cash on me. Will you take a check?"

"You know, Eli, you are not coming across as completely sincere."

"And they said you couldn't do your little mind-reading act over the phone."

Fine. I didn't really expect him to fold. We'll do it the hard way.

While pulling the hard drive out from the desk, I accidentally bump the keyboard, and the giant HD screen flares to life. There's a simple password prompt over the OmniVore logo.

That's not what I need. I already know it's a waste of time to try Max's passwords and logins. Like the door, there's only one wizard with the magic words to open this gate.

And he's not sounding very cooperative.

Fortunately, I have another, more reliable method to get what I want out of the computer.

I take my last tool from the cart: a high-speed, handheld rotary zip saw. Slices through sheet metal quicker than a knife through a beer can in those infomercials.

I put the phone on speaker and turn on the saw. "Just remember," I say, "I tried to negotiate."

I fire up the saw and cut into the computer's casing. Then I carve the hard drive out of the machine.

I can hear Preston yelling, even over the sirens and the metal-on-metal shriek of the saw.

"What the hell do you think you're doing?" he yells over the speaker as I turn off the saw.

"I'm sure you've got a link to the cameras in your office. You should be able to see."

The drive is huge, at least compared to the off-the-shelf units you can buy at Staples. It still fits easily into a small messenger bag, however.

I look up and find the camera. I smile, and hold up the bag.

"I know what you keep in here," I tell him.

The source code for Cutter. The core of his business. The engine to his Ferrari.

Maybe it's just a huge coincidence that both Sloan and Preston came up with software that can sift so brilliantly through trillions of bytes of raw data. I've got a theory about that. Maybe I'll get to test it someday. Maybe I'll never know.

Either way, I've got years of Preston's work—his entire life—in this little box. Without what's on this hard drive, he's got to start all over. Without this, he loses the bleeding edge.

"I've got the heart of Cutter," I tell him. "I've got the key to your whole world, right here."

There's a long pause. Then Preston erupts into howls of vicious laughter.

"You can't really be that dumb," he says. "Are you a fucking moron? Do you really think I'd be so stupid as to keep something like that on one computer? With no backups? Oh my God, you idiot. I can't believe you had me worried for a second. I've got multiple copies of my software throughout the office, on every machine. How else do you think we operate? We back up every day to a central storage facility. That hard drive is just one place I keep the data. Honestly, have you never used a computer?"

He goes on like that. I'm distracted by other things.

The alarms stop blaring. Almost at the same time, the pounding on the outer doors stops. Then I hear muffled orders, followed by the sound of heavy equipment moving.

That's a bad sign. The real professionals have arrived.

I hear a loud, high-pitched whine. I stand up and look toward the doors. There's a bright flare of light. Sparks flying from the doors. Someone thought to bring an angle grinder. They must have been Boy Scouts in an earlier life.

I've got maybe five minutes before they breach the doors.

I check my watch. It's going to be close.

"You're going to want to order your men to back off now," I tell Preston.

"Are you listening to me? You have no leverage, dipshit. All you've got is the sharp end of the stick, and I am personally going to jam it so far up your—"

"Preston," I snap, cutting him off. "I'm sure a computer genius like you knows how to do a remote-access login on a server."

That stops him short. "What? Yeah. Of course."

"You say you have everything backed up? You might want to take a quick look at that. Just to check."

There's a pause. Then I hear the quiet clacking of a keyboard.

"No," Preston says quietly. "No, no, no, no, no, no, no . . ."

"Lose something?" I ask.

"Son of a bitch," he shouts. "Where is it? How did you do that? You son of a bitch, where the hell is all my *data*?"

I NEVER MEANT to use Max's knowledge to get inside OmniVore's offices.

It never would have worked. He was too low on the totem pole. Only Preston would have access to the source code and the algorithm.

But Max's passwords and logins were more than enough to get me access to the remote server farm where OmniVore keeps all its backups.

Of course I knew Preston would have a remote storage facility. Everyone in the industry does, because it's cheap and efficient. Instead of the expense and hassle of maintaining their own huge banks of computers, they rent out space on a rack of servers kept in a warehouse. Then they upload their data to the servers on a daily basis, usually on an automated schedule. That way, if there's a power failure or a virus or a fire, the company's data is safe and sound, miles away.

It's common practice, even for a guy who's using classified, black-ops-level software. Almost everybody knows about remote storage facilities.

What most people don't know is that their security is god-awful.

As soon as I had the information I needed from Max's brain, I dropped Kelsey at a hotel and drove straight to OmniVore's server farm.

There was one security guard working the desk that late at night. The facilities have to be open 24-7 so their clients can get access at any time.

The guard was playing Angry Birds and reliving a little family drama when I showed up.

<why do I always have to be the bad guy?> <she gets to say yes to everything, I always have to say no> <crying over a damn cookie> <I don't like it either> <dammit, kills me every time> <just a damn cookie> <maybe I could be the one who says yes be the good guy for a change> <bring some cookies-and-cream ice cream home, maybe> <no, kid's going to weigh two hundred pounds if we don't draw the line somewhere> <dammit>

I had a clipboard and a suit jacket. That and a confident wave took me right past him. He barely looked up from his iPad.

There was a glass door leading back to the racks of computer servers, separated by mesh metal cages. Each company has its own sector of the farm; the more data the company stored, the more floor space. OmniVore's servers took about half the warehouse. Its cage was helpfully labeled with its name above the door.

I put my clipboard into my bag, took out a pick gun, snapped it twice in the lock, and the cage popped open.

A moment later, I used a USB cord to hook my laptop to the nearest server. That's when I tapped Max's knowledge. My fingers flew over the keys, just like his would. For a few seconds, it was like having his talent. I flew past the login prompts, entered the right passwords, and got access to the server's main memory.

Then I uploaded a file from the laptop into the server and inserted the virus. Nothing too fancy, really. You can get the program from the Internet yourself, and customize it with a few keystrokes. It instructed the servers to wipe their own hard drives, and then overwrite them with random gibberish. Once it was done, all of OmniVore's backup data would be irretrievably lost.

The whole errand took less than ten minutes.

On the way out, I waved at the security guard again.

"Have a good night," he said.

"Next time, just give your kid the cookie," I told him. "Life's too short."

He gave me a strange look as I went out the door.

"You son of a bitch," Preston says again. "I am going to make sure they keep you alive until I can get there. Then I am going to put a fucking ice pick right into your fucking eyeball—"

"Focus, Eli. We're on a bit of a clock. Order your guys to get back from the doors."

He laughs, but he sounds a lot less amused now. "Why the hell should I?"

I check my watch again. Getting down to the wire.

"Because I've got the only copy of your life's work here in my hands."

"I told you: every computer in there has the algorithm in one form or another. The building is surrounded by my people. You are trapped inside. As soon as my guys get in there, I get everything back. How do you not get this already? *You've got no hand.*"

"Preston, I'm not screwing around. Get them back right now."

He starts screaming again. "Are you retarded? They're going to be through the door in *two minutes,* and then—"

"And the bombs go off in one," I shout back. I'm yelling at the phone, because I'm running for the fire exit.

I yank the wedge from the doorframe and pull the door open in one move. Whatever Preston says next is lost in the scream of the fire alarm. The door slams shut behind me.

I take the stairs four at a time, but even so, I'm barely down two floors when the explosion hits.

A REGULAR BOMB isn't enough to destroy all the data in a computer. There are tools that can scrape lost bits of information from hard drives that have been smashed with a hammer.

What you need is an EMP bomb: a weapon that releases an electromagnetic pulse as it detonates, frying the circuits of anything electronic inside its blast radius.

This sounds like it should be science fiction. It's actually disturbingly easy to find the plans for one on the Internet. Sure, you'll probably end up on a terrorist watch list, but by the time the FBI gets around to visiting you, you could build a couple hundred of the things.

It took me only about half a day to make six. I had help from Tidhar, who kept a whole box of construction-grade Semtex, the civilian version of C-4 plastic explosive, inside his storage unit.

Basically, an EMP bomb is an electromagnetic coil wrapped around a simple pipe device. The detonation of the explosion releases electromagnetic waves in a single strong burst. The pulse fries anything with a computer chip that's inside the blast radius—and the shrapnel destroys anything else that's left.

The effect is a lot like putting your laptop in a microwave. And then dropping the microwave off a cliff.

The inside of my messenger bag is lined in metallic foil. Zipped closed, it will keep the hard drive safe from the EMP.

But everything else inside OmniVore's headquarters has just been reduced to smoking, high-tech scrap.

I REACH THE first floor running, out of breath. The sprinkler system is going full tilt and the air is full of smoke. Fire engines and police cruisers are already outside the building.

I'm not the only guy in a janitor's outfit to emerge from the fire stairs. A couple of OmniVore's security goons try to keep us penned in the lobby, but the cops and the firefighters won't have it. We're all released into the courtyard in front of the building and quickly hustled to a safe distance.

I spare a quick glance upward. The windows on the top floors are all gone, and smoke pours from the building's empty sockets. OmniVore's headquarters looks like a cheap cigar set on its end.

Maybe I used too much Semtex. It's been a while since Bomb Building 101.

I walk away from the crowd while everyone's attention is fixed on the fire.

Kelsey waits in a car at the corner. Her eyes are wide, her pulse is hammering. *<holy crap> <so that's what a bomb looks like in real life>* But once again, she holds it together.

"You okay?" she asks.

I nod, and she pulls out into traffic. Smoothly, not too fast, not drawing any attention to us. The CIA really screwed up when they passed her over. She would have been great.

We drive away, the building still smoldering in the rearview.

[21]

We drive back to Los Angeles, just one of thousands of cars on the highway. I get a little paranoid about satellite surveillance. I don't seriously believe Preston's influence goes that high. But if it does, we're already screwed, because there's nothing we can do about it.

We make it back to Tidhar's safe house without being hit by a drone strike, so I assume we're in the clear.

In the morning, I watch coverage of the explosion on CNN. Tidhar brought us a TV and hooked it up to a cable feed. It's fairly kind of him, considering he's going to have to break down this whole place after we leave. You never use a safe house twice. They're not meant to be permanent installations or hotels for spies. They're a temporary refuge at best.

Someone recorded the explosion on his phone—because someone always does. The smoke pours from the office tower on continuous repeat while the talking heads find a hundred different ways to say they don't know anything.

OmniVore's PR crew is surprisingly tight-lipped. Usually they have an answer for everything, but today, it's a simple statement about cooperating with the authorities.

"Luckily, no one was hurt," the reporter says.

"Yeah. Lucky," Kelsey says, watching from the bed next to me. She's been wound a little tighter since we left San Jose. I've been trying not to peer into her head, like she's asked, but sometimes she thinks pretty loud.

I don't reply to her. Her irritation grows. "'Luckily, no one was hurt,'" she says, more sharply this time.

"That was always the plan," I say.

"Remind me, how many things have gone according to plan so far?"

I can see where she's going with this. It's like a highway closing down to only one lane. But I don't see a lot of choice.

"This was your idea, remember?"

"Don't. Don't pretend you're doing all this for me. I didn't ask you to blow up a building."

"I didn't start this fight. Preston did. And like you keep saying: nobody got hurt."

"Would it have made a difference to you?"

I'm starting to get a headache. I want this to stop. "Can you do me a favor?" I ask. "Can you just say out loud what's really going through your mind? I already know what you're thinking. I know why you're angry."

"Don't be too sure about that," she says.

This is an argument I can't win, so I settle for the truth.

"Of course I do," I snap back, angrier than I intended. "I know exactly what is going through your mind. You're frightened, you're pissed, and you're worried that you're going to get some blood on your Jimmy Choos. I can't control that. Not any of it."

She surprises me, once more, with how calm she is in the face of my outburst. "Wow, that must save a lot of time. Having both sides of a conversation."

"It's what you were thinking."

"Do you mind if I talk now? Or can you do all of this by yourself?"

I nod. Whatever.

"You have this gift. You could do almost anything with it. You could be so much more. And this is what you choose. This is what you want to be. Remember when we were talking about other jobs you could do? You could find other ways to survive. A lot of them would be safer, and some of them would even pay better. But none of them would give you a chance to hurt people."

I consider that for a second. "So now you're psychic too?"

"I don't have to read minds to see that you were badly damaged, and you're angry. Maybe that's inevitable, for someone who has your abilities. But that's why you do this. Someone's got to pay for what's been done to you. You do this because you need someone to punish."

That sounds like her Psych 101 credit from college to me. I struggle for patience as I reply. "You're right: I don't care that much about other people being hurt. I care about you, and more importantly, I care about me. Right now those are my priorities."

She looks at me for the longest time. Her thoughts don't make it to the level of words. There's just a raw feeling, something that's hard for me to name.

"You need to be careful," she says. "I know you want to think you're not human. That you've crossed some line, or that you were born different. I don't buy it. You're still one of us. But if you work really hard at it, you might get what you wish for, John."

I've got five or six smart-ass replies I could make to that, but even I'm not stupid enough to say them out loud.

She's done talking to me anyway. She turns away and starts singing in her head again, a greatest-hits medley designed to shut me out.

<we built this city on rock and roll> <fun, fun, think about fun> <believe in life after love> <who let the dogs out> <and you're gonna hear me ROAR>

Jesus God. Where does she get these songs?

I step into the corridor, close the door, and call Preston. If I'm looking for someone to punish, then he's a pretty good candidate.

PRESTON SURPRISES ME. There's no abuse, no foaming at the mouth, no screaming. He doesn't even raise his voice when I call him.

"What the hell," he says. "We've been meaning to redecorate anyway."

I assume he's trying to trace the call. Good luck. Thanks to Tidhar, I'm piggybacking on Mossad tech, my cheap mobile riding a signal that's bounced all over the world through an anonymizing VoIP network. That won't stall him forever, but it should give us enough time to talk. Preston's CIA backers could probably identify the source of the call, if they worked at it. But I suspect Preston isn't running to them with his problems right now. I bet the Agency is asking him a lot of questions he's reluctant to answer.

Maybe that's why he sounds so reasonable.

"You're taking this awfully well," I say.

"I've been doing some Zen sitting with a Buddhist monk lately. Trying to understand my karma, you know. That sort of thing." Then he laughs. "Ah, you don't believe that for a second, do you? Of course I'm pissed. But there comes a time when you've got to cut your losses and stop chasing a losing strategy. We can still negotiate."

"Glad to hear that. You know the terms: call off the hit on me and Kelsey. Restore our property. Throw in two million for my trouble, and you get the hard drive."

Slight pause. "You said it would be one million before."

"Did I? I meant three million."

"Hey, wait a second—"

"And now it's four."

He makes a noise, almost like a growl. "You know, John, I'm not a complete idiot. I mean, you seem to have this idea that I'm a fraud, that I can't write my own code. But you must know better. You were in my head, or so you keep telling me. You must know I can rewrite everything we lost. Sure, that's a pain in the ass—I am not exactly nostalgic for those twenty-hour coding sessions wired up on Red Bull and Adderall. That's why I became a CEO, so I wouldn't have to do that crap anymore. But I can do it. I'm the guy who wrote it in the first place and you're trying to sell me something I already know how to make. That's fine. I'm willing to pay for that convenience. Still, there's something you should keep in mind: I don't need Cutter to keep a price on your head. You've proven you can hurt me. Great. You're very impressive, I get that now. But I can hurt you much worse. Right now I'm being a grown-up. You keep pissing me off, I might just kick over the game board completely."

I wait. He doesn't say anything else. I assume he's had his badass moment, so I ask him the question.

"How long do you think you can stall them, Eli?"

"What? Stall who?"

"All of them. Your clients. The Agency. All of the people you're supposed to be monitoring and protecting and analyzing. I bet you'll get a little slack, because, after all, you just had your offices blown to bits on national television. But sooner or later, they're going to expect to see your mojo working again. Do you think you'll be able to rebuild Cutter before they notice you're completely fucked? You can't even tell your best programmers, because if they knew how bad it was, they'd run screaming to the competition. So I bet you're pretending it's business as usual while you try to re-create everything, all by yourself. How's that going for you?"

Silence. I'd swear he's pouting.

"I could be wrong, of course. What did your friends at the Agency say? How'd they take it when they found out you've lost all the secrets they wanted to steal?"

He swallows loud enough for me to hear it over the line.

"You said three million, right?"

"Four."

A bitter laugh. "Right. Four. What was I thinking? So where do you want to meet, John?"

I give him the details for a public meeting. This could turn into a fairly profitable job after all.

[22]

Screaming children and exhausted parents wander around us. Hipsters with multiple piercings sneer at the chain restaurant and the rides, trying hard to kill whatever childlike wonder they've got left inside them. There's a polyglottal soup of languages and accents in the air as tourists compare what's in front of their eyes with what they've seen on TV. Homeless people sift through the trash cans and beg spare change, their hunger and exhaustion numbed a little by drugs. And from all sides, all around me, there's pressure, like the water in the deep end of the pool, a heavier atmosphere pressing on me, the weight of a few thousand minds, all gathered in one spot, all of them filled with need and want.

This is where we agreed to meet: the Santa Monica Pier at noon. Broad daylight, big crowds, hundreds of potential witnesses.

Ordinarily you'd never get me within a thousand yards of a place like this. It's up there with Disneyland in my nightmares. But this should keep both sides honest.

Preston agreed a little too fast, with a minimum of bitching. That makes me think either I made a mistake or he really has given up. From my perspective, it's about as safe here as possible. There's no good sniper position within a half mile, and too many police and civilians for an ambush. Even if he could get a guy on a roof somewhere, the fixed attention on me would instantly set off my alarm bells. Anyone in the crowd who targets me should wake me up to immediate danger as well.

I have to have faith in my talent. All the mental noise around me is worth what I'm gaining in safety. This is about as good as I can get.

The pier starts with a long bridge sloping down from the street to the structure. There are two concrete walkways on either side for pedestrians—never enough room for all of them—and a two-lane road for the cars that are early enough to get a space on the pier's parking lot.

I put Kelsey at a spot on the walkway, well above the place where I'm meeting Preston's men. She can watch the crowd and watch my back from here.

"Almost done," I tell her. "Just this last bit, and then it's over."

"Then what happens?" she asks.

"You can't be serious. You want to talk about our relationship now?"

She smiles. "Guys always get so scared when it's time to talk commitment," she says. "Don't be a jerk. When this is over, I'm going to run away from you as fast and as far as I can. No offense."

"Some taken."

"Well, if you ever get that island, I might come visit. If you think you could use a friend."

I look at her. "Might be nice," I admit.

I check my watch as an excuse to look away. Almost time for the meet. Now comes the tricky part. I've done this only a few times, and it's never easy.

I look at her. "Do you trust me?"

She gives me a look back. *<what a stupid question>*

She's right. She's already trusted me more than anyone should.

I lean close and touch my forehead to hers.

This isn't necessary, but it makes things easier. Physical proximity always makes my talent work better. I'm sure there's a whole theory behind that, but I've never been interested in the process much. Just the results.

I look inside her head. Really look. I push past the surface thoughts and her memories and her buzz of anxiety. I submerge myself inside her physical responses, the sound of the pier and the ocean, the brightness of the sun through her closed eyelids, the slight breeze carrying the scents of fried food and salt water. I'm hearing what she hears. Seeing what she sees.

It's as intimate as being in bed together, but out in public, in broad daylight. She shakes, just a little bit, and grips my arms as if to maintain her balance.

I swim back to the surface and pull out. But I leave a chunk of myself behind.

When I open my eyes, I have to split-screen my consciousness. On the one side, everything that I see: Kelsey, standing there in the sun, with people streaming around her as they head down for fun and frolic.

And on the other side, I see myself through her eyes. I look worried. And older than I remember.

She can feel it, that piece of myself still inside her head. Without my talent, she can't see it the same way. All she can feel is her end of the link, like a telephone connection left open after one person hangs up. She doesn't get the visuals or the words or the inside of my mind. But she knows I'm there.

She could break the link if she wanted. I could claw hard and try to hang on, but there's really nothing I can do to keep her from shaking me out of her head when she's had enough. That's why this requires trust.

"Oh man," she says. "That's weird."

"Just take it easy. I'm right here."

She nods. She turns her head, and my perspective shifts. The world tilts on one side of the split screen. She looks down and sees the meeting spot, the tables outside the carousel on the pier.

On my side of the screen, I'm still looking at her. Her perspective jumps around while she checks the crowd.

I have to fight the urge to try to direct her vision. That just leads to migraines. She looks where she looks. I'm a passive rider. It's like wearing 3-D glasses or talking on the phone while driving. It takes a little getting used to at first.

Kelsey is smarter than I am, and tougher than I thought possible, but she's still basically a civilian. She doesn't have my training. She doesn't know what to look for or how to pick an enemy out of the crowd. So I'm going to have to do a ride-along. With her up here, I can look for anyone else working for Preston through her eyes. I can watch my back at the same time she does.

It might also have occurred to me that this is also the best way to keep her away from Preston's men and still be with her.

Before I pull away, I kiss her.

Again, not necessary, but we need all the luck we can get right now.

I check my watch. Time to go.

Half of my mind is filled with the picture of me walking away from her.

. . . .

THE CAROUSEL IS just to the left of where the road levels out and meets the pier. There's a deck outside the entrance with metal tables.

Preston's men are there, as arranged, holding down a position at one of the tables. Three of them. Wearing baggy shorts and T-shirts, scowls on their faces as if daring any happy families to try to take their seats. People give them a lot of space. Ice cream melts, uneaten, in little paper cups in front of them.

Never trust a man who doesn't like ice cream. If that's not a saying, it should be.

On the other side of the split screen, Kelsey watches the crowd as they stream past her, on their way up and down the bridge to the pier. *<kids going past with balloons> <baby crying> <teenage boy and girl holding hands, she looks like a model, he can barely grow a mustache> <brown-haired man, muscular, yellow polo shirt buttoned at the neck> <toddler surrounded by cheap stuffed animals from the games, fast asleep in his stroller> <tourists speaking German get way too close before detouring around her, sunburned, weird European sandals on their feet>*

Nobody looks hostile. I'm not getting that telltale prickle on the back of my neck that tells me someone is lining up a shot. I'm not a target. We're good.

I sit down at the table.

"Join you?"

"Free country," the lead guy—Adkins, his name is Adkins—says.

"Nice day, huh?"

"If you like seventy degrees and sunshine," Adkins says.

"Beats the hell out of a hundred and twenty in the shade in

Fallujah." I'm trying to be nice. Two vets, talking about the war. What better way to bond?

"Fuck you. Let's just get this over with."

So much for bonding.

<baby still crying like a car alarm> <bodybuilder in a muscle T and a parrot on each shoulder, smiling at everyone who stares> <jingling chimes as a Mexican ice man wheels his cart down the ramp>

I feel Kelsey's anxiety growing. Something wrong, out at the periphery of her senses. Nothing conscious. But enough to make her nervous.

Meanwhile, Iggy and the stooges are already screwing up the deal with me.

"All right. Nice doing business with you," I say. I try to take the duffel.

Adkins won't give it up. He puts his foot down on the bag. Hard.

"No way," he says. "Not until you give us the drive."

"That's not how this is supposed to work," I say quietly.

He smirks. "I'm telling you how it works."

<minivan rumbling down the ramp, stressed-out dad behind the wheel, carful of kids bouncing around behind him> <Parrot guy standing in the middle of the road, won't get out of the way>

He's improvising. He actually thinks it's a good idea. Showing initiative as a way to impress both Preston and the people behind him.

"Adkins," I tell him, "the people who hired you are most impressed by men who can follow orders."

<how did he know my name?> <they said this guy was serious> <take him down, bring in a scalp, prove I can do better stuff than this> <I can do this> <I can!>

"Adkins," I say again, as patiently as I can, "this is not the time for you to show me your dick. Follow the rules, we'll all go home happy."

He gets defensive. I'm embarrassing him in front of the other two. Their names pop up as well: <*Wylie*> and <*Gill*>.

I can feel the weapons they're carrying, under their baggy shirts, snug against their hips.

"All right," I say, trying to project <*calm*> and <*reasonable*> into their atrophied little frontal lobes. "Let me look inside the bag. See if Preston fulfilled his end of the bargain. Then we can talk about where you can get the drive."

"No. You tell us now."

Jesus. Even the five-year-olds waiting in line for ice cream display more patience than this guy. I'd have better luck negotiating with them. Why did Preston send the B-team for this meet?

<the dad lays on the horn, trying to get the Parrot Man to move> <the Parrot Man talks to two young girls, can't be more than fourteen> <pervert> <enjoying their attention> <Parrot Man turns and scowls> <Dad hits the horn again, a long pissed-off blare>

I'm starting to get a headache keeping it all separate.

<Parrot Man is pounding on the window of the minivan now, taunting Dad> <Dad looks terrified, he reaches for his phone> <the birds are squawking loudly>

Wait a second. Who was that?

I close my eyes and try to focus.

<Parrot Man hits the window so hard the safety glass cracks and stars> <Dad has the phone to his ear, yelling into it now> <kids crying in the backseat> <bystanders begin to get involved, tell Parrot Man to calm down> <birds are trying to fly away, tethered by straps to Parrot Man's arms>

At the edge of Kelsey's peripheral vision. <*brown-haired man*> She's not completely conscious of having seen him, that's why this is hard. She knows him, even if she's only aware of it as a nagging feeling of unease.

"Hey," Adkins snaps. "You taking a nap on me?"

Oh right, this asshole. "Let me open the bag. Please."

Focus. At the edge of the crowd. Dammit, Kelsey, turn your head. *<brown-haired man, muscular>*

"Not until you tell us where you've stashed the hard drive."

<yellow polo shirt buttoned to the neck>

Oh no.

I get up from the table so fast that Wylie and Gill both twitch for their weapons. Adkins nearly jumps up with me. "Hey, man, what the hell are you—"

I'm up and sprinting away from him, toward Kelsey, screaming inside my head.

<Kelsey> <RUN> <RUN> <RUN>

Because of our link, she hears me.

<Why?> comes back at me. But she starts moving. Slowly, but she moves. I try to kick her legs into gear.

She's not used to it, not used to trusting the voices in her head. That's a sign of schizophrenia in the world where she usually lives, but she has to move.

I push as hard as I can, because I know his body language, even if Kelsey doesn't. I know the threat.

In her memory, at the edges of her vision, there he was. *<yellow polo shirt buttoned to the neck>*

<God DAMMIT, Kelsey, will you just RUN?>

She trusts me. She takes a step, prepares to run.

And finally sees him again. About six feet away from her.

<brown-haired man> <muscular> <yellow polo shirt buttoned to the neck> <still not high enough to keep the edges of his tattoo from peeking out>

Snake Eater.

He's broken away from the crowd. Everyone is fixated on the Parrot Man reaching through the broken window of the minivan. Cars are stacked up behind, honking. The birds are flapping their wings madly, as if they're trying to pull their owner into the sky with them.

He sees Kelsey. That's why I never felt anyone targeting me. I wasn't the target.

She was.

She turns, and starts to run in the other direction.

Too late.

He's already made his decision. He pulls the gun and fires.

The fastest a human being has ever run is about twenty-seven miles per hour. A 9mm bullet fired from a gun moves at just under seven hundred miles per hour. It doesn't matter how much of a head start she has. The bullet catches up to her in a split second.

Entangled with her as I am, I feel it hit the same instant she does.

It breaks her shoulder blade, tears a hole through the top of her lung. She falls.

I stumble, and trip, and fall down with her.

Not real, I remind myself. Not real. It only feels like I am coughing up blood. It only feels like I am dying.

It's only real for Kelsey. She's in pain. She needs help. She's dying, every second I waste.

Get up. Ignore the signals. Get up.

I limp, and then stagger, and then run.

She can barely lift her head. She can feel her shirt, suddenly heavy and wet. <*so much blood*> Everything she sees is surrounded by a black mist, darkness pushing in around the edges. She can't feel her legs now.

Mine threaten to go numb too, but I tell myself it's not real, and I keep on moving.

I round the corner, and this is what I see, from her perspective and mine.

Some people are running. Others stand around, looking almost bored. Everyone heard the shot, but no one saw it. Gunfire isn't enough to get a crowd running, not just one shot, not in L.A. They'll still hang around to get pics on their phones.

Parrot Man is covered in bird shit, his parrots clawing and scratching at him as they try to escape. The doors of the minivan are open, and the father is shielding his children with his body. Other people lie flat on the asphalt, covering their heads.

The police are already at the top of the ramp.

Snake Eater walks right past them, looking straight ahead. Like about half the people in the crowd, he has his phone out.

From Kelsey's rapidly dimming vision, I see him pressing buttons.

Then the explosion hits.

Down by the carousel, and I feel Adkins, Wylie, and Gill wink out of existence. They never saw it coming. They weren't allowed to look inside the bag either.

Now I know why Preston sent the B-team to the meeting.

Now there is true panic, a collective scream going up from everyone at once. People in Los Angeles might be bored by gunfire, but a bomb definitely gets their attention. My brain rings with deeper, more primal fears, and ghosts that go all the way back to the cave and the forest and the creatures at the edge of the firelight possess everyone, and reduce them to animals fleeing a predator. People run in every direction, leaping from the pier to the beach and even into the ocean.

I knock down everyone in my path, but it still seems to take forever to move a dozen yards.

I'm praying to a god I never believed in by the time I reach Kelsey.

I've got my hand on the wound and I'm screaming for help when her half of the split screen finally goes dark.

GAINES, TO HIS credit, shows up at the hospital. He must have used the corporate jet.

I've been sitting in the visitor area for about twelve hours, exuding a steady stream of don't-fuck-with-me vibes. Even the paparazzi and the local TV crews won't bother me, despite the compelling visual of a man sitting with dried blood coloring half his shirt.

The police have accepted my initial story that I was just one of the many bystanders, that I happened to reach Kelsey first.

Gaines finds me in my chair. He's scared shitless, but he still walks up to me. I should give him points for that, but I'm not feeling generous.

"They say she's going to make it," he says.

"I know."

There was an ambulance already scrambled to the pier because of the dad in the minivan's panicked 911 call. I carried her straight to it, my hand plugging the entry wound. I rode with Kelsey the twenty blocks to St. John's. Some of the finest trauma center surgeons in the world work in Los Angeles. The medics back in Iraq used to do their training here, since there are few other places that offer so much experience with such a wide variety of gunshot wounds.

In some ways, you could say she was lucky.

I haven't paid much attention to the TV bolted to the ceiling in the corner, but I've seen enough of the news to know that nobody died, aside from Preston's men. Wounded and maimed, probably. But nobody died.

I suppose they were lucky too.

Gaines looks for the right words. "Mr. Sloan is on his way back from Geneva now. He told me to spare no expense looking after Kelsey."

"How big of him."

We sit in silence for a long moment. Then I sense the real reason he approached me, growing like a mushroom. As always, he's on an errand from his boss.

"Mr. Sloan also wanted me to ask you—"

"You have got to be fucking kidding me."

"—he wanted to know if you, in fact, were able to recover the algorithm from Mr. Preston."

I have to smile at that. Amazing what seems funny when you've been awake long enough. "Seriously? You canceled the contract, remember?"

"It seems, perhaps, I was premature in that."

"You said you were going to call the FBI."

"It seems that the people I spoke with may not have actually been federal agents."

"Yeah. No shit. Maybe if you had anything other than real-estate law and bad TV stuffed into your head, you'd have figured that out sooner."

Gaines chokes back some more bile. "I acted without Mr. Sloan's authority in this matter. I overstepped my bounds. Mr. Sloan instructed me to apologize to you as well."

"You're doing a hell of a job so far, Lawrence."

<fuck you, you bastard> "I am sorry. As I said, I was premature and reckless. But you shouldn't use my mistakes as a reason to hold any animosity against Mr. Sloan."

"Oh, I shouldn't. Good to know."

There's a long pause before Gaines speaks again.

"So, were you able to do the job? Mr. Sloan would still be prepared to pay you if you were able to recover his intellectual property. And we can hopefully get past all of this unpleasantness."

"What about Kelsey? How's she supposed to get past it?"

"We will see that she gets the very best of care. She is still our employee. Any legal problems she might face because of her involvement will, of course, be handled by our attorneys—"

I cut him off. "—a little something extra in the Christmas bonus, maybe a twenty-dollar gift card at Starbucks . . ."

Some semblance of pride rears up in him. "Hey. I didn't get her involved in this."

"No. You were just the guy who abandoned her."

His anger overrides his fear. "And you were the one who let her get shot."

I turn and face him. He shrinks back from whatever he sees there.

"I'm sorry," he says quickly.

I can think of five or six ways to punish him, but I'm too tired. Besides, he's not wrong.

"Don't worry about it," I say.

He waits a whole thirty seconds before asking, "Can I tell Mr. Sloan you have what he wants?"

God. What a little corporate weasel. Of course, I took Sloan's money, too. So what does that make me?

It doesn't matter. We left professional in the rearview a long time ago. Now this is as personal as it gets.

I ignore the question. "They're going to try for her again," I say. "You need to get the police here. That should be enough to discourage them. And then, when she can move, you need to have some professional security ready. I mean professional. Not like those two idiots you had in the office before."

"I'll take care of it."

I stand up. "You'd better."

"Wait. Where are you going?"

"Don't worry about that," I tell him. "Worry about what happens when I come back."

I walk away from him and head out the door.

I tried being civilized with Preston. Now we do it the other way.

Now I burn it all down.

[23]

I take a bus from Los Angeles to El Paso. Bus stations don't have the kind of customers that OmniVore wants to track. If you can't afford a car or a plane ticket, you're too far down the food chain to matter. So there are none of the mechanisms Preston could use to find me. No credit cards, no free Wi-Fi, not even that many surveillance cameras. People still pay cash in bus stations, still get their lunches out of a vending machine.

I'm dressed in clothes I got at a Goodwill. Ordinarily, I'd be thinking about who wore them before me, and who died in this seat.

But something has happened. Somewhere along the line, I slipped into mission-mind. It happened all the time back in Iraq. Somehow the distractions—like the hangover of the alcoholic across the aisle, the one who doesn't realize that pain in his gut is the impending collapse of his liver's ability to function—recede far into the distance. It's not like meditation or the intense focus that comes with actual combat. It's more like the opposite: a kind of enforced dullness where I'm simply observing everything. Asleep on my feet, but ready for the alarm that will wake me up again and turn me loose.

I stay in this zone as I trudge in line across the Stanton Street Bridge into Juárez. There's no requirement to show a passport or a visa to enter Mexico from this side, so there won't be any record of me leaving the country.

On every side of me are people. Their thoughts and babble barely register today.

Once I'm on the other side of the bridge, I know I've dropped off OmniVore's radar entirely. Juárez is too poor, too racked with violence and murder, for Preston's tools to follow me around. Even the CIA would have some trouble finding me here if I chose to disappear.

Preston might even think I'm dead. He's that kind of optimist, the kind who assumes it will always work out for him, just because it always has. It's a reflex more than an actual philosophy. Even though there's no body, no confirmed kill, I'm willing to bet he's written me off the books already because that's the reality he prefers.

The smart play would be to let him go on thinking that.

There's a guy selling cheap phones from a kiosk on the other side of the bridge. I hand over a few dollars and pick up an old iPhone. The screen is cracked, and there's a picture of someone else's kids as the wallpaper, but it works. I make the call.

He picks up, because a guy like him cannot let a phone or email go unanswered.

"Hello, Eli," I say.

There's a pause, almost a hiccup, as he draws a sharp breath.

"Well," he says when he finally recovers. "Didn't expect to hear from you."

"I won't keep you long."

"No, we should talk," he says. "Things have gotten a little out of hand. I want you to know, I didn't authorize that. That was a rogue employee, and obviously, he's already had to pay for his mistake—"

There's furious tapping on a keyboard in the background. I imagine he's trying to trace the call, round up the troops. It doesn't matter.

"Oh, at least try to be a man, Eli. Admit it. It was your idea. You thought you were being bold. You saw yourself as Alexander with the Gordian Knot, didn't you?"

He could go on denying, but he can't resist. He wants to take credit. I was in his head. I know him.

He snickers, just a little. "Lateral thinking. Admit it, you never saw it coming. How often does that happen to a psychic?"

"Maybe you should ask Kelsey for a gold star."

"Hey, that's what happens when you want to play with the big boys. Sometimes there's collateral damage. I was told to snip the loose ends, and she was one of them. It's the cost of doing business."

For an instant, my vision goes dark around the edges. I bite down hard and shift topics. I don't want him to think he can get to me.

"You still haven't told your friends in the CIA."

"What?" That throws him. "What makes you think that?"

"Because your plan was idiotic. You brought civilians into a private business dispute and put the entire country on terrorist alert. They would have slapped you down instantly if they knew you were going to blow a hole in a nationally known landmark."

"You used bombs first," he says, voice sullen.

God. What a toddler. "You didn't tell them because they still don't know you lost everything."

Silence. I can imagine how hard he's working. Years of work, lost in an instant, no backups. I doubt he's slept much.

"Have you still got the hard drive?" I hear a tiny hint of hope in his voice. "We could still make a deal."

"Negotiations are over," I tell him. "You've got nothing I want."

"Oh, that's a load. You must want something. Otherwise, why did you call? You have to want something. Come on. Tell me. We can make a deal. Just tell me what you want. What do you want?"

There it is. The edge of panic in his voice.

"I want you to be afraid," I say. "See you around, Eli."

I hang up and toss the phone into a nearby trash can.

THE STACK OF bills from the meth dealer has gotten thin, so I have to settle for a chain hotel near the U.S. consulate. It looks like the setting of a crime-scene photo, but the phone works, and that's all I really need.

I call the contact number of an old client and give my information. I begin with my terrible Spanish, but the person on the other end answers in barely accented English. Then I sit on the bedspread and stare at the stain on the wall.

I don't have to wait long. Within two hours, two men—both younger than me—show up at my door and ask me to come with them. They're both extraordinarily polite. They don't even show me their guns.

They take me to a waiting black Mercedes, and from there, to the airport. We board a small private jet, where I'm installed in a plush leather seat. One of the young men asks if I want anything to eat or drink. I decline.

They take the seats opposite me and spend most of the short flight looking through magazines or checking their phones. Occasionally, one or the other will look over, just to check on me. He will usually smile, eyebrows raised, silently asking if I need anything. I'll smile back and shake my head. And he'll go back to his magazine or his phone.

Their minds are remarkably clean and untroubled for hired killers. The ghosts of all the victims trailing them barely make a sound.

WE LAND IN Cancún. The airport is filled with college kids on vacation. They all think they're on MTV, and they all believe everyone is watching. It's like I've traveled to a different planet, a happy little biosphere populated entirely by healthy young mammals in the prime of mating season.

But this isn't just a tourist trap. It's also disputed territory in the drug war. The Zetas used to hold the entire area, but over the last couple of years, two other cartels have united to try to kick them out. At least the Mexican army isn't involved here, like they are in Juárez and the poorer areas. The government understands that decapitated co-eds are not exactly a boost for the tourist industry, and so do the cartels. That keeps the war simmering offstage, where it doesn't interfere with the gringos getting sunburns and STDs. The blood only boils over into public view occasionally.

My client, Juan-Gómez Olivarez, is the Zetas' top man here. To the outside world, he's one of the chief lieutenants in the cartel, a ruthless drug lord, and a leading candidate to assume control over the whole operation since the arrest of the Zetas' former leader, Miguel Ángel Trevino Morales.

He's also a deep-cover DEA plant. His real name is Nathan Giles, and he was born to immigrant parents in Tucson, Arizona. He joined Special Forces after high school, which is where we met: he was on a team that backstopped a couple of my jobs in Afghanistan.

After Nathan got out of the army, he joined the DEA and was sent to infiltrate the Zetas. I think even he was surprised how fast he rose in the leadership, but there's nothing like a bloody war to advance your career prospects when you're a soldier. Everyone ahead of you for promotion keeps dying.

His rapid ascent earned him more than a few enemies. Some of his people began to suspect him of being a traitor as his rivals and competitors were busted one too many times. Not long after he was given responsibility for Cancún by no less than Morales himself, Olivarez thought his cover was blown. He heard a corrupt official on the U.S. side of the border might have leaked his true identity.

He was alone. He was afraid. He didn't have anyone on either side of the law to turn to. But he did have a stupidly huge pile of money. So he hired me to find out who else was keeping his secrets.

I went to Mexico for a week, pretending to be just another soldier for hire looking for work. I met with his men and scanned their minds. Three of them knew who Olivarez really was, and they were all holding on to the secret, waiting for the right time to reveal it and take his place. Cartel politics. I gave their names to Olivarez and went back to L.A.

A few days after that, I saw an item on the Web about a dozen Zetas turning up on the steps of the Juárez courthouse. Their heads had been severed and placed neatly in front of their bodies. The picture that accompanied the article was grainy, and the faces on the heads had been through some serious abuse, but I recognized three of them.

So I have no compunctions about calling in this debt.

THE BODYGUARDS ESCORT me to a suite at the Ritz-Carlton. The Gulf is painfully blue through the patio doors. I barely see it. I fall on the bed and sleep like the dead until there's a restrained knock on the door.

When I open my eyes, it's night. The bodyguards are waiting. They escort me downstairs, back into the car. We drive through the streets, out to the edge of the hotel zone, where we turn into a small driveway almost hidden by twenty-foot walls topped with razor wire.

There's no need to frisk me at the front door—I left my gun at the hotel—but a new bodyguard does it anyway. It's important to observe the protocols in this world. It's like exchanging business cards in Japan or trading email addresses in Silicon Valley.

Olivarez himself meets me in the foyer. He looks better than ever: slim, smiling, well dressed.

"You look like shit," he says pleasantly.

"Been an interesting couple of days."

He nods. "Tell me about it."

INSIDE THE HOUSE, everything looks like it's just been removed from plastic wrap. There's not a speck of dust on the Saltillo-tile floors or a single painting hanging askew on the walls. The archways over each door must have cost a fortune in man-hours to build. I should tell Tidhar, if I ever see him again: apparently someone does remember how to plaster those.

A pair of extraordinarily beautiful young women appear at Olivarez's side, not saying anything, just following him from room to room. He finally finds the right setting: a huge living room with the air-conditioning on high and a roaring fire in a central fireplace. He installs himself on a white couch and gestures to a leather armchair for me.

"Still a whiskey drinker?" he asks, and says something in rapid Spanish to one of the girls, not waiting for a reply. She brings me a tumbler with dark liquid and a single sphere of ice.

I sip. Something single malt, appropriately aged, a little spicy. Gorgeous.

"Good Lord," I say. "Lagavulin?"

He nods. "Thirty year."

I tip the glass in his direction. He shrugs and pours himself a glass of Herradura.

"I still prefer vodka, but you try drinking anything other than tequila around here, you get shot."

I admit, it's fascinating to watch him up close. He's compartmentalized himself so completely it's like there are two people sitting with him. I can almost see their shadows.

There's Nathan, the kid who grew up in a crappy part of town and made something of himself, who still believes in truth, justice, and the American Way, who came down here to fight the bad guys.

To do that, he became the bad guy. He turned into Olivarez, the enforcer, the drug lord, the nightmare supervillain of the cartoonish propaganda of the War on Drugs. He's racked up a body count maybe thirty or forty times greater than his kills in Afghanistan, directly and indirectly. He's been responsible for millions of kilos of drugs crossing the border.

There is even a part of him that enjoys the excess. He is rich beyond measure. There are beautiful women who will do anything for him, installed like expensive fixtures in his home. He is respected and feared.

And at the same time, he's considered a hero, because he is stopping the people who do the very same things he does every day.

The DEA allows Olivarez to get away with the things that Nathan is supposed to be fighting. Nathan allows Olivarez to do horrible things because he believes in the greater good. Olivarez goes on killing.

But no one will stop the cycle. The information he's getting is too good. The DEA has never had a source this highly placed. They're finally arresting the big names, the top cartel leaders. No one wants to turn off the spigot.

Nathan knows he is stuck here until someone finally kills him—both of him. And he's quietly going crazy in the middle, wondering who is real and who is the invention.

I do not want to be around when the strands of his personality, pulled in competing directions for so long, finally snap. But he's holding it together for now. And he owes me. Which is all I really need.

"So what's up?" he asks. He's enjoying using the voice of the kid from Tucson. A decade or so has dropped off his face.

I look at the women. He waves a hand. "Please. They don't speak any English."

I smile. "You sure about that?"

The kid vanishes. The drug lord returns. He's suddenly all business. "Which one?"

I incline my head toward the girl on the right. Her eyes go wide, but otherwise she manages to keep her composure.

Olivarez doesn't say anything about it to her in front of me. He dismisses them in Spanish.

The woman is worried as she leaves the room. She doesn't know what Olivarez will do to her. Neither does he. Not yet.

I try not to think about it. It's not why I'm here.

"Well, you've earned your drink," he says. "So now you can tell me what you really want."

There's something liberating about being able to tell your secrets to someone who's forced to keep them. Olivarez is one of the few people in the world I can trust, because what I know about him is so much more dangerous than what he knows about me.

I explain what has happened as best I can. He listens to the whole tale of woe, asking questions at the right time when he needs clarification. Then he delivers his verdict: "You're fucked."

I smile at that.

"Sorry, I know you're a psychic ninja and all that, but you're never going to get close to Preston. You probably scared him away from you forever."

“Not as long as I’ve got the hard drive. He’ll keep coming until he gets it.”

“If what you say about his business is true—if he needs what you’ve got so badly—he’s got maybe six months, tops, before he can’t hide his problems anymore. The CIA will dump him. He won’t make payroll. Why not just hide out for a while? Let him disintegrate on his own.”

“Is that what you would do?”

He looks at me darkly. “You don’t want to know what I’d have to do. I play by different rules.”

I shake my head. “Not this time,” I say. “I am going to end him.”

He sighs and rubs his eyes, but he gets it. He doesn’t need any further explanation, not with his life. Once there was a kid from Tucson who believed in justice, but his career, like mine, has taught him better. Justice is too much to ask from primates like us. We’re not wired for it. You can talk about abstract concepts and we’ll nod and smile, but as a species, we’re barely five hundred years from tearing the hearts out of virgins to ensure a good harvest. When it comes down to the limbic system, where our bodies do the thinking for us, all we really understand is an eye for an eye. We try to codify that, farm out the hard work to the cops or soldiers, dress it up with language. It doesn’t matter. We need to see the blood in the dirt, or it just doesn’t count.

Olivarez knows that there’s an economic value to revenge, which is why we always talk about it like we’re talking about money. No matter what it costs, the lesson is worth it: here is a line that must not be crossed. Touch me and mine, and this is what will happen to you. You owe me for what you did. And I will make you pay.

“You must already have a plan,” he says.

“Got a computer around here?” I ask.

He opens a drawer in an eighteenth-century desk and pulls out a laptop. It's slow to boot up—"Took me forever to get the fucking Wi-Fi working here," he mutters—then he hands it over.

I type in a site address and show it to him.

Preston will be the keynote speaker at the FutureTech conference next week. In Dubai.

"Dubai?" Olivarez looks skeptical. "Come on, Smith. Dubai? If there's one place in the world he could expect to be safe, it would be Dubai."

"Exactly," I say.

He snorts. "You think I can get you into the country without anyone else noticing?"

I sigh. It's late, and I'm tired. "Nathan." I use his real name. Just to tell him I'm serious. "Why do you think I'm here? I already know you can."

I'VE GOT A few days before my transport will be ready. Olivarez keeps me at the hotel, stations a bodyguard nearby, and arranges for a black credit card with a fake name. He sends over a tailor, who cuts me three good suits. I take the sheen off the card in the malls and shops until I look like a respectable traveler again. I accept a brick of cash as well, roughly twice as thick as what I got from the meth dealer, all crisp new hundreds. A bodyguard brings it to my hotel room. He even has me sign a receipt.

We call it a loan. We both know that there's very little chance Olivarez will have to send someone to collect.

If I don't pay him back, it's because I'm already dead.

[24]

I arrive a little after 5:00 A.M. local time at Dubai International.

My plane lands with the other cargo flights. I wake up with a jolt as we hit the tarmac. The heat is already pressing down through the steel skin of the aircraft. I undo my straps and finally get out of the battered little seat where I've spent most of the last eighteen hours. It's not exactly business class. The seat is airline surplus, salvaged from a junk heap and bolted down as an afterthought behind the cockpit for the crew on the flight. I exit the plane with the pilots, wearing a coverall. No one looks at me as they start to unload the cargo.

In fact, no one wants to pay much attention to this particular flight at all.

An airport employee waves me over to an electric cart, then drives me to the main terminal.

The last time I was at LAX, there was a TSA agent napping on a stool at the security line, an overflowing toilet in the men's room, and a garden hose coming down through a hole in the ceiling for no apparent reason.

In Dubai, it's like walking into a high-end luxury hotel. There are overstuffed couches. Every surface in the terminal gleams. A flock of women, wearing hijabs and carrying Coach bags, passes me on the right. In the shops, you can pick up a $10,000 bottle of Cheval Blanc, a Cartier Tank watch, or a solid gold bar to take home to the kids.

It's the same almost everywhere here. Dubai makes Vegas look like a trailer park. They both started as patches of desert. But in 1966, Dubai struck oil. The man who owned the country, Sheikh Rashid bin Saeed Al Maktoum, knew the oil wasn't limitless. He decided to try to create something that would last after the sands ran dry. So he, and later his sons, poured their wealth into creating a center for high-dollar tourism and finance. Their idea was, if you build it, preferably with lots of chrome and marble and tax incentives and underpaid foreign workers, the rest of the world will come.

I've got no idea if it will last, but right now it's Disneyland for billionaires. The country's economy stalled badly during the global financial crash, but now it's humming along again as if the meltdown never happened. Everything is larger than life, all beginning with the words "the biggest," "the best," or "the most expensive." There's an underwater hotel out in the Persian Gulf, right next to the custom-built islands. The airport just passed Heathrow as the busiest on the planet. They're putting up five hundred new skyscrapers to keep pace with the demand for office space, and construction just started on an entire indoor city, complete with replica versions of New York, London, and Paris. The conference where Preston is speaking will take place in the Burj Khalifa, the tallest skyscraper on earth. Even the police drive Ferraris and Bentleys.

And even though Dubai sits at the edge of four or five different war zones, violent crime is almost unheard of, at least in public. Islamic jihad checks its suicide vests at the border. The current ruler of Dubai, Mohammed bin Rashid Al Maktoum, the previous sheikh's son, goes out in public without bodyguards and drives his own Mercedes G-class everywhere.

All of which proves, once again, my golden rule: Nobody screws with serious money. Nobody wants to upset the cash flow. It's like the entire country is a VIP lounge and the bouncer at the velvet rope keeps out anything unpleasant.

There's a rumor that half the world's arms sales go through Dubai airport, but nobody would think of bringing a gun off one of those planes. That's why Olivarez wouldn't let me bring my gun with me, even though he put me in a cargo flight stuffed with illegal drugs. I'm okay with that. It means that Preston's bodyguards won't be carrying either. I'm walking onto a level playing field.

I can see why Preston thinks he's safe here.

He's wrong, but it's an easy mistake to make.

I DON'T BOTHER with customs. Instead, I find one of the travelers' lounges. The man at the door makes a face at my coveralls, but I pay the fee with the black card, which eases his mind considerably.

My changing room includes a full-size shower and bath. The coveralls go into a trash bin. I open my bag and get to work. Twenty minutes later, I emerge freshly showered and shaved, wearing an Armani suit. Then I exit the terminal into the 120-degree heat.

I spot my contact immediately. It would be hard to miss her. She's over six feet tall in her heels, with masses of blond hair. She looks even better than her picture from the website.

She goes by Katya, but that's not her name. She's a prostitute.

Dubai is Islamic, but unlike, say, Saudi Arabia, it's not medieval. There are thousands of unattached men here, from the foreign workers actually building all the new construction to the first-class passengers and tourists looking for temporary companionship. Most of them are willing to pay, and the authorities are willing to look the other way on all manner of sins—including the kind that Olivarez is importing. That means in the tourist and expat zones, anything goes.

Within reason, of course. I suspect not even Allah would help you if you tried to form a labor union or started bad-mouthing the sheikh. Report a rape to the police and you could be the one who ends up in jail, or, at best, on the next plane back home. And failure to pay your debts can still get you thrown in prison here. Again, it's all about keeping the money flowing, and anyone who might disrupt that is ejected from the country so fast they leave vapor trails.

That's why I'm keeping as low a profile as possible. I know that Preston will have people looking for me. I might have crippled his operations in the States, but I'm sure he still has all kinds of clever programs watching for my name or picture on a passport or a hotel registry.

So I figured out a way to sidestep the whole process. I went on the Net, Googled "Dubai escorts," and found someone willing to offer me a full package—tour guide, girlfriend, transportation, and, included in her fee, her apartment near the Burj Khalifa.

Katya is one of a small army of professionals—mostly Russian—who live in Dubai and service the high-end clients. She linked to a page full of reviews that described her as professional, reliable, and discreet. Among many other, more colorful terms.

I tell myself I'm not interested in her other talents as long as she provides cover and a place to stay. Then she greets me like a boyfriend gone for too long, with both arms wrapped around me and a long, lingering kiss.

There's disapproval from some of the men and women nearby, envy from others.

Screw them. I'm a rich foreigner, and this is how I blend in.

I let her guide me to her car. We have trouble finding it at first. Only in Dubai would a Mercedes SLK be as generic as a Toyota Corolla. Katya presses the button on her keys until one of the cars finally beeps and flashes its lights. I throw my bag in the trunk, and we blast off for a week of impossibly expensive decadence.

I'm only partially faking it when I grin like an idiot.

We get to Katya's apartment, and she handles the exchange of cash like everything else: professionally and elegantly. The envelope I hand her disappears in an instant.

That's the only moment I get any anxiety from her. She had to clear her schedule for a week to accommodate me, and there's always a chance that a john will try to rip her off, or worse. She has been lucky so far—she's twenty-three—and she's smart. But lurking in her mind, always, are the possibilities of what could happen to her, what she has seen happen to other women in her line of work. Her smile never wavers, but her mind turns hard as stone. It's impressive. I've had people shoot at me, cut me, and try to beat me to death, but I don't think I'll ever be able to imagine what it takes to be a woman forced to trust a man.

Once that's over, however, she's back on familiar ground. She shows me around the apartment—beautiful, tasteful, and impersonal, as devoid of any real identifying touches as a catalog photo. It pops into my head that she doesn't actually live here. This is just for work, and she splits the rent with another couple of escorts. Her real life is safely contained in a much smaller place a little farther from the tourist zone.

There's a computer, with high-speed Net access. Katya takes my bag and offers to unpack once she sees me zero in on the machine.

I sit down before the screen and go to the conference's official site. The main page comes up: FUTURETECH DUBAI—THE SILICON DESERT.

Someone in the sheikh's brain trust, or the sheikh himself, must have decided that Dubai needed its own version of Silicon Valley, and this is their attempt to jump-start a digital economy. Aside from the speeches, Preston and the other up-and-coming CEOs will judge entries from hopeful start-ups. If they give their approval, it could mean millions of dollars in venture funding.

According to the schedule, Preston is supposed to give his big talk on Wednesday, two days from now. He's staying at the Burj Al Arab, away from the conference. But he'll have to make a few appearances in public, for photo ops. I can't imagine the conference would let him get away with ordering room service and watching pay-per-view.

I need to get over to the Burj and do recon. But first I need sleep. Jet lag has landed on me like a sack of dry cement.

Katya is rubbing my shoulders. I must be tired. I didn't even hear her, let alone sense her thoughts. She's had a lot of practice at being unobtrusive, fading into her surroundings until she's ready to be noticed. It's a survival skill.

"So what brings you to the conference?" she asks.

"You don't really want to know."

She laughs. "You're right."

She really doesn't. It's almost refreshing, after all the fear and anxiety, after all the caring and concern. I don't use those emotions much, and now they feel like atrophied muscles, sore from a sad, middle-aged return to the gym.

"I should sleep," I tell her. I turn off the computer. She keeps kneading my back, then her lips are at my ear.

"You're not just paying for the room, you know," she says. She doesn't care about me. I know it for a fact. This is her job. Her calm, professional indifference is like standing in front of an open refrigerator on a hot summer day.

I can't help but think of Kelsey, who's still in a hospital bed right now.

It doesn't stop me.

CAMOUFLAGE.

After sixteen hours of sleep—with some exercise in between—I'm ready to hit the conference. Which means looking the part.

I unroll a pair of jeans and a T-shirt from my bag. They're brand-new, but the kind of expensive that looks cheap from a distance. Frayed and faded. Wearing them, I'm indistinguishable from every other brogrammer here for his shot at greatness.

Katya's seated at the breakfast nook in a robe, drinking a cup of black coffee so slowly that it seems she's absorbing it by osmosis. She flares her nostrils in an elegant display of distaste when she sees me.

"I'm trying to fit in," I say.

"You succeed," she says, and shifts her attention away. I think I've disappointed her.

I leave the condo and catch a ride to the conference in a hired car. In this part of the city, it looks like the future showed up a century too soon. Everything shines like polished chrome. Even the cement looks vacuumed. There's not a single person walking—just a steady stream of gleaming cars moving in clockwork precision.

When I get out of the car, the death-ray heat of the sun is cut by a strong wind. This is not a good sign. There was a warning earlier in the conference weather report about a shamal—a sandstorm with winds as high as fifty miles per hour.

I remember a shamal from Iraq. Air traffic was completely shut down. Being outside was like walking into a sandblaster. All you could do was sit tight and let it blow over. When it was gone, you discovered sand in crevices you didn't know you had.

But the relentlessly optimistic conference website assured me the winds will probably blow right past the tip of Dubai, out into the Gulf, so no one will be inconvenienced by a high-speed sandstorm.

I don't have any of the proper badges or cards to get me into Future-Tech Dubai. Fortunately, the Burj Khalifa is also a tourist attraction—tallest building in the world, remember—and my prepaid ticket to the observation deck gets me past the red-scarfed security guards. Once I'm inside, it's fairly easy to wander away from the tour group and join a group of tech nerds clustered together. The elevator takes me a half mile into the sky, and the doors open into the conference center.

This is where the illusion of the future breaks down. Despite the water of the Persian Gulf visible through the windows, this could be an insurance convention in Reno. The space is filled with row after row of stalls, fronted by booth babes—models for hire wearing company logos on tight T-shirts. They draw in the men wearing dishdasha. Then the nerds get up from behind the tables and do their best to convince the Arabs that Bazoomercom or TwitWit will completely revolutionize cloud-based social-media integration. Or something.

Ordinarily, I'd find clients in a place like this. Dollar signs are dancing in the eyes of everyone here, and anyone willing to drop a few million on a tech start-up is usually my target demographic.

Instead, I blend into the background again. No one sees me. One guy walks into me and bounces off. He looks a little confused and annoyed, as if he tripped over a power cord. But he never says a word, just keeps going, with barely a pause.

I cruise the exhibition hall for almost an hour before a buzz of excitement rises. I feel the shift in the mood as everyone turns and looks at a group that's just arrived at the main entrance.

<judges> <look sharp> <judges are here> <who's that?> <Preston> <OmniVore> <guess they couldn't get Zuckerberg> <doesn't look that smart to me>

I head over to see for myself.

Preston and the other judges are at the center of a cluster of people. They cruise down the aisles, checking out the competitors. This isn't the actual judging; according to the schedule, that's not until tomorrow. I have no doubt this is a mandatory public appearance, a requirement made by the conference organizers for the judges to go out and see the sights.

The other judges at least pretend to enjoy it. Preston can't even manage that.

He's forgotten to bring one of his novelty toys with him, so there are no fart noises or funny catchphrases. He has aged half a decade since I last saw him. His face is tight with stress, and his grin looks like a dentist's experimental treatment gone wrong. His clothes look slept in, and his hair doesn't have the usual application of product. He flinches if someone comes in too close for a selfie or a handshake.

More important, he's got three bodyguards with him.

This is considered tacky, if not actually rude. As I said, Dubai is supposed to be completely safe.

But Preston is scared. I made sure of that. He's not going anywhere without protection.

The judges trail an entourage of reporters and cameramen and fans with phones held up high. I slip in and follow them all the way down to the lobby.

. . . .

A QUICK SHUTTLE-BUS ride and then we're all herded inside the Mall of the Emirates, the largest mall in the Middle East. We're here for a photo op. The sponsors and organizers want the world to know that Dubai is the Next Big Thing in the tech world, and they're going to get photographic proof. Specifically, they're going to get shots of Preston and his fellow billionaires acting cool.

So they take the whole entourage to Ski Dubai. It's the perfect symbol of what unlimited money can do: an indoor ski hill in the middle of the desert. Manufactured snow covers a giant ramp in a room the size of three football fields. A small chair lift takes skiers and boarders to the top of the room, where they have their choice of five runs. There's even a penguin habitat and a sledding hill for the kids.

Outside, workers regularly collapse from heatstroke as they struggle to complete the latest new building in triple-degree heat. Inside, a kid in a snowsuit and mittens just ran past me with an idiot grin and pure joy radiating from his mind. It's obscene and a miracle at the same time.

And in the middle of all this impossibility, Preston is finally starting to enjoy himself. He's a pretty good boarder, at least in his own mind, and this fits his self-image. He's still young enough to be extreme. He's looking forward to showing off in front of the other rich guys.

The entourage is kept outside, on the other side of big glass windows that contain a view of the entire slope.

I walk inside with Preston, the judges, his bodyguards, and their escorts. Again, nobody really sees me. Their eyes skate over me in the crowd. It takes work to stay this hard in the background, and I'm starting to feel the strain.

Still, nobody notices when I take a suit from the rack, pick up a snowboard, and get on the ski lift with the others.

Preston goes down, bodyguard on each side, about three people ahead of me. It's not a long slope—even with Dubai money, you can do only so much—so I've got to be quick if I want a chance at him. Fortunately, he's hotdogging, pulling tricks, half-assed jumps, cutting wide swaths back and forth across the powdered ice.

Two of the bodyguards are on skis, and they grimace as they keep up, looking like impatient parents chasing a rebellious tween.

I push ahead in line, and by stepping out of the scenery, I give up my invisibility. I hear it several times—*<hey, who's that?>* *<dude, uncool>* *<who's that guy?>*—before someone finally says it out loud: "Hey, who the hell is that?"

By then, I'm cutting a straight line toward Preston. His bodyguard at the top of the run shouts something. It's hard to hear over the blast-force air-conditioning.

The other bodyguards see me headed for Preston. He's too far away from them.

I slice straight through the snow toward him. I'm not a great boarder, but this is a bunny slope, and all I have to do is pick up speed.

"Preston!" one of the guards finally screams. "Look out!"

Preston turns, sees me barreling toward him, and just manages to skid to a halt.

I hit him as I race past, knocking him flat on his ass.

It only hurts a little. But it's incredibly humiliating. Everyone starts laughing.

Everyone except Preston and his guards. Preston recognizes me. He thinks he just dodged an assassination attempt.

"Get that son of a bitch!" he screams.

And here they come.

I'm already at the bottom of the hill, kicking off the board and the boots, pulling off the ski suit, and running as fast as I can.

I burst through the doors and into the mall. I get a few strange looks, but no one stops me or says anything.

Preston's bodyguards come out of Ski Dubai, two of them still in their stifling ski outfits.

I stay where they can see me for just long enough, then I turn into a service corridor, and effectively vanish.

I paint myself right out of their perceptions, covering their minds' images of me with scenes from the background again.

Several times, they scan right over me, then continue searching, getting more and more agitated. Their faces are locked into the usual action-hero expression of grim certainty, but I sense their panic and confusion. They've lost me. They're nervous. They've talked about me. They know the rumors. They've got to split up, and for a long moment, they're afraid.

I can't help grinning. That little jolt of fear is better than cocaine.

But they're soldiers, so they get over it. I can feel the adrenaline surge. It tastes like metal at the back of their throats. I get a glimpse of the reward that Preston is offering to whoever brings in my scalp: <*ten million*>. They repeat it to themselves, like a chant, like a prayer, over and over: <*ten million, ten million, ten million*>. <*Ten million dollars!*> Images flit around their heads of fast cars, new houses, nearly naked women on pristine white beaches.

That's when they find the nerve. They each take a different direction, and each one is determined to kill me, whatever it takes.

I don't care about the other two in their snow gear. Sure, they're far more dangerous than they appear right now, clomping around in their ski boots. But they've never gotten close enough to me to do any damage. I don't owe them anything.

I let them stomp away.

Then I follow the other guy.

He jogs forward, looking for me.

<*Right behind you, genius*> I send, like flinging a dart at the back of his head.

He turns around.

I would know him by his stance, by the unique tang of his thoughts and the echo of his feelings. I'd recognize him anywhere, even if I couldn't see the edge of the tattoo.

Snake Eater. The man who shot Kelsey.

I sprint for the doors of the shopping center. He follows.

I've gone from 105 degrees to climate-controlled 68 to below zero in the ski hill, all in less than an hour. So for a moment, when I hit the open air, I wonder if my sense of temperature has been completely screwed.

Then I look up, and I realize what's happened.

Snake Eater exits the mall a few steps behind me, and he stops dead as well. For a moment, we both look at the sky.

A great gray wall appears, blotting out the sun, dwarfing even the sky-high tower of the Burj.

It looks like a biblical plague. It's impossible not to feel a little awe.

The shamal will not miss us. It hits the center of Dubai, and it hits hard.

There's rain at first, fat drops that evaporate as soon as they hit the parched cement.

Then the wind comes tearing down the concrete and glass canyons, howling like a motherless child.

Those people still dumb or unlucky enough to be outside rush for the nearest shelter. Their movement breaks me out of my daze, and I begin sprinting away again.

Snake Eater races after me.

I run around the corner and find a construction scaffolding that leads to the roof, temporarily abandoned by its crew in the storm.

Then I make what looks like a rookie mistake. I go up the ladder.

Snake Eater follows me. He's thinking <*dumb fuck*> because he knows there's no escape up there. He's already spending that $10 million.

I reach the top of the scaffolding, then pull myself onto the roof and wait. This section overlooks the plaza below, but I can't see any of it from where I stand. The shamal is growing worse. It carries whole sand dunes from the desert and all the dust from Dubai's never-ending construction along with it. Visibility is maybe a dozen yards at best. The rest of Dubai is huddled inside their homes and offices, waiting for the storm to pass. It's possible to feel like the last man on earth up here.

But I don't have to wait long.

Snake Eater lifts his head over the edge of the roof in achingly slow increments, waiting for an ambush or even a bullet.

But I let him make the climb. He gets on the roof safely. I let him stand up and get his balance.

He waits for a moment, alert, on guard, and then he sees me.

I want him to see this coming. I want him to know.

I knew Preston would bring Snake Eater with him. It's not easy finding employees who are both willing to kill and halfway competent at the job. I don't know if that's a good sign or a bad one for the future of the human race. But when you find a guy who's proven he can blow up three men and put a bullet into an unarmed woman, no questions asked, you tend to keep that guy around.

Especially if you think you've got a pissed-off black-ops veteran coming after you. You want some reliable backup, preferably someone who's already got blood on his hands.

Preston thought he was my target. He was wrong.

Oh, I intend to get around to him. Eventually. But this is the main event.

Even in the sand and grit, I see Snake Eater smile. He's actually stupid enough to be happy to find me. He thinks this is going to end well for him.

I'm going to enjoy proving him wrong.

THE WIND KICKS up again. The shamal fills the air with more sand and dust. It's like walking into a fog made of ground glass. Snake Eater stands less than a dozen feet away from me, but he's a just blurry outline now.

That works for me. I can use my talent like radar, zeroing in on his thoughts. He'll stumble around with grit in his eyes, the wind howling in his ears, deaf and blind, while I cut him to pieces with elegant kicks and punches, then dance away before he can touch me. I'm not sure if I'll beat him to death or only cripple him. I should win without raising too much of a sweat.

I've already got a little mind game planned for him—quadriplegic paralysis. I'm going to convince his brain that his body has lost its ability to move below the neck. He should be helpless. It means my own legs and arms will go numb for a while, but I figure it will be worth the cost.

At least, that's the plan.

But just before the shamal kicks into high gear—just before the entire rooftop goes dark as the dust blots out all but the most feeble sunlight—Snake Eater stops thinking like a conscious human being and turns into a creature of pure rage.

He remembers being shot back in Pennsylvania, and remembers

seeing me behind the gun. He remembers, with humiliation, how I froze him in a nightmare in the hotel lobby. And he remembers how I simply walked away from him both times, as if he was nothing, no threat at all.

He has not felt that helpless since he was a child, and every time he remembers it, his shame has only grown, until he has created a tank of pure hatred for me, down deep in the center of himself. It's why he volunteered when Preston asked for someone willing to go after me. It's why he had no hesitation about shooting Kelsey or triggering the explosion he thought would kill me.

I scared him. I stole the only thing he's ever been able to rely on—himself—and he hates me for it.

It takes him only a split second to tap into that fuel. He's operating on instinct, so I don't get an inkling of his plan before it happens.

He leaps forward and tackles me. I try to twist out of his path, but he still gets an arm around me. He takes me down on the roof. Before I can use my talent, he shifts position, punching me in the face with one fist while simultaneously pressing down on my throat with his forearm.

That's when I realize: Snake Eater is a grappler.

I hate grapplers.

My talent is close to useless once they get a grip on me. They use Brazilian jujitsu and judo holds, and keep everything right in their hands, so I can't fool their eyes. They've got lots of experience at handling pain, so I can light up their brains with all kinds of terrible memories and they just take it. I can see what they've got planned, but slipping out of a choke hold is a lot tougher than dodging a punch.

All of my advantages just vanished. It's hard to focus and cast my thoughts when someone is pummeling my face over and over. At least I won't have any trouble finding him. He's right at the other end of the arm that he's using to crush my windpipe.

I try to flip him off me, but he rolls with it and comes up on top. So I do it again. We end up tumbling along the roof, neither of us willing to slow down or give up an advantage.

Suddenly the roof ends. I open my eyes and get a good look down into the swirling wind and sand. I twist with everything I have, feel something pop in my back, and nearly shrug Snake Eater right over my head and over the edge.

But he doesn't go. He must have figured out where I was headed when I slammed on the brakes, so he suddenly shifts his weight and hauls back. His grip loosens on my neck enough for me to break his hold and scramble sideways, palms shredding on the gravel. I choke on the dirt as it clots inside my nose and mouth. He's slapping at me, trying to find a handhold, to keep me close.

I'm almost free, halfway to my feet, when one of his hands clamps on my ankle like a vise. I spin and kick, but he dodges it. Then he yanks my leg out from under me, and I hit the roof on my back.

He leaps into the air, ready to come down on me with his full weight.

But this time, some dimly remembered move comes back to me from my training, and I get my feet up to block him. He grunts, and I know I've just kicked him hard in the solar plexus.

It doesn't slow him down much. He drives downward, hands still scrabbling for a grip. Then he finds one—around my throat.

He starts choking me, going for the kill.

I punch him twice in the head. It's like hitting a cast-iron skillet. I try to fill his brain with spiders, but he shakes it off. He knows it's not real. I feel the glow of triumph start to build from him. He figures he can take whatever I dish out until he crushes my throat.

So I decide, finally, to fight him on his own terms.

I slide my right hand between his arms and find the edge of his collar. I get the left in there as well, and I cross my arms and start pulling.

I've just turned the collar of his jacket into a noose.

We are no more than arm's length from each other, the shamal blasting us both. He's got gravity on his side, pressing me down, but I've got the better grip. He's choking the life out of me at the same time as I'm strangling him. Now it just comes down to who can last. Who can live.

While we're waiting to find out, his mind and memories open and spill into mine.

Snake Eater's real name is Eric Schaffer. He's thirty-two. He grew up in a small house in Kansas City. <*Not that one. The one that's actually in Kansas.*> He joined Special Forces like his uncle Ken, his dad's older brother, who came back home from Vietnam and showed him the cool tattoo under his sleeve. When he got out of the army, he got the same one done on his neck. It took a long time to find a guy who could do it just right, who knew the history.

He increases the pressure. I do the same. I can hear him grunt, feel the collar cut into the skin of his neck. His thumbs slide around, trying for my carotid.

The ceiling of his bedroom was painted blue. He had a dog named Barkley. Some kind of Lab mix. One day the dog ran off and never came back. He cried so hard he thought something would break.

I jerk my head back, keep him from getting his thumbs in. Jam my elbow into his, trying to break his grip. Twist the collar harder. His face is going deep red now.

He took a girl named Christy to prom and had sex for the very first time in a hotel room he and his friends rented together.

I keep applying pressure, pulling as hard as I can with both hands. His hands are greasy with sweat. They slip. I get a little slack and I make the most of it, ratchet my noose even tighter.

He spent the morning after his thirtieth birthday hungover, looking at the number for his parents on his phone, wondering if he should call them back.

He's fading out, but his grip is still tight. He won't let go.

He spent the night of his thirtieth birthday in a bar where he beat a guy half to death over an insult he can't remember now. He never called his parents back.

His throat is burning red and spots are dancing in front of his eyes now.

<God damn, there was this one song, what was it?> He can't remember. *<Christy really liked it. She had it on repeat on the CD player the whole time.>*

His face is purple and blue.

It occurs to him that he's really thirsty. He'd really like a cold drink of water right now.

I see a blood vessel burst in his eye. I pull harder.

<Man, that water sure would taste good.>

It's the last thing he wants.

His hands only unclench a second after he dies.

It takes me a long moment to disentangle myself from him. Mentally and physically.

I shove his body aside and spend a few minutes panting for air. It feels like sucking down hot mud. None of my limbs are working right.

But it's worse inside my skull. His whole life is right there. Right next to the knowledge that I ended it. When I'm that close to someone at the end, it all gets badly mixed together. He still sent his mom flowers on Mother's Day and once dragged a friend from a flaming Humvee in Iraq.

And here comes his death. That all-too-familiar black hole filling my head with darkness thicker than quicksand, threatening to drag me down with him.

Nobody's ever the villain in his own story. Aside from trying to kill me for money, Schaffer wasn't such a bad guy. And at these moments, it becomes incredibly hard for me to justify why I'm the one still breathing and the other guy's a corpse.

All he did was take a job. Not so different from me. Up close and personal, there is no way to lie about it, especially to myself.

I am almost ready to let the blackness suck me down. To give up, and give in, and stop breathing. It seems so easy.

But as always, I find a straw to grasp.

There's the knowledge, tucked in the middle of all of Schaffer's memories, of Kelsey, and how he was ready to kill her. How he put the crosshairs of a target on her and pulled the trigger.

In his memory, there is a tiny sliver of disappointment at how she turned at the last moment so he could not see her face. He really wanted to see her face.

There's the difference, slim as it seems, but it's enough. I never would have done that. I have done shameful things and hurt people, but I never would have done that. Sloan and Cantrell may not be right about me. I might not have a conscience. But I have limits.

Schaffer didn't. That's enough for me to drag myself back from the abyss where I sent him.

A moment later, when I can feel my arms and legs again, I get up. I tear Schaffer's suit off his corpse and dress in it. I dig through his pockets and find what I need. The storm has passed, and I know where I'm going.

Along with his memories, his clothing, and his keys, I stole one other thing from the last few moments of Eric Schaffer's life.

I know where to find Eli Preston now.

. . . .

Ordinarily, the staff at the Burj Al Arab would never allow someone looking like me into the lobby. It's supposed to be the only seven-star resort in the world. It sits on its own man-made island, connected to the city by a private causeway. It's the only hotel in Dubai with a reputation for serious security, which is why Preston chose it.

I'm wearing a suit, but I'm literally trailing grit and dirt. The horrified concierge snaps his fingers, and a young woman rushes out with a broom and dustpan. She follows along behind me, sweeping up the sand, right at my heels with every step.

It should take all my Jedi mind tricks to get to the elevators looking like this, and unfortunately, I am exhausted. But everyone knows about the shamal. And I have a room card.

This makes me an honored guest. As soon as I bring out the hotel key, the concierge is all grace and solicitude, asking if I'm all right, expressing sorrow at my misfortune at being caught outside. He emphasizes that a storm like that is very rare.

I thank him for his concern and walk past security to the elevators.

I swipe Schaffer's card, and I'm on my way to Preston's suite.

One of the remaining bodyguards is at the door. I don't really remember which one. Or care. I am utterly out of patience.

He sees me coming, wearing the dead man's suit, and for a second, he sees Schaffer. Then his brain catches up, and he opens his mouth to shout something.

I don't let him. I send a mind strike right to the Broca's area of his brain. Instead of what he meant to say, he blurts, "Flanges! Turnips and antifreeze!"

He's so shocked at what comes out of his own mouth he drops his guard completely. While he struggles to figure out if he's having a stroke, I hit him hard enough to bounce his skull off the frame of the door. His eyes roll up into his head, and he sags to the floor.

I pause at the door and scan the room, stretching my talent, listening for stray thoughts.

I sense two people inside.

One man is off in a side room, his brain deep in the regular delta-wave rhythms of sleep. That's got to be the bodyguard. Makes sense. Three men to cover a single person, twenty-four-hour day, eight-hour shifts. One of them has to sleep sometime.

There's nothing there for me to read. He's completely unconscious. Nothing short of a gunshot is going to get him up now.

Then there's the other mind in the suite, very much awake, scurrying like a rat in a maze, running down possibilities, discarding what doesn't work, streams and streams of data flowing all around it.

Preston.

Schaffer's key card opens the door. I walk into the main room.

The suite is half the size of a football field. There are floor-to-ceiling windows framing the sky and the Gulf, and the moon. The view is utterly magnificent.

Preston has his back to it, his entire focus riveted on the screen of the laptop on his desk. There are pill bottles and empty cans and coffee cups. He is typing furiously. I can see him racking his brain, trying to dredge up memories of code he wrote two years ago.

It's not going well.

He barely glances at me. Like the guard at the door, he's fooled by the suit. He puts a can of Rockstar to his lips, finds it empty, and flings it across the room. It bounces off the wood paneling.

"Get me another one of those," he snaps. "Is it done? Did you get him?"

"No, Preston," I say. "He didn't."

It takes him a moment to disengage from the virtual world and come back to this one. He looks up, and his eyes shift their focus from the screen. Then he sees me standing there.

"Holy shit," he says. Not exactly eloquent, but a pretty accurate read on the situation.

He leaps up, knocking over his chair, and fills his lungs to scream for help.

With resources I didn't know I still had, I cross the room at a fast run and put my fist in his stomach.

He folds in half, unable to breathe. I grab his right hand, twist it back in a two-finger grip, and put him in an armlock. He drops to his knees and I pull his arm above his head. He's not going anywhere.

"Please," he gasps. "I'll pay whatever you want."

"I told you already," I remind him. "Negotiations are over."

"Wait, wait, wait," he demands. Even cornered, even trapped, he wants to deal. "Looking into your past. I found something. Something I can give you. All you have to do is let me go. Just let me go, and I'll tell you."

I'm mildly curious now. "Tell me what?"

"I know the names of your real parents."

He says it with a little smile of triumph. If I weren't so sick of him, I'd want to laugh. He thinks he's dug up a secret that I have to know. It's what he does, after all. But I made my peace with this issue years ago. There were times, I admit, when I went to bed wondering who they were, and I might have even fallen asleep with tears and snot on my face from crying about how they didn't love me. But that was a long time ago. I left that baggage in junior high. I've had far worse traumas than my mommy and daddy issues to keep me busy since then.

"Eli," I say. "What makes you think I could possibly give a damn?"

He's speechless for a moment. He thought he had a way out. When I shut it down without discussion, his mind ignites with desperation.

"Money. Stock options. You could be a millionaire—no, a billionaire," he says. "You know how much I'm going to be worth. All you have to do is let it happen. You could own a piece of the future."

I hesitate. Because I'm not an idiot. Sloan's offering an island. A billion dollars would buy a whole chain of islands. Or maybe even a small country.

But Preston cannot ever quit while he's ahead. Even if he could shut his mouth, he can't keep his brain quiet.

"And I swear, nothing will ever happen to Kelsey in the future. I promise."

I see it then, in his mind. He's got the location of the private clinic where Sloan has moved Kelsey from the hospital. He has performed some of his usual hacker bullshit to find her, and he's got people he can call who could be there before morning. He hasn't carried out any of these plans yet—he's been too busy trying to save his own ass—but he's got them ready. Just in case.

"You promise?" I ask.

He nods so hard I think his head will shake off. "She'll be safe. I swear. She'll never have to worry about me."

He says it in the same tone a magician would say "abracadabra" and reveal the girl whole and unharmed despite all the swords he has rammed through the box.

But as I keep saying, this is not a Vegas act. This is real.

And he will never put her in danger again.

I tighten my grip.

"You're right," I tell him. "She won't."

He sees the look on my face and closes his eyes. He's braced for a bullet to the brain, or worse. But he still finds the air to beg. "Please don't kill me."

"I'm not here to kill you, Preston," I say.

He opens one eye again. For a moment, hope sparks inside him.

"I'm here to take everything from you," I say. Then I concentrate. I don't really remember how I wiped out my drill sergeant's mind. But I've figured out a way so it doesn't matter. Just like the computer virus I planted in OmniVore's servers, deleting memory by overwriting it, I'm going to give Preston a few new things to think about.

"What's the name of your company?"

"What?" He's baffled. He knows I know the name. But I don't want the answer. I want him to *think* of the answer.

There it is, lighting up that corner of his mind. The part that thinks about OmniVore, and all his cool little apps and his software.

As soon as I see it, I send him an explicit memory from a soldier in Iraq who saw his right leg go flying off into the distance, along with the shrapnel from an IED.

Preston screams in shock and horror. He clutches his own leg, as if he can't believe that it's still there.

"OmniVore," I say. "It eats everything. You thought that was clever."

"What?" he says again. But his pride is wired deeper than that. He goes right back to those memories. Adapting the algorithm. Watching it peel apart data, finding the hidden secrets, the stuff people didn't even know they were revealing. I see strings of code in his mind, lined up in neat and orderly rows.

I send him another memory. This is what it feels like when your foster father stops using the belt and starts hitting you with a bottle.

He ducks like he's feeling the blows himself, curling inward from both the betrayal and the hurt.

"OmniVore," I say again.

He thinks of his company, his computers, his programs.

This is what it feels like when a four-inch piece of jagged metal from a mortar blast buries itself in your abdomen.

He hisses in pain and wets his pants.

"OmniVore."

This is what it feels like when someone holds your head down in four inches of water and your lungs fill and you pray to God he'll let go, but he doesn't let go.

Preston's eyes go wide and he goes deathly pale and he gasps for breath.

"OmniVore."

This is what it feels like to have someone choke you to death with the lapels of your own jacket.

He begins crying.

I release him and he collapses onto the deep-pile carpet. He's got no fight left in him.

I decide to test my work.

"OmniVore," I say.

Preston's mind explodes with pain. He yells out, and he shakes like he's in the grip of an epileptic seizure.

It won't last forever. But he's going to have a hell of a time ever touching a computer again without PTSD.

Then, just out of curiosity, I probe around, looking for the answer to the one question that's still nagging me. It's not in his memories of Sloan, which is why I had such a hard time finding it before.

And there it is. It seems so obvious in hindsight. Once I dig it out, everything else falls into place.

Now I know what started this whole mess.

I'm almost finished here. But I've got one last thing to tell him before I go.

I kneel down next to him and say a single word, loud enough to be heard over his crying:

"Kelsey."

And at the same time, I let him know what it feels like to have a 9mm slug of copper-jacketed lead tear through your chest, your lung, and your shoulder.

Just like she felt.

He begins screaming, and he doesn't stop. I'm glad the walls are thick.

"Don't even think about her. Ever again," I tell him.

That's where I leave him.

[25]

We are back where we started, in the office in Sioux Falls. Sloan sits behind the desk this time. I'm in the chair facing him.

I flew out of Dubai on Schaffer's passport. Nobody looked at it too closely, and I dumped it in a trash can at LAX as soon as I got back. His memories were harder to lose. I spent the past week in a cabin at Big Sur, letting my body heal and sweating out a dead man's nightmares. Now my bruises have almost faded, even if my tie still irritates the places on my neck where he left handprints.

It's just me and Sloan in the room. His bodyguards are nowhere I can sense them. Gaines picked me up at the airport himself, and he's waiting on the other side of the door.

Sloan has the good sense to look embarrassed, even if he's not particularly feeling it.

"I wanted to tell you, in person, that I had no idea any of this would happen," he says.

"Do you think we'd be having this conversation if I didn't already know that?"

I can't keep the scorn out of my voice. He might be the world's smartest man, for all I know. But he can't read minds.

He looks down at the desk, upset at being scolded. Here's how I know he's scared: he's practically transparent, compared to our first meeting. There's no ice wall, no high barrier of equations and lofty thoughts. He's focused on me. And what I might do.

"I just want you to know I am sorry," he said. *<not my fault not going to grovel for this person> <does he have his gun? is he armed?> <still unfortunate doesn't hurt anything to admit that> <pacify him> <he won't shoot me> <will he?>*

"I know," I tell him. I open the bag by my feet and take out Preston's hard drive, then place it on the desk. This is more ceremonial than anything else. OmniVore is already going down in flames. There's only been a short press release, saying the company's IPO has been postponed indefinitely. Preston hasn't been seen in public since last week in Dubai. Bloomberg News ran a piece saying he's in a high-dollar psychiatric care center, where the doctors have him on a steady diet of tranquilizers. Top talent is already running for the exits. Within three months—six at the most—OmniVore will be a memory.

"There's just the matter of my bill," I tell Sloan. This is why I'm here.

He nods, and I feel the relief like a cool breeze. *<pay him off>* "Of course," he says out loud. "I will honor our agreement." *<a mercenary in the end> <just like everyone else> <just business>*

"I know you will," I say. "I expect the contract for Ward Island and the residence to be signed and delivered to my attorney before end of business today. But I've added something to my fee. For the inconvenience."

<fucking grifter> The thought escapes him before he can lock it down. "I'm sure we can come to an arrangement. I know this job took some turns neither of us expected, and we can compensate you for that."

I have to marvel at his cool. It's like he's reading from a script a lawyer prepared for him. "I'm glad to hear that," I say. "Would you call Mr. Gaines in here, please?"

Sloan's a little surprised by that, but he does it anyway. Gaines has been eavesdropping the entire time. I can sense the anxiety coming off his thoughts like sweat. He enters immediately when Sloan says his name.

"Mr. Smith," he says, not waiting for anything. "I want you to know how deeply sorry we all are—how sorry I am—that things got so, well, fucked up, pardon my French. Obviously, I didn't know or understand the depth of the issues here—"

"No," I cut him off. "You didn't."

"I want you to know that we've had Kelsey moved to a top-flight facility. And of course we're taking care of all her bills. She'll receive only the best of care."

"I didn't ask." That sits there for a long moment.

I focus on Gaines. "How much are you worth?

That catches him off guard, and I get a nice shot of his financial status. A guy like this, his portfolio is never far from his thoughts anyway. Assets versus liabilities all tallied up in big black letters; the total at the bottom when he adds up all his bank accounts and stock holdings and even the cash in his wallet.

Plus one more big debt, as of right now.

"About three-point-two million," I say. "That's fine. We'll round it off."

He's baffled.

I turn to Sloan again. "Here's my last condition. Three-point-two million."

<*oh hell no*> "Now just a moment. There was some unpleasantness, yes, but you're paid to assume certain risks—"

"I'm not finished." I point at Gaines. "I want *his* three-point-two million. Everything he has. All of it. He writes you a check, you write me a check."

The blood drains out of Gaines's face. "What?"

"What?" Sloan echoes.

"Your employee's incompetence nearly cost me my life. Several times. All of this could have been avoided if he had fulfilled your obligations to me. Or even made a simple phone call to you."

<*Not my fault not my fault not my fault*> Gaines is squealing inside.

"Yes, it is, Lawrence," I say. "You think I really believed that there was no way to get hold of Sloan? There's always a phone number. Kelsey didn't know it. You did. But you got scared. You thought it would be better to cut us off."

<*the government*> <*they told me*> <*had to protect Mr. Sloan*>

"I don't care," I say. "You had an obligation. You failed. This is how you pay for it."

Sloan snaps his fingers so I look at him. He's able to hear only one part of this exchange, and he hates being out of the loop.

"What makes you think I'll bankrupt one of my most loyal employees for you? You're asking too much."

"I don't particularly care if you keep employing him. I'm not asking you to fire him. I simply want everything he's got. Because he cost me everything I have. Or do I have to remind you that everything I owned is now the property of OmniVore? We both know that I'm not going to be on the list of creditors when they go into bankruptcy."

"That is unfortunate, but there are other ways to make you whole," Sloan says. "We can reimburse you."

"No," and I let him know with a sharp prod that I am not budging on this. I point at Gaines again. "He pays."

Gaines looks to his boss. <*please*> <*you can't*> <*you won't let him*>

"No," Sloan says, shaking his head. "I will not do that. You can't bully me. I realize this must seem foreign to someone like you, Mr. Smith, but I have principles."

Cheap shot. That makes it a little easier to pull out the big gun.

"That is, of course, your choice," I say. "And, of course, I can always go back to the NSA and let them know you've been using classified software for private gain."

That hits him like a heart attack. His blood pressure jumps so fast I'm afraid I did some real damage there.

One thought echoes in the sudden stillness in his mind: *<how?>*

"Preston never stole anything from you. He was given your algorithm by the CIA. Who got it from the NSA. The ones you made it for. The ones who paid for it."

He doesn't say anything. He's waiting to see how much I know. Which is not smart, because I'm psychic, remember? I know it all.

"All those years ago, the NSA hired you to make something that could break Soviet codes. That's when you found your algorithm. Then you realized you could make more money with it in the private sector. You gave them an early version of your work; then you resigned, waited a decent interval, and began trading with it. You turned it into Spike. And your old bosses at the NSA, they never knew it was the same program. Back then, nobody understood algorithmic trading. You were so much smarter than they were. You thought they'd never catch on. And you were right. Since then, there's been so much turnover, so many changes of administration, nobody even remembers where the original software came from. Who would put code breaking and stock trading together? Only a genius like you, right?"

Sloan's face is slate gray, but he's recovering. He's glaring at me, letting me spin this out as far as I want to go while he desperately tries to come up with an answer. It's not going well.

So I keep telling the story.

"Then Preston came along. He's not as smart as you are, granted, but he's still pretty smart. Or he was, anyway. Once he saw how you'd used algorithms to find patterns, he figured out another business model. He knew he couldn't get your code, though. It was locked down too tight. And he didn't have time to build something so brilliant from scratch. That kind of research takes years. It's for the losers in academia. He wanted to get rich quick. Fortunately, he knew just where to find some really serious, brain-busting algorithms. He used to do code breaking too. It was one reason you hired him. So he went to the CIA and offered them a deal: give him some code-breaking software, and he'd turn it into a Trojan horse and smuggle it inside every big corporation in America. It was sort of brilliant, really. So the CIA gave him your original work, and he turned it into Cutter, his data-mining engine. They had no idea you'd think he stole it from you. Because they didn't know you'd stolen it from them in the first place."

Everything I'm saying is true. For Sloan, hearing it out loud is like seeing his own name on a tombstone. He's churning inside, trying to manage the sudden rush of fear. He never thought anyone would figure it out. It's been years.

Sloan musters some dignity. "I did not steal it. I created it. You can't steal your own property."

"I'm sure your attorneys will say that. Still, I don't think the government will agree. You were being paid by the feds when you wrote the original source code for Spike. I'll bet you even signed something that said anything you made was their intellectual property. They're probably going to want a cut of every dollar you've earned since then."

Sloan recovers from the shock fast. He opens his mouth to argue with me. Dozens of excuses and reasons fly through his head. But none of them masks the truth as we know it. If I take this knowledge to our perpetually cash-hungry government, Sloan is going to find himself on the receiving end of a very big bill from Uncle Sam.

He could fight it out in court, spend years and millions of dollars, and still lose. Or he could give me what I want for a fraction of the cost. Sloan's decision is easy. He really is a smart guy.

He closes his mouth. Swallows. Then he smiles at me.

"I thought you said you didn't believe in blackmail," he says.

I shrug. "I make an exception, every now and then."

Sloan uses some words in his head that he'd never say out loud, and then turns to Gaines. "Lawrence," he says. "Please leave the room. We'll work this out."

"What?" *<oh no no no no no no>*

"It's not the end of the world, Lawrence. You'll still have a job."

Gaines hears it. He just can't believe it. He thought he'd do anything for Sloan. He was willing to throw himself on his sword for his king.

He didn't realize that loyalty went only one way.

"You can't," Gaines says. "You can't make me. That's my money. I earned it. I've given you years, given your company the very best I have—"

Now Sloan has a place to focus his anger: an employee who won't do as he's told. The blast furnace opens. "I gave you that money," he shouts, voice suddenly huge, echoing off the walls. "I have all of your assets in my fund, under my control, and I can do whatever the hell I want with them. Now, if you want there to be a company for you to work for, you will listen to me and leave the goddamn room!"

Gaines trembles. He considers rebellion. He could screw this up for Sloan in a dozen ways. He could go public and fuck up Sloan's life considerably. He's got better secrets about the company than the ones I know.

But in the end, he folds. He goes out the door, his mind hollow. He'll do what he's told. He doesn't know anything else.

As he closes the door—carefully, trying very hard not to slam it—he wonders what he's going to tell his wife.

At least he doesn't have kids. I wouldn't have done this if he had.

Sloan watches him go. He turns back to me. "There," he says. "You have a deal." *<bastard>* *<white trash>* *<trailer-park piece of crap>* *<freak>* *<God damn you>* "Happy now?"

"Getting there," I tell him. I take the lease drawn up by my lawyer from my suit jacket and place it next to the hard drive. "Close of business today," I remind him.

He snorts. He's not bothering to hide his contempt or anger anymore. That's good. Starts the healing process.

I stand up. "I'll skip lunch and head straight back to the airport, if that's all right with you."

"Why did you do that?" Sloan asks when I'm at the door. The intellectual in him is already taking over, rebuilding the ice wall. He looks at what just happened like a math problem. "Why would you ruin a man like that?"

I could say something about accountability. Or Kelsey. Or the carelessness with which people like Sloan and Gaines make decisions, and the costs they never see. Instead, I opt for the truth.

"I really, really, really hate being shot at," I say.

That raises a small smile. "Be serious," he says.

"Oh, I am. But you already know the real reason. Somebody always has to pay. Always. Would you rather it was you?"

He shakes his head. "You've made an enemy out of Lawrence, you know."

"But not you."

"No," he admits. "Not me. Just business."

"Just business," I agree.

I close the door behind me.

Epilogue

The boat is late. I can see it cutting across the waters from the beach. I've been here for a bit, drinking my coffee, watching the sun burn through the morning clouds.

No Vicodin. No Oxy. Because no migraines. I don't even have any whiskey in the coffee.

The house is everything Sloan promised and more. There are moments, when I stand here on the beach and watch the waves and the sun, when I wonder if this is what it's like to be content.

I'm not an idiot, of course. I know this is not permanent. And even if I didn't, I got a call last week to remind me.

Cantrell's accent was thick. He was in a good mood. "Nice to see you can still perform when your back's against the wall, son," he said.

I didn't bother asking how he got my new number.

He wanted me to know that behind the scenes, the CIA had withdrawn its support completely from OmniVore. Government contracts were canceled, and the entire investment written off as a loss.

"So do I need to look over my shoulder?" I asked.

"I thought you never needed to look over your shoulder," he said.

"Figure of speech."

"Nah," Cantrell said. "That Preston kid is still gibbering in a rest home. He's done. No point in coming after you now. Nothing valuable left to protect."

"That's what I thought," I said. "Bureaucracies don't really hold grudges."

"Oh, but they do have long memories, John," Cantrell said. "You might want to keep that in mind. After all of this, I wonder if maybe you'd be safer back on the inside. You know. With a responsible adult looking after you."

"I'm taking a long vacation," I told him. "I've got a pretty large cushion in the bank right now. Maybe I'm even retired."

Cantrell laughed. "That's a good one, John. You always did crack me up."

Then he hung up.

Aside from that call, it's mostly been blessed silence for a month.

The one exception is when the boat comes out on Friday mornings with the groceries and the housekeepers. A nice couple. Very quiet, inside and out. I barely even have to avoid them. The wife cleans the house, the husband brings his gardening tools and keeps the forest from swallowing the place completely. Last week, we repaired the pump that feeds the sprinkler system from a century-old freshwater cistern. We hardly spoke, just handed tools back and forth and worked.

I was almost sorry to see them go.

Today, there's someone else with them when they pull up to the dock. I felt the new presence long before they got close enough to cast the line.

She hops off the boat before I finish tying it up.

Kelsey has lost some weight, and she's pale. Hospital food and a lack of sun. But very little pain. She's healing.

"How's it going, Gilligan?" she asks.

"I like to think of myself more as Robinson Crusoe."

"You don't have the beard for it. Maybe the Professor, on a good day."

My face hurts. Unfamiliar muscles moving. I'm smiling. I try to wipe it off my face.

"Sloan send you?"

He didn't, but I can at least pretend to have a conversation.

"No. I'm still on vacation. Getting used to it, actually."

"Me too."

She looks around. "Yeah. Seems like you have everything you need."

"Pretty much," I say.

An awkward pause follows. "So what are you doing here? We don't get many tourists."

<what do you think?> <moron>

She looks in my eyes and says, "I thought you might need a friend."

Something happens. For the first time in years, I see blue, all around her. And I feel at peace.

"Yeah," I say. "Why don't you stay for a while."

Acknowledgments

Many thanks are due:

As always, my brilliant agent, Alexandra Machinist; my peerless editor, Rachel Kahan; Alexander Maldutis, who explained algorithmic trading and quantitative analysis in terms so simple that even I understood them; Laura Hiler, who served as my long-distance tour guide to Dubai; Jonathan Sander, strategy officer at STEALTHBits, who helped me figure out how to steal data from a secure server network; Dan Chmielewski, who continues to teach me about security, as well as friendship; the legendary Beau Smith, my personal armaments consultant; Phil Roosevelt, who served as a first reader and gave valuable feedback; Levi Preston (no relation), who gave me information on the military as well as notes on the story; Britt McCombs, who gave me great advice and ideas for Kelsey Foster.

And to Jean and Caroline and Daphne, for being the reason why.

The quote from Allen Dulles about mind warfare is from Jon Ronson's brilliant and invaluable *The Men Who Stare at Goats,* about the American military's and the CIA's real-life efforts to harness psychic powers. I also relied on my friends John Whalen and Jonathan Vankin's massive and massively useful *The 80 Greatest Conspiracies of All Time.* (Again. It's a really great book.) I used Will Storr's ridiculously smart

The Unpersuadables: Adventures with the Enemies of Science as a reference for all the ways our brains work and the ways they don't. The stories about Wolf Messing originated from several sources—I first read about him in my junior high library, in a book I have never been able to track down since. But you can learn more about him in the biography *Wolf Messing: The True Story of Russia's Greatest Psychic* by Tatiana Lungin. I also quoted reporting from Donald L. Barlett and James B. Steele's article on American cash in Iraq ("Billions over Baghdad," *Vanity Fair*, October 2007).

Any mistakes are mine, despite the best efforts of everyone listed here.

About the Author

A former journalist and screenwriter, Christopher Farnsworth is the author of the Nathaniel Cade/President's Vampire series of novels, which was optioned for film and TV and has been published in nine languages. Born and raised in Idaho, he now lives in Los Angeles with his family.